Frances Paige wa
married to a psychiatrist whose thinking, she admits, has greatly influenced her approach to characterisation in her novels. A prolific writer under her own name, *Lost Time* is her second novel under the pseudonym of Frances Paige. Her first, *Three Girls*, was also published by Corgi Books. She and her husband live in Lancashire and travel regularly to south-west France, her second love.

Also by Frances Paige

THREE GIRLS

and published by Corgi Books

Lost Time

Frances Paige

LOST TIME

A CORGI BOOK 0 552 12699 3

Originally published in Great Britain by Souvenir Press Ltd.

PRINTING HISTORY

Souvenir Press edition published 1985
Corgi edition published 1986

This book is set in 10/11 pt Plantin

Corgi Books are published by Transworld Publishers Ltd., 61–63 Uxbridge Road, Ealing, London W5 5SA, in Australia by Transworld Publishers (Aust.) Pty. Ltd., 26 Harley Crescent, Condell Park, NSW 2200, and in New Zealand by Transworld Publishers (N.Z.) Ltd., Cnr. Moselle and Waipareira Avenues, Henderson, Auckland.

Printed and bound in Great Britain by
Hunt Barnard Printing Ltd., Aylesbury, Bucks.

All of the characters in this book are fictitious, and any resemblance to actual persons, living or dead, is purely coincidental

The author is grateful for permission to quote several lines from the poem 'Barbara', from *Paroles* by Jacques Prévert, © Editions Gallimard 1949.

Some people say that the heart is the organ with which we think and that it feels pain and anxiety. It is not so. Men ought to know that from the brain and the brain alone arise our pleasures, joys, laughter and jests, as well as our sorrows, pain, grief and tears.

Hippocrates.

Lost Time

CHAPTER ONE

'I can hardly believe I'm on a boat going to Dieppe,' Karin said. What she meant was that she could hardly believe she could find herself going anywhere with this girl she hadn't seen for eight years.

'When I phoned I'd no intention of asking you.' Barbara smiled nervously.

'Let's say I asked *you*.' Perhaps it was unusual to cross the Channel in February, although looking round the well-filled bar, there were obviously other people who'd had the same idea. Skiers, Karin decided. She smiled reassuringly.

Barbara shied from the smile, lowering her head.

'No . . . I had this sudden wish to see you. I *needed* to see you.' Why was she looking so apprehensive? 'I only thought of dinner at first . . .'

'But when you said you were going to Dieppe for the weekend I barged my way in.' She hoped that would be the end of it. All she'd felt at the time was a slight rush of French clichés to the head, not specifically *Dieppois* ones – accordion music, Gauloises, remembrance of a café in Paris where the waiter had left a saucer every time he brought a fresh cup of coffee. 'His personal abacus', Gerald had said. Weekends were when she missed him most, even his risqué jokes in bed, 'I'm a rising young consultant . . .' He's my real reason for being here, she thought. What was Barbara's?

'I'm glad you came.'

'So am I.' How awkward they both sounded. But then eight years was a long time, and they hadn't been close friends at school. If she'd thought of Barbara at all it was of a quiet, withdrawn girl, somehow different from the others because she had a French mother. But the nervousness, the apprehension were new, or was it that one became more perceptive at twenty-six?

The girl's looks hadn't changed, the Gallic set of her features, the width across the eyes, the pointed chin, and the sad hair. Even at school it had been that pale grey colour, as if there were no pigment in it. And the hands she remembered too, the long narrow hands which seemed to come to a point like the chin. Now they were twining together, nervously. 'Would you like a drink?' Karin asked briskly, thinking how like her mother she sounded; she also had a talent for jollying things along. 'A gin and tonic?'

'I don't usually . . . well, yes, please.' It was as if she'd had to convince herself. 'I'll pay for it.' She unzipped the lining of her duffle coat, or was it a velcro fastening, and produced a slim wallet.

'No, no!' Karin waved it away. 'You're wise not to carry a bag.'

'It was Don's idea, my husband. A long time ago. He was afraid I might be mugged when . . . if . . .' her voice trailed away, then brightened, 'But it's my turn next time.'

'Don't worry. I'll give you plenty of chances in Dieppe.' Karin got up and walked with a certain sense of relief to the bar.

'Two gins and tonic, please.' The man smiled at her and she smiled back. This was familiar country.

'Off for a naughty weekend, then?' He poured gin into two glasses, slid two bottles of tonic water along the counter.

'Far from it. An Old Girls' Outing.'

'Come off it. You're not old! Ah, I get it. All the better, then, without the lads.' He had a cockney voice, hair plastered back from his forehead, bold eyes beneath thick eyebrows which met above his nose. 'One sixty to *you*,' he said. She gave him the money, thinking her tight jeans and voluminous sweater, combined with her short hair and swinging earrings probably constituted body language to bar tenders. She only dressed to look like a solicitor when she was on the job. Someone touched her arm. It was Barbara.

'Let me help.'

The man's eyes changed, flattened. He lifted the two tonic bottles, handed them to Barbara, like a barman.

'Thank you, Miss.' His voice had become subdued. When they were back at their table she said to Barbara, 'You haven't changed a bit. You always looked so . . . fragile.' She had found the right word.

'I'm quite tough. I've had to be.' Her voice was bitter, and then she was saying quickly, 'You've got very slim. You used to have . . .'

'Big boobs?' Anything to make her laugh. 'I still have, in comparison with the rest of me.' She clowned a little. 'I remember writing an *anguished* letter to Mother, imploring her to send me a bra, something to *bind* or *flatten*.' She laughed, pleased to see the shadow clearing from Barbara's face. 'I got a long lecture back saying I ought to be thankful I wasn't *deformed*, blind, deaf, or FORCED TO WEAR RAGS! Capitals. Mother has a missionary zeal when it comes to comparisons with the haves and the have-nots.'

'I liked your mother so much.' She was smiling now, naturally. 'I remember you taking me home for tea once, and your family were all so jolly, especially your mother.'

'Bossy's the word. She bosses father, James and me – even the dogs. She always wants you to be doing things, topping and tailing gooseberries, chopping up vegetables, pushing the barrow to the compost heap, taking chicken broth to invalids in the village. She sees herself as the queen bee in a hive of activity.'

'You were like that at school.'

'Bossy?'

'No, always doing things, errands for teachers, marking registers, looking after new arrivals, sticking up notices . . .'

'You make me sound terrible. I didn't realize . . .' In fact she had; sometimes she'd thought they treated her like an adult when she was still a child.

It was the way her mother had brought her up, to be self-reliant, to offer help always to the needy. Gerald had said she came from a long line of matriarchs. Father had been happy enough with the petticoat régime, saying in his dry way that it was at least benevolent, but not so Gerald.

'The fear of women lies deep in the mythic consciousness of men,' he'd quoted. 'Women are more carnal. They turn men's eyes away from heaven.' When they were first married, before he'd started studying for the Membership and working overtime, he'd tended to read worthy books in bed, copying excerpts from them into a notebook. He'd said it was the equivalent of the post-coital cigarette.

'I'm separated from my husband,' she said to Barbara. 'For a trial period.' She didn't have to elaborate, but she did. 'His background was different from mine. On certain basic questions we don't see eye to eye.' She still went on. 'His mother is more dangerous than mine, a bit of the D.H. Lawrence syndrome. She's a widow, strong-willed, but men and especially sons are in her eyes superior beings.' She laughed in case she sounded bitter, which she was. 'When you've been put on a pedestral you're not used to listening to women.'

'Have you been married long?'

'Three years. I was working in London and my brother introduced me to him. They were sharing a flat before James went off to Australia. It was a whirlwind courtship, as they say.' She was trying to be amusing to conceal her hurt. 'I'd been so busy at university that I hadn't had time for an affair, well, a long one, and besides, I was in the tennis team. Gerald bowled me over . . .' She laughed. 'I'm mixing my metaphors. Doctors learn an authoritative manner early on. I wasn't used to it.' She thought she must sound boring and complaining, and changed the subject. 'I vaguely heard you were a child bride a year after you left school.'

'Yes. It didn't work.' She looked away.

'Are you divorced?'

'Yes.'

'Any children?'

'No.' She saw the pinched look round the girl's nostrils in time.

'God, I've been haranguing you. I'm sorry. I'm so used to firing questions at clients.' She watched the conscious attempt at a smile. It was a charming smile, an unused smile; it altered her whole face, broadening its planes, making the chin piquant.

'It's all right. Your job must be frightfully interesting. I often wondered what had happened to you. You seemed to be so in command of yourself.'

'Command? Me!' People said it all the time.

'I shouldn't have known where to phone you, only Liz Cuthbert . . .'

'Oh, Liz!' Karin yawned exaggeratedly and patted her mouth. Barbara giggled. For the first time they were natural and girlish with each other. Karin remembered the girl's suppressed giggling, so unlike her usual serious expression, the reddening of her face, the eyes spurting tears. She'd had a sense of the ridiculous.

Barbara was wiping her eyes. 'That was good . . . but you remember what she was like. She still sends me a Christmas card plastered all over with newsy items about old girls.' She spoke in an affected voice. 'A little bird tells me Karin Armstrong, Karin Elliot that was, has landed a super job as junior partner in the well-known City solicitors of Saithe and Saithe . . .'

And antagonized her husband by doing so. She saw for a second Gerald's hurt white face when she'd told him. She wouldn't go on about Gerald. 'Poor Liz.' She laughed. 'She never misses a trick.' It was strange how being with Barbara Charles . . . she hadn't said what her married name was . . . brought back school memories. Although she'd had a 'good shot at it', (her mother again), she'd disliked the restrictions, the closeness of living with girls, their habits, their smells. Gerald had said once she was a natural lover and good to sleep with as well. 'Because I like men,' she'd said.

But all the same, since they'd split up, she hadn't accepted many of the invitations which came her way in Saithe and Saithe's. Only one, she remembered, the Harvard man who'd come to the firm for a year. What a lot of people didn't realize, she thought, was that under her air of confidence she could feel very frightened indeed. When she and Gerald had parted she'd lain awake all night, shivering and miserable, like a cowering dog, or bitch. It had been a basic thing, quite apart from his body absence, an unfamiliar female feeling of being left unprotected, and the knowledge that outside there were dark shapes and shadows which she would now have to face up to alone. Over and above that there had been the crushing sense of defeat. With all her so-called cleverness, she hadn't managed to get over to Gerald that she needed him, fundamentally.

She looked at Barbara. The brightness had died out of her face. She was sitting, her hand round the glass, her eyes fixed on something above Karin's head. There was a rigidity about her posture as if she were holding an inward trembling in check. She felt a creeping sense of unease, knew it had been there from the beginning. 'It's quite a good crossing,' she said, falsely cheerful. Through the windows she could see the small choppy waves of the Channel, bad-tempered little waves because it was too early for calm seas. It was a ridiculous time of the year to go to Dieppe; they'd probably creep about in the streets in the cold, or hide themselves away all day in cafés. How had she got herself into this situation? What would they talk about all the time? 'Of course, France is your favourite place.' She tried again. 'We all envied you, speaking the language so well. Is your mother still there?'

'No, she died.' She said it in a flat voice, head lowered again, tensing away. It was unnerving. Mrs Charles could only have been in her middle forties. Karin remembered her as a dark, elegant woman, pale-faced, exceptionally large eyes. It's stupid, she thought, two girls setting off like this, nothing in common. If I'd wanted a break I should have gone home to Kent and been swept into the domestic maelstrom round mother. She wouldn't have asked about Gerald. She'd refused to take the separation seriously.

You didn't give it time, she told herself now, made more miserable by this girl. 'I'm sorry, Barbara,' she said. 'She was young to die. What was the . . . ?' She met her eyes before she completed the sentence. They were full of something deeper than sadness, a kind of desolation. 'Let's go and have lunch,' she said. She felt out of her depth.

Then, as they went up the wide staircase with its rubber treads, stopped to look politely, for each other's sake, at the duty free shops, whisky, Nina Ricci perfume, king-sized cigarettes, asked each other politely outside the ladies' toilet if either wanted to 'go', an uneasy compassion for the girl rose like indigestion in Karin's gorge. The pale profile stirred her in an unaccountable way. No one should look that miserable, so bowed down at her age. I must do something for her, she thought, show her sympathy at least. I'll show her a good time. She echoed the words of Sam Kapec, the American who'd come to learn English jurisprudence at Saithe and Saithe's. He'd shown *her* that, with no expense spared, but she'd jibbed at the last part of it. Gerald had spoiled her for Ivy League romps.

Dieppe was more crowded than Karin had imagined, forgetting that it came into its own as a fishing port in winter. There was a bustling workaday air about the town which pleased her. Barbara knew a hotel which was within walking distance of the Henry IV Quay where they disembarked, and they took their time along the Grande Rue, glad to stretch their legs, window shopping when the fancy took them. She seemed more relaxed than on the ferry. Perhaps it was the fact of being on French soil.

'It's better not to be on the plage,' she said. 'We'd get blown to bits by the wind in February. This hotel is near the shops and the Place de Puits Sale isn't far away. There's a good café there.'

'Suits me,' Karin said. 'We'll sit and watch the world go

by. I hope your hotel's got central heating.'

'Yes, it has.'

'We can always save by sharing a room if you like; two for the price of one in France. Once, James and I, when we were small, Ma and Pa, the four of us, crowded into an enormous room with three beds. We laughed a lot, took turns at undressing in the shower room . . .'

'I prefer to be alone.' Barbara's voice was cold, final.

The hotel was warm, and French, and welcoming, its Renaissance exterior concealing its modern comforts. When Barbara had spoken to the woman at the desk they were shown to separate rooms adjoining each other on the first floor. Now that she thought of it, Karin was glad of the privacy.

'I'll probably read for ages,' she said. She'd discovered insomnia for the first time in her life. 'I'd only have disturbed you.' She wouldn't mention the nights when she'd walked about her flat, made unwanted cups of tea, thought of Gerald with longing . . . 'And I've brought some work to go over. Coming away at such short notice . . .' Barbara's eyes went bleak.

'I'm sorry. It's my fault.'

'I invited myself, remember?' She said the words in a sing-song voice to conceal her irritation. 'You go and unpack, then we'll walk round the town to work up a good appetite for dinner.'

'All right.' Barbara slid away.

What am I *doing* here with this girl, Karin asked herself as she shut the door behind her. She had an instant's depression but rallied herself, looking round the room instead. Inevitable flock wall-paper, crimson velvet curtains, white-painted furniture, gilt-beaded, mock Louis Quinze. She walked into the bathroom and saw with relief that the fittings were modern. She turned on the hot tap, found it lived up to its name. She was glad to be alone. Barbara was hard going.

Maybe she's like me, she thought, back in the bedroom, lifting out her night-dress and dressing-gown from her hold-all, laying them on the crimson quilted bedspread. The night-dress had been a small bow to convention. She never wore one at home. Gerald liked her naked . . . why did everything make her think of Gerald?

Barbara could have some kind of emotional problem with a man. Who hadn't? And then there was her mother. Perhaps she'd died recently. She couldn't imagine life without her own bustling mother in the background, although that's where she liked her to stay. 'Mother's like a ship's figurehead cleaving the waters of life,' James had once said. 'At least she doesn't make waves.' That was true enough. There wasn't the narrow obsessive love which might have existed between Barbara and her mother. She remembered the pale elegant woman, how she'd kept apart from the others at speech days. And her restless eyes, large, blank . . .

She placed the bulky file headed *Smithers V. Smithers* on her bedside table for reading later. Novels were no panacea, she'd found. Details of the characters' personal relationships could start a train of thought, of remorse, or sadness, worse still, an explicit description of a love-scene sometimes overwhelmed her with vicarious feeling which surprised her by its fierceness. She'd had to bury her face in the pillow before now until the heavy beating in her body subsided. She sat down on the bed, feeling exhausted, suddenly, defeated. The memory of that night flooded over her, she had it give way to it, live through it again, be tortured again by remorse . . .

She managed to unlock the door, her arms full of the shopping she'd done on the way home, the bag topped by a bunch of hot-house spray chrysanthemums, costly at this time of the year but she loved their vivid colours – acid yellow, cyclamen pink, tangerine. She felt vivid this evening herself, she thought, as she plumped everything on the hall table and looked at herself in the mirror.

Michael had cut her hair even shorter at the sides, lightened its darkness with a russet rinse. 'You have lovely lobes, Mrs Armstrong,' he'd said. 'Doesn't your husband ever tell you?'

'Sure,' she'd laughed, 'all the time.'

How could he notice, far less tell her, when he staggered into the flat at all hours, dazed with work, crawled into bed beside her and went out like a light? Sometimes he woke up in the middle of the night and made love to her, hungrily, as if his consciousness had surfaced enough to tell him he needed her. Like a baby at the breast, falling away when replete. She responded always, felt resentful sometimes, but still loved this overworked husband with the pale face and the gut which played him up.

'Medicine isn't a nine to five job, Ka,' he'd said more than once. You're telling me, she'd thought. 'You have to slave at it, give your soul to it.' He seemed oblivious to the paperwork she brought home in her brief case and often spent a part of the evening studying, and he didn't know of the hours she sat up in bed with it when he was on night duty.

But it had borne fruit. Her heart jumped with joy. Twenty-six years of age and today old Mr Reginald had told her. 'I'm going to be bowing out soon, Karin, withdrawing from the fray. I'm making you and Sanderson junior partners.'

She unwrapped the packet of convenience food she'd bought in the French delicatessen because she'd been late after all. When she'd telephoned Gerald to ask him when he'd be home he'd said, 'Anything up to midnight. I'll be awash with Sister's coffee. Something light to eat, please.'

'Okay,' she'd agreed, but added, 'Hurry up, darling, I've a marvellous surprise for you.' He hadn't caught her enthusiasm. 'A tray in bed and you is all I ask.' He'd hung up.

She read the instructions on the packet, translating with difficulty. Monsieur Robert in the shop had explained. 'It says here, *Croque Monsieur*, but we say *Croque Madame*.' He had laughed, rolling his black eyes. 'I'll leave you to guess why.' She looked at the picture of the round egg smiling on its roasty platform. Perhaps Gerald would be quicker to see the point.

She was having a quick shower, being careful with her hair, when she heard the door bang. Gerald lumbered into the bathroom, looking wan. He always lumbered when he was tired. 'Hello, darling!' She stepped out and wrapped a towel under her arms. 'Can't kiss you properly when I'm wet.'

'What's wet?' he said, drawing her against him. 'I was covered with blood not so long ago. The chief asked me to help with a . . .'

'No ghoulish talk before eating. Rub me dry.' She stood like a small girl while he set about it like a nanny. 'Don't be so fussy about the corners,' she said, smiling at him.

'It's the corners I like.' He dropped the towel on the floor. 'Oh, God, I love you so much. Let's go to bed.'

'Soon. I've got a light supper for you and a bottle of that Sauvignon you like. Go and open it and we'll have a glass as an aperitif.' She turned him round, gave him a push towards the door and he lumbered out again. His back was in a long curve, his arms hung tiredly. He looked as if he hadn't the energy to pull himself straight.

She put on her dressing-gown, stuck her feet into mules and went into the kitchen. Gerald was opening the bottle. 'You've spread yourself tonight,' he said, looking up. 'I hope you haven't got a lot of food. I'm not hungry.'

'You will be when you've had some wine. Sit down and drink it while I make something. I'm hungry if you aren't.' She lit the oven, put the *Croque Monsieurs* into it on a tray, broke two eggs into a pan. 'Busy day?' she said, trying to look wifely. Wait till she told him her news.

'You must be joking.' He gave her a glass of wine, sipped his appreciatively. 'Yes, delicious. This was the stuff we had on our honeymoon, wasn't it?'

'Yes.' That week on the Loire three years ago seemed as distant as the last war. 'Happy days!'

'Happy days.' He got off the edge of the table where he was perched to kiss her. 'You're lovelier than ever and your eyes are shining like a naughty child's. What have you been up to?'

'Wait.' She freed herself to slide the cooked eggs on to a plate and put them on top of the oven to keep warm. 'While you're eating supper I'll tell you why they're shining.' She could scarcely contain her joy. She'd worked hard, harder than Gerald knew or appreciated, but she'd never thought advancement would come so soon. Don't lay it on too thick, a voice inside her warned.

Gerald sat down at his place and she put the *Croque Monsieur* in front of him with its crown of egg. 'What's this?' he said, poking at it suspiciously.

'It's as light as a feather and it's called *Croque Madame*, Monsieur Robert tells me. Can you guess why?'

'No?' He looked at her, blank-faced.

She shaped her breasts with her hands, looked enquiringly at him. 'The egg?'

'I get it.' He was not amused. He poked at it again, took a forkful of the toast interlined with cheese and bacon, chewed. 'As tough as old rope,' he said, and seeing her face, 'well, nearly. Still, I haven't eaten all day except one mouldy sandwich. I'm so sick of bread. Everything's between bread, convenience food, I've had it up to here with convenience food – on the hoof, on the run, using bread as a plate, as a vehicle – I'm stuffed with bread, I'm going to be like those loaves mother used to make: she set this dough stuff in a great bowl on the side of the stove, covered it with a cloth and it began to rise till it nearly filled the kitchen.' His truculence faded, he looked at Karin, rapt. 'Still, it had a lovely smell. The whole house would be filled with it, and when I came home from school I used to think, "Yummy, Mum's been baking." She'd cut me a great doorstep slice when it was ready and lather it with fresh butter and homemade strawberry jam and I would sink my fangs into it . . .'

'Gerald . . .' she interrupted. She knew his ethnic yearnings of old. According to him his mother had lived in a pinny in a floury kitchen from morning to night . . . a different picture from the smart Newcastle matron she knew, who was sharp, ever so slightly wary of her southern daughter-in-law.

'I've been made a partner in Saithe and Saithe.'

'You've what?' His jaw dropped open.

'You heard me the first time. Old Mr Reginald told me today. He's going to retire in stages.'

'I suppose you've got an increase in salary too?'

'Yes.' She put down her knife and fork. 'I'm almost afraid to say it, but it must be true. I've been upped to the tune of £3,000 a year more with a promise of yearly review.'

'That's great.' His voice lacked conviction. She was stung.

'You don't sound as if it was great.'

'I said it was, didn't I? You're a clever girl. Old Reginald must have a soft spot for you.'

'It couldn't conceivably be because I'm good at my job?' she said, her temper rising. 'I didn't sleep with old Reginald to get it, nor young Reginald come to that . . . although that would be a change of direction for him!'

'I'm sure you're good at your job.' Again he was not amused. 'You're efficient, pretty, you're being paid commensurate with your abilities.' He pushed the mutilated toast and egg away from him. 'It's a pity we aren't all in the same league.'

'Your turn will come, darling,' she said, mortified, 'it's a steeper hill, that's all.'

'I'm not after money, you know that. I'd like to stay on the hospital staff for a time, to do research. All I want is more time and enough money to keep you. All I want is to have exams behind me and think, not cram . . .'

'It will come,' she said, looking at his miserable face. 'We'll both be busy. I expect I'll bring even more work home. I don't get paid for nothing, you know. We'll look back on this time with pleasure, you'll see, both . . .'

He got to his feet abruptly. ' . . . working shoulder to shoulder, except that you'll be paid five or six times as much as I am. We could have managed. I thought that while I was struggling out of this situation you would get into your role of wife and mother. Then when I emerged with a decent appointment in the hospital our family would be growing up. That would have been the time for you to go back to Saithe and Saithe, become a partner.'

She snatched up his plate, scraped the contents into the bin, followed it with her own, her disappointment bursting into anger. 'You can't bear my success, that's what it is! You want me to be hassled along with you, bringing up children in a poky London flat on a pittance of a salary, struggling to make ends meet, while I have the potential . . .' It was an old argument. They'd never seen eye to eye on the issue, and she recognized in her calmer moments that the big mistake they'd made was not to have discussed it fully before they were married. But he'd never attacked her with such virulence. She saw his eyes sparking in his white face.

'You're also twenty-six. You'll soon be twenty-seven, twenty-eight, getting too fond of your career, the fleshpots, getting too cautious, too old to have children.'

'Girls are having children all the time in their thirties. Science has improved, or hadn't you noticed? I'm not alone in my attitude, I've discussed it, thought about it. Why should I leave my experience to crumble and then spend years trying to claw my way back again? I *might* have, in fact I *was* coming round to your way of thinking, but this offer has changed everything.'

'I don't want children when I'm grey-haired,' he said, sulkily. She gritted her teeth in exasperation.

'Oh, for goodness sake! I'll send you to Michael and he'll dye it for you.' She looked at his sullen face. 'That North Sea stubbornness of yours! I thought working where it's civilized would have changed your ideas a bit, but it hasn't. You live in the last century. If you're like that in your work I'm sorry for your patients, that's all I can say!' She realized she was talking wildly now because he couldn't bring himself to congratulate her.

'So you're now saying I'm a bad doctor, is that it?' She

had struck where it hurt most. He kicked his chair out of the way and began to pace about the kitchen. His anger came to her in waves. This was where it had gone far enough, where she knew the soft answer would turn away his wrath, where the proffered cheek would be kissed. But it was a special day, he should have been rejoicing with her . . .

'I didn't say anything of the kind, but if the cap fits . . .'

'You implied it. Oh, yes, I knew what you really thought of me would come out some day. Just as I don't need reminding that you've sailed through all your exams and I failed my Membership. Even got the gold medal at your college, didn't you . . . roses, roses, all the way, the best divorce lawyer in the business, and now the final accolade, a partner in that well-known firm of Saithe and Saithe . . . at twenty-six, if you please, salary upped to . . . what was it? Those figures make my poor brain dizzy!' The misery in his face made her want to weep for him, if she hadn't been so angry.

'You can't take competition!' she shouted, incensed. 'That's what it is. You have to be king-pin all the time. Why don't you clear out of here and go back to the hospital, back to the milieu you like – with all the little nurses twittering around you in their daft hats . . . shades of Florence Nightingale, isn't it, fawning, saying, "Yes, doctor, no, doctor . . ."?'

'Is that what you want me to do?' he said, his voice quiet, dangerously quiet, 'clear out?'

'You can't imagine I'd want you to stay after this?' She was trembling. 'I thought you'd be glad for me . . .'

'Crown you with laurel leaves, bow at your feet?'

'Don't be stupid,' she said.

'So it's all coming out now.' He thrust his fists into his pockets, hunched his shoulders. 'I'm a bad doctor, I'm stupid, I can't take competition. Have I forgotten something? I wonder why you married me in the first place?' Here it is again, she thought, the sarcasm, the old rock on which we perish, after the anger. It's not that I don't recognize my own stubbornness, my own brashness, but this was a very special night to me, becoming a partner; I would have rejoiced with him if he'd got his Membership. She made up her mind.

'I've had enough. I can stand your perpetual tiredness, your irritability, but what really sickens me tonight is your dog-in-the-manger attitude. I think you should go back to the hospital . . . and stay away.'

'You mean, split?' His voice was like ice. His skin was pallid.

'I mean, not see each other for a time. We're hurting each other too much. I can't take it, nor can you. My working days are spoiled. I can't imagine yours aren't.' There's still time, she thought, looking at him. You could put your arms round me, say you can't live without me . . .

'You're chucking me out?'

'I'm suggesting an amnesty, a halt, a time to think . . .'

'That's the advice you'd give to your clients?' he said, his fists still in his pocket, his foot tracing the design of a tile.

'Since you ask, yes. We always advise the two parties to reconsider before starting on proceedings . . .'

'For divorce, you mean?' He had an air of wishing to acquire knowledge.

'That's it,' she said, brashly, wanting to die of the pain, to curl up somewhere dark.

'Thank you. Far be it from me to turn down the advice of a partner in that well-known firm of Saithe and Saithe, especially,' he smiled at her, eyes cold, 'when it's given free.'

She stood straight to prevent herself from swaying on her feet. Through the cloud of resentment in her brain, the anger and the self-righteousness, she heard noises in their bedroom, the bathroom, then heard the outside door slam, shaking the flat. She emerged from the cloud into deep pain at her own inadequacy in dealing with this misguided man, because she was a misguided woman.

She went running from the kitchen to the bedroom to fling herself on the bed, realizing how she was conforming to the idea of femininity which Gerald held. Girls always threw themselves on a convenient bed to weep. Men stalked out. She tried to fight against her prototype, even said aloud to herself, jokingly, 'So much for the *Croque Madame*,' before she burst into a fit of weeping which lasted for hours, it seemed. The new partner of Saithe and Saithe is a sorry sight, she thought, but it didn't stop the tears . . .

CHAPTER TWO

Later, the two girls were sitting in a leather-padded banquette in the Café des Tribunaux where Barbara had led her companion with confidence. Its fin-de-siècle air pleased Karin, the ornate ceiling, fringed lampshades, the panelled walls inset with gold velvet, crystal wall-lights, wrought iron balustrade. 'Oscar Wilde might come strolling in at any minute,' she said, and scored a bull's eye.

'As a matter of fact he used this place often,' Barbara said, and a flicker of humour appeared in her eyes, 'with or without Bosie, I'm not sure.'

Karin was having a Pernod, to suit the ambience, she said; Barbara a black coffee. She had been adamant about that. She hardly ever drank. Why come to France at all, Karin had thought, but now she smiled brightly at the girl, prepared to make fresh efforts. 'Show her a good time . . .' shades of Sam Kapek.

What a pretty girl she was with those large grey eyes, the breadth of the upper part of the face accommodating them, the pleasing contrast of the narrow chin, and then that colourless hair, sheenless, its weight and thickness making her face look smaller and somehow appealing. 'It's fun, isn't it?' she said. 'We'll let our hair down, tell each other all our worries.'

'You don't look as if you had many,' Barbara said, chin lowered, shyly smiling.

'I'm a tragedy queen, I'd have you know, buffeted by fate. Would you like to hear the story of my life?'

'Proceed.' Barbara giggled. The pale complexion became suffused with red; the eyes screwed up, became moist.

'My downfall is all due to my losing weight.' She pulled a

sad face. 'You know what I was like at school, huge calves, great hams, a bust like Platform One at Charing Cross.'

'That's not true.' The eyes were now swimming with laughter. 'You were only plump, with rosy cheeks and glossy black hair. I envied it; mine is like tow.'

'Thick hair is the sign of a sexy nature. All the great courtesans had it. And how about that generous girl in the fairy story who let down her hair for her lover to climb up it into her room? But to get back to me. Young men used to tease me at university about my plumpness, especially my *derrière* which would have been a riot in France; bikinis on me became obscene . . . and then I met Gerald and fell hopelessly in love with him, ridiculously in love with him, a fat girl in love.'

'Is he still working in a hospital?' Barbara put her narrow hands together to support her chin. She looked relaxed, there was a faint pink still in her cheeks.

'Yes, St. Thomas's. He's a registrar. He used to say he was a rising young consultant.' In bed. Her cheeks grew hot at the immediate image in her mind, the warmth, the closeness, skin against skin. She coughed and took a sip of Pernod. 'I was desperate for him. The fat simply fell away from me; I languished; there was no rigorous diet, nothing like that. I went off my food till we got married.' It was good to talk. 'A complete personality change. The thin girl who emerged was quite different, not nearly as nice.'

'You aren't serious?'

'Truly; I got narky. It must have been a metabolic thing. It affected my brain as well.' She was piling it on a bit for effect, but there was more than a grain of truth in what she was saying. 'I discovered Gerald was an out-and-out, dyed-in-the-wool male chauvinist. He thought my Saithe and Saithe partnership was the death-knell to his hope for our marriage. He wanted to be the chief provider and I had outsmarted him. If I had it was unwitting, but he couldn't see that. I said he should clear out for a bit . . .'

'And did he?'

'Like a shot.' She smiled at Barbara to dispel the memory

of his hurt, pale face, 'Maybe I'll look back on it as just a bad patch. The loving at the beginning was super. Did you feel like that, the wonder, the sheer enchantment of it? If only we could have kept it going . . .' Too much Pernod, swallowed too quickly. 'Did *you* feel like that?'

'I can't remember. It's a long time ago.' The heavy eyelids dropped, concealing the eyes which had gone bleak again. Shop closed. Don't ask questions.

'How long?'

'Three years.' The reply was reluctant. The head remained lowered.

'That's comforting, at least. We've only been separated for three weeks. I miss him, especially at nights, however tired and irritable.'

Barbara looked up at her, all the colour gone now from her cheeks, even the eyes were a washed-out grey. 'It isn't the main thing in marriage, bed. There's a simple kindness . . .' she pushed back the dun-coloured hair impatiently, her voice becoming sharp. 'How did we get on to this subject of men? We're here to forget them, aren't we?'

'Are we?' She wasn't aware of any agreement. But this strange girl was right. Any thought of Gerald was hurtful. It would go on being hurtful. She'd listened to too many couples at Saithe and Saithe telling her about the heart-break and remorse and guilt. 'Those who say divorce is easy nowadays should try it,' she remembered one client saying, 'it's a small death.' I mustn't get to that stage, she thought now, and then to Barbara. 'We ought to think more carefully before we embark on marriage.' The remark sounded pedantic in her ears, and to keep it light she bent forward, 'Don't look now, but behind you, no, slightly to the left,' of course she'd looked round, 'there's the most peculiar woman. She's got one of those French lap dogs in her arms, and it has the same face! And she's wearing a knobbly white wool sweater and a black leather strap round her neck with an initial on it. Pretend to be looking at something else . . .'

Dining with Barbara was easier than she had imagined. The French had a way of getting the ambience right, the feeling of the importance of food, a willingness to share that feeling. They chose *petites fritures de la Manche* to begin with, and Barbara translated *raie* for her as skate, which she recommended because of its butter and black pepper sauce. If they had room after that, she said, they should have hot apple tart because the apples would be cooked in calvados.

With its curtains drawn against the darkness, the hotel dining-room had the air of a cosy velvet-lined box, and the candles on each table gave Karin the feeling that they were guests rather than customers. Only two other tables were occupied, one by an elderly couple who studied the menu carefully, and the other by a middle-aged woman who sat alone with a book on her knee. Barbara said they might be *pensionnaires*.

Schooldays seemed to be a safe subject. They reminisced as they ate, Karin remembering how she'd cycled willingly uphill on Sundays to church because of the lure of the handsome young curate. 'Calf love,' she said, laughing, 'all plaits, wired teeth and sweaty armpits. Do you remember him? He was like Byron without the limp. I looked up the word "sensual" in my dictionary and had dark dreams about him.'

Barbara listened, interested but surprised. She'd had a poetic view of Kent, she said. She remembered the brass rubbings, the oast-houses, and the long guided walks which had been anathema to her. She hadn't had a close schoolfriend. Sects and secrets and handsome curates seemed to have passed her by.

'Why did you think of Dieppe?' Karin asked her when she felt she'd scraped the barrel. 'Was it just more or less the nearest French place?'

'I feel at home in France, especially Normandy.'

'Nothing more?'

'My grandfather was killed in the Normandy landings. He was English; his name was Norman Sanctuary.'

'Norman Sanctuary?' Karin repeated the name, liking

the sound. 'It's very English.'

'Yes, but his wife was French. She liked me to call her *grand-mère*.'

'That's interesting, both your mother and grandmother marrying Englishmen.'

'Maybe my mother was influenced. And then my father was a Francophile. They met while he was studying Norman churches.' She was looking away as she spoke, as if the subject held no interest for her.

'We could hire a car tomorrow if you like and go to the landing beaches; it wouldn't cost the earth.'

'No, no.' She shook her head.

It was coming back to Karin. 'You went to Normandy for your school holidays, to your grandmother's house, didn't you? Wouldn't you like to go back there?'

'It's better not to go back. Besides, it's been locked up for ages.' She turned a flat gaze on Karin. 'It's better just to remember.'

'I suppose so.' She didn't really understand. 'What age was your mother when her father was killed?'

'Eight. I was eight too when my father died . . . the same for both of us.'

She remembered now that the mother had been a widow. 'So now you're alone?' She shouldn't have said that; no one liked pity.

'Isn't everyone alone in the end?'

'I suppose so. I thought I was independent until Gerald and I split up . . . perhaps it would have been easier if we'd never met.' She didn't believe it, but it sounded more sympathetic. 'Let's plan what we'll do tomorrow, shall we?' The conversation was becoming too heavy. Barbara looked at her, unsmiling. The candlelight had hollowed out her eyes, and the density of her hair was unrelieved by any reflection.

The next day passed surprisingly quickly as they walked about the town, window-shopping, sitting in cafés when it became too cold. They went to the fish market, and Karin had a fishy French lesson from Barbara as they went round the stalls – *crevettes, maquereaux, moules, harengs, huîres, merlan, langoustines, roussettes, carrelets*. Some of them she recognized, but the French names made the colourful mounds in their beds of ice seem more exotic then their English counterparts. The unknown ones she christened 'creatures of the deep'. If she could make Barbara laugh she felt rewarded.

It seemed they were becoming attuned to each other. Although Karin did most of the talking, she found herself growing fond of the girl in a strange way. There was an acerbic sweetness about her, and she had a sense of humour which flashed out occasionally. She's like an iceberg, she told herself. I'm only being allowed to see a tiny part of her.

In the afternoon they walked along the narrow Rue de Chastes and climbed up the steep hill to the old castle which overlooked the town. Barbara said there was a museum housed in it, and after wandering around the various rooms of pictures and pottery with not too much interest, they came upon an unusually fine collection of ivories. She was immediately enchanted. The habitual sad cast of her features had disappeared; the pale skin glowed. Karin thought her delicate profile was in a way as exquisite as the ivories themselves.

She talked animatedly about them on their way down to the town again. They were heading for the Puits de Salle and their favourite upstairs seat in the Café Tribunaux. 'Do you think there might be carvers still here?' she asked Karin. 'It's a shame if the art has died out.'

'Why don't we look around first?' Karin suggested.

They wandered into the network of streets off the Rue de la Barre looking for antique shops. It wasn't long before they found one on a corner facing a ruined church, perhaps bombed in the last war.

'*Objets trouvés*,' Barbara said happily. They put their noses to the window and peered in. Karin was the first to see the ivory earrings.

'See, on the little shelf behind the shepherdess with the

crook . . . and the broken nose . . . beside the glass bell covering waxed flowers. They look genuinely old. They're carved like the ones in the castle museum.'

'Where?' Barbara twisted her neck. 'Oh, yes, I see them. You're quite right. Do you think they're really antique?'

'Why not? They look old. The setting's lovely, and the carving's intricate, even from here . . .'

'Would you like them?' Barbara turned to her, her eyes wide, pleading.

'No, thanks.' She wasn't sure if she was being offered them. 'I've far too many already. That's the thing with having your hair short: they're absolutely essential.' She peered at the earrings again. They were rather fine, ivory balls intricately fretted, on long ivory drops like miniature Gothic spires.

'I'd like to buy them for you.' Her eyes were still wide, her smile tentative.

Karin shook her head firmly. Gifts often left you with a sense of obligation. She'd learned that in Saithe and Saithe. 'No, I wouldn't hear of it,' she said. 'I've a much better idea. We'll go to the *Salon du Thé* in the Grand Rue instead of the Tribunaux and have some of their raspberry torte.'

Barbara didn't reply. She was silent as they walked along, and when Karin glanced at her she saw the sad cast of the features was back again. Was it self-pity, or was there something badly wrong? She had enough to worry about with Gerald. 'What's French for sod off, Barbara?' she said. And seeing the girl's startled look, 'I might need to use it if I have to fight off a randy Frenchman.'

This amused her, a faint wash of pink took away the paleness, she even giggled. 'Why bother to fight him off? Frenchmen, they are the great *lovairs* . . .' They chattered happily now as they walked quickly along the street. The air was icy; the ancient houses, tall and narrow, made tunnels of cold air. When they came to the busy Grande Rue again, and Barbara had pushed open the door of the tea shop with her almost foreign politeness, Karin saw the pale mask was back.

When they'd chosen their cakes, not raspberry torte as they'd planned, she said, 'Once we're back in London we must meet.' She felt hypocritical as she said it.

'I don't live in London; I'm in Surbiton.' The flat voice.

'That's not the end of the earth. Do you work there too?'

'Yes, in an estate agents; but I only do temporary work; it suits me.' She looked distracted, unhappy.

'Well, if you ever want to have a chat, or a meal . . . it's better than being alone.'

'Whatever gave you the idea I'm alone?' Now her voice was high and bright. 'All the same, I did want to have a talk with you. That's why I phoned you. You always seemed so . . . mature at school.'

'It was my figure.' She waited.

'You see,' the narrow hands were twining on the table, 'I thought there was something I could ask . . .'

'Sure.'

'It's . . .'

She really looked at the girl. Her face was grey, her eyes frightened. Had she murdered someone, for God's sake? 'Go on, Barbara.' She used her voice for nervous clients.

'It's . . . it's this man I live with . . .' the words came away with a rush. 'He wants to marry me; he's nice, fair-haired, smokes a pipe. He has a lovely house. That's one of the attractions.' She laughed, too gaily. She's lying, Karin thought. That isn't what she was going to ask me at all. 'Quite a country cottage, in fact. It must be one of the old ones. Lovely garden . . . he adores gardening . . . casement windows, a touch of Gloucestershire about it. Do you know that golden stone?

'The only thing I don't like is that above the front door there's a stone plinth suspended by chains, and I'm always afraid to go in that way in case it falls on my head. I've a jinx about it. He laughs at me, says, "Barbara, you are *full* of terrors; you have to face up to things." But I don't risk it. I use the cobbled path which leads directly into the kitchen. It's much more convenient and you can dump all your shopping on the table right away and make a cup of tea. Is there anything nicer than doing a good shop, putting away the stuff in cupboards and making a cup of tea? Cave-womanish. You have to get pleasure out of the simple things, that's the way to do it. Push the big things to the back. My friend never wanted a flat; he adores gardening . . . did I say that before? There's a funny monkey puzzle tree at the front and he prunes it beautifully.' She stopped suddenly.

'So what's the problem?' Karin said. 'He sounds ideal, garden and all.' Quite apart from the pipe and the monkey puzzle tree.

'It's just that I don't want to make the same mistake twice. I told you my first marriage wasn't successful.'

'In what way? Did he leave you?'

'Oh, no. Well, yes he did . . .'

'Was there someone else?'

'Yes . . . you see, there was this one thing he couldn't stand about me, just couldn't stand . . .' She stopped speaking again, looked away, but not before Karin saw that her mouth was trembling. She leant forward and put her hand over Barbara's twining hands.

'If it would help, please tell me.' The hands moved under hers. 'Barbara, it might help to talk . . .'

The eyes she turned on Karin surprised her. Terror-filled. 'Well, I . . .' and then the words came like a rush of water. 'I lost the baby I was going to have. I got . . . upset.'

'Upset?' Who wouldn't get upset? But not terrified. 'That was sad for you. Still, it wasn't the end of the world.'

'Wasn't it?' Her mouth was ugly for a moment.

'Didn't you try again?'

'No, we didn't get on so well after that; those terrible scenes . . .' Some weekend, Karin thought. I might as well be back at my desk, listening to a client.

'What were the scenes about? Was it his fault, you losing the baby?'

'What makes you say that?' Her voice was sharp.

'I just wondered . . .' The case she'd dealt with before Mrs Smithers had been about a woman who was being battered by her husband. 'So, was it because of that, you losing the baby, that the marriage broke up?'

She looked almost grateful for the suggestion. 'Yes, that's it. That's exactly it. It finished the marriage. He didn't show me any sympathy, none at all.' Her voice quickened. 'I don't like to talk about it. I don't know why I did just now. But you can see, can't you, why I don't want to make the same mistake twice?' She looked away.

It didn't follow. 'The one you're living with sounds ideal: a pipe-smoker and a garden-lover.' She smiled, trying to keep it light. 'What's his name?' To her surprise Barbara's face flamed.

'You keep asking me questions!' Her hands clasped like a vice. There was dead silence, and then she said, her voice low, looking down at her hands, 'I'm sorry. I don't mean to be rude. You've been so kind.'

'Rubbish. Look. I know what I'm like. I ask questions because I do it in my job. Or maybe I'm like that in any case. Remember how my mother went on when you came to visit that time? "And this is your little friend from school? Where is your home, Barbara, dear? Have you any brothers or sisters? How long have you been friends with Karin? Don't you find her very naughty at times? Do you wear a sensible woollen vest under *your* blouse, Barbara?"' For my next trick I'll stand on my head . . . but she'd at least made her smile.

'She was kind. It was a home, your home. I remember when I lived with my grandmother it was like that. I could *feel* the warmth, although I must have been very young. Isn't it strange, I can remember her house, the sunniness, the pink carpet, a flower border outside the open window, but not my own home then.'

Karin was confused. 'You mean your Normandy grandmother?'

'No, no, *she* was always *grand-mère*, and I only spent holidays with her. But right at the beginning of my life it's my father's mother I remember, my English grandmother, soft, bosomy, a pink clove smell . . . when she died it was father, mother, and I; then *he* died. That was when my mother moved with me to a flat in Gloucester Road and sent me away to school. But the flat was never a home, like yours. You were just like your mother at school; a tower of strength.'

'A leaning tower, more likely. You should never go by appearances. Look, you haven't eaten your cake. What did you call it?'

'A *réligieuse*.'

'Why is it called that?'

'It's like a nun with her coif.'

'Bite her coif off then.'

'All right.' She giggled.

'You could eat half-a-dozen of those and it wouldn't make any difference to you.' The girl was on the edge of painful thinness. 'You haven't any problems with your weight.'

'Not with my weight.' She ate obediently, like a child.

Karin lay awake for a long time in bed that night, thinking of the girl in the adjoining room. It was as well they weren't together. It was as if they existed on separate islands, not fully trusting each other.

It was difficult to sort out her thoughts fairly between Gerald and Barbara. Her own mood was lowered because of him, and that in itself might make her imagine or see too much in Barbara's behaviour. There was no doubt her problems were real enough: her mother dead, a broken marriage, the loss of the child.

Mine is a flea-bite in comparison, she thought. She knew through her job the terrible despair which existed below the surface in some marriages, the recriminations, the misunderstandings, the jealousy, the hate. Children often made the situation worse since they were victims too. We'll have to sort out our problems before we have any, she told herself.

She was sure Barbara was holding back something.

Hadn't she experienced this feeling often when clients came in, sat down, wasted half-an-hour talking about trivialities, and only when she said, 'Shall we leave it there for the time being?' did they let it all spill out. As Barbara had done this afternoon . . . but had she? The man she'd talked of wasn't important, or if he was, she was capable of dealing with him. The crux of her problem had been reached at the end when she'd talked about losing the baby. *How* had she lost it?

No one tells the truth, the whole truth and nothing but the truth, she cautioned herself. You hardly ever tell the truth to yourself about Gerald although you're aware of the dichotomy. There's the Karin who wants to be loved and cherished, and the other Karin who wants to run her own life. You should have discussed this dichotomy with him before; you didn't strip yourself down to the bone of truth. You should have bared your soul as well as your body.

She suddenly heard a noise from the other room, a choking, a gasping, like someone being sick. She was out of bed in a flash, reaching for her dressing-gown, when she stopped herself. This was another island, a private person. If Barbara wanted help, she'd call. She herself had no territorial rights. She wasn't happy with that. If I hear another noise, she told herself, I'll knock on her door . . .

She sat tensely on the side of the bed until her feet were like ice, but she heard nothing more. At last she gave in and crept between the sheets. Just as she was turning on her side into her favourite sleeping position, she heard another noise, no retching this time, but for all the world like a loud sigh, and then what sounded like a distant humming of some kind of tune. A shudder of fear went through her. She lay rigid, listening.

It was the wind moaning. Relief flooded her. Of course that's what it was. It had sprung up suddenly, and as if to justify this thought the wooden shutters in her room rattled and an eddy of cold air played on her face. She was wide awake now. Or had it been a seagull? She heard a faint mewing, remembering how she'd seen them circling above the tall houses as if seeking refuge from the wind. She sat up and switched on the bedside light, lifted the book from the table which Barbara had given her when she'd said she might want some light relief from her paper-work.

Jacques Prévert, she read. *Paroles*. Poems by a Frenchman. Not in her line of country at all. What a French face he had, the low jowls, round cheeks, the bold nose, and the ubiquitous flat cap. She flicked through the pages and it fell open as if it had done so before. She said the words slowly, translating as she went:

Rappelle-toi, Barbara, N'oublie pas . . . Do you remember, Barbara. Don't forget . . .

Why did the words strike such a strange chord inside her? She sat up in bed, her black hair rumpled, her face wan from lack of sleep and felt the sadness around her, as if the girl next door were surrounded by an aura of sadness which had crept like a vapour through to her. She put her hand to her mouth in the grip of a deep unease, something inexplicable, pervading, and connected with Barbara.

The next day she wondered why she'd been so stupid. Barbara was downstairs before her, and she waved, smiling from their table. She was pale, but unusually cheerful. When Karin sat down opposite her she said, 'I hope I didn't disturb you last night. I have a stomach which doesn't stand too much wine. I must have overindulged.'

'I nearly came in. I was worried.'

'I'm glad you didn't. I'm fine now. What do you think we should do today? We've to catch the one forty-five boat. It's been far too short, but I expect you're regretting it already.'

Karin, tetchy from lack of sleep said, buttering her croissant, 'I told you before it was my idea.' She might well have struck the girl across the face with a whip, judging by the effect of her words. She winced, apprehension flooded her face with colour, her mouth trembled. Karin was mortified at her clumsiness. 'Next time we'll plan it better and have longer.' *Nothing* would persuade her . . . she made herself smile. 'You've whetted my appetite for Normandy.'

'I'm glad.' The colour had gone, she was deathly pale, but she spoke gaily. 'There's Honfleur, although it's too determinedly touristy now, but beyond Cabourg, where the little resorts are, is my favourite part, Franceville, Ouistreham, Lion-sur-mer . . .'

'Is that the coast the landing beaches are on?'

'Yes, but I don't think of the war. Nor of when grandfather was killed.'

'Norman Sanctuary?'

'Yes. He never knew it as I did at *grand-mère's* house. I think of when I was a schoolgirl there, the long hot summers . . . how sunlit they are in my memory . . . the warm grainy sand between my toes in the dunes, or hard and damp when I ran down to the sea. And shrimping and collecting cockle shells; there are millions when the tide goes out. And bathing when *grand-mère* said the tide was right. We had a bathing cabin, larger than the others. She used to . . . *preside* there, that's the word, wearing her broad brimmed straw hat because she didn't want to have her complexion ruined . . . it was like Limoges china. And she'd see that Sophie, that was her maid, had hot chocolate ready for me when I came running out, and wrap me in a soft towel. She was regal, small and delicate-looking with narrow hands and feet, but she created atmosphere . . . my God, how she could do that!' The voice was bitter, then it changed.

'Some people, like my Aunt Berthe, for instance, say they like it inland, the *Pays D'Auge*, and that's nice too: thatched barns, shaggy horses, cows, orchards, orchards and more orchards; one thinks of a pink mass, no green. Or apples, as if they'd been polished. But the sea's better. I could show you secret places where I played.' She looked shyly at Karin. 'That is, if we came back.'

'Oh, we'll do that sometime.' Not if she could help it. 'There's only time to do our shopping, worse luck. I want to take back some wine, and tins. Where's the best place?'

'The cheapest is the hypermarket on the Rouen Road,

but I wouldn't even attempt that if I were you. There's no way of getting out and back in time.'

'I wouldn't risk it without a car. Besides, there are plenty of shops in the town. Are *you* buying any wine?'

'No, there's no point. I drink so little.' What about last night's upset, Karin thought. 'But I'll come with you, if you like.'

'Have you anything to do?'

'I'd like to go back to that junk shop where we saw the earrings.' She looked slightly pink, and shy.

'Don't tell me you've succumbed and you're going to treat yourself?'

'Maybe.' Her eyes were hidden by a heavy swatch of hair. 'Let me pour you some coffee.'

The morning dribbled away through their fingers. They had to have a look at St. Jacques Church to see the rose window and the carving, and have a last coffee upstairs in the Tribunaux before they went back to the hotel to pay the bill and collect their cases. It was getting on for midday when they were leaving again.

'There isn't a lot of time for shopping.' Barbara looked doubtful. 'We'll have to be there half an hour before the boat leaves.'

'One fifteen? Why don't we go our separate ways?' Karin said. 'You go off to your *Brocanteur*, isn't that what you call it, and I'll get my wine, etcetera. We'll meet at the boat.'

'Are you sure you'll manage on your own?'

'You couldn't be questioning my command of the French language?'

'I meant if you got lost.' What a pretty girl she was when she smiled!

'You can point me in the right direction. One fifteen, then, at the boat.'

It was a relief to be on her own, even for a short time. Barbara had become too much of a puzzle for her with her sudden changes of mood. But eight years was a long time, she told herself. A lot could have happened. A lot had happened to *her*: university, Saithe and Saithe, Gerald . . . her heart gave a sudden twist at the thought of him.

She found a good shop in the Grande Rue where the young man took a more than casual interest in her, and she pretended to take more than a casual interest in him because he could speak excellent English. He sold her two bottles of *Côtes du Rhône*, told her he was a German student from Frankfurt on a working holiday and asked if she were staying long. She said no, unfortunately, giving him a sad blue beam, and asked him to direct her to a delicatessen. At *Gamard's* she filled a plastic bag with tins of *rillettes, pâtés, quenelles, cassoulet*, and such like, all with such speed that without hurrying she was at the *Quai Henri IV*, had climbed the stairway, shown her passport and stationed herself at the foot of the passenger gangway by one o'clock.

She wasn't surprised that she was first. She was early, and she stood waiting, her case by her side, the two plastic bags of groceries and wine leaning against it, feeling comparatively pleased with life. What was it Barbara had said when she was talking about the house where she lived in Surbiton? Something about there being nothing nicer than a good shop, putting away the stuff, having a cup of tea . . .

It was the kind of feeling Gerald would like her to have. Men got on with their jobs, but expected their wives to give up a hard-won career and wallow in domesticity to suit them. You're not being fair, she told herself. He only wanted you to *entertain* the idea. And you shouted at him that it should be a thing of your own choice, not a demand. Then you both shouted. Her heart twisted again. She remembered his pale face, the misery in his eyes.

People were beginning to go up the gangway now, trailing in twos and threes; then there was a lull. She looked at her watch: five past one. No need to get worried. Barbara had only to walk from that little square behind the Rue de la Barre. But when it was half-past one and still no Barbara she spoke to the officer at the gangway who'd been glancing at her from time to time. 'I'm waiting for a girl friend. It's getting near the time of departure. One forty-five, isn't it?'

He nodded. 'She wouldn't have gone on board?' He had a sharp profile, a big chin and nose with a long smile which seemed to get lost between them.

'I don't thing so. I said one fifteen at the boat.' Perhaps she should have said, 'at the gangway'.

'What was she like?' the man said. 'As pretty as you?' The smile came and went, a wolfish smile.

She hadn't time for this. 'Quite different. Sort of . . . silver hair . . .' that made her sound like an old woman . . . 'no, not silver, gun-metal.' She had to smile at him then, 'very slim, wearing a navy-blue duffle coat and a grey pleated skirt'.

'I'm pretty sure I saw someone answering to that description. I think you'll find her there already.'

'Do you think so?' She was hesitant about boarding. The minutes were like hours. At one forty-two there was no sign of Barbara, and the officer was beginning to loosen the netting round the gangway with the help of a sailor.

She made up her mind, and lifting the plastic bags in one hand and her case in the other, made her way precariously along it. She'd find Barbara already on the ship. She'd be standing near the passenger entrance. That was one good thing about not being in a car; there wasn't that steep climb upstairs from the bowels of the ship.

But she wasn't there. Her first feeling was of intense irritation. She hovered at the foot of the gangway, watched the last passenger hurry abroad, felt the ship moving under her before she would give in. She saw the officer sliding past, no face, just a wide grin. I'll wring her neck, she thought, fanning her irritation. She'd have to start combing the boat now. But they'd meet any minute and then laugh and say to each other, 'Where did you get to?'

She went through the ship, including the ladies' toilets and the bars, and then, realizing it would be better to become stationary, collected her bags and case and went to the same bar lounge they'd been in on the outward crossing. Occasionally she found difficulty in breathing. I won't allow myself to become afraid, she told herself.

But an hour later she *was* afraid. She had an ache in her shoulders through keeping herself from trembling. It was so damnably irresponsible of Barbara to do this. She got up when she couldn't bear sitting any longer and made her way to the purser's office to ask his help. Halfway there she met a woman wearing a duffle coat and a grey skirt, a middle-aged woman with grey hair. She had to accept it: Barbara was not on the boat.

Newhaven is not the best of towns in which to kill time on a winter's evening; unlike its bigger neighbour, Brighton. Karin hung about waiting for the next boat from Dieppe, the last one that night, in a strange mixture of annoyance with herself for getting into a situation like this and annoyance at Barbara, which towards nine o'clock became a kind of foreboding centred in the pit of her stomach. And above all, a feeling of inevitability. Something like this had been bound to happen. She'd known it in her bones.

At first she walked aimlessly about the shopping centre, peering sightlessly through the windows, but when the lights went out there, she sat in a small hotel bar in the main street and tried to be reasonable about the whole business. It was a damned nuisance, that was all. She would have been better not to have set off on this foolhardy expedition with a girl she hadn't seen for so long, but however she rationalized her feelings, she was always left with the same deep sense of unease.

She could have sworn that Barbara had every intention of catching the boat. She knew exactly where the junk shop was. She had even cautioned Karin not to venture out of town to the hypermarket in case *she* missed the boat. What, then, had prevented her? As the coffee grew colder in her cup, (she hadn't wanted a drink), and the feeling of being the only one alive in the whole place became stronger, Karin's conviction grew. Barbara wouldn't be on the next boat either . . .

But long before it was due, she had left the hotel and made her way once more to the docks, her plastic bags and weekend case growing heavier by the minute. Everything had a *déja vu* feeling by this time. There were few people about. The place wasn't too well-lit. Even the word 'docks' had a seamy sound. One thought of knifings in the dark, the splash of a body falling into the water. She was hungry, tired and dispirited.

She watched the few passengers on foot coming through the customs barrier, tired men with tired suits and heavy suitcases, possibly reps, a British family with two crying children, three red-faced Frenchmen chattering unintelligibly, but no one remotely like Barbara – a slight girl in a grey pleated skirt and navy blue duffle coat. The purser came off last, carrying a suitcase, then trailing far behind a lone Pakistani in workman's overalls. A few cars appeared and disappeared, their rear lights twinkling red; the official shut the barrier. The boat was empty.

She had been unsuccessful in finding a taxi in the town, but now she saw one cruising outside the dock gates, looking for night fares. She hailed it, and sank back into the seat, momentarily exhausted, dropping the case and the plastic bags on the floor beside her.

'You didn't tell me where to, Miss,' the man said, partially sliding back the glass divider.

'Sorry.' Leaning forward, she spoke through the small aperture. Taxi drivers were careful nowadays. 'The police station.' She was following the advice of the purser on the *Valençay*.

CHAPTER THREE

The sergeant at the police station was sympathetic, but not inclined to take the matter too seriously. He agreed that to miss two boats was unusual, but he was sure there would be a perfectly good explanation. Karin thought he was trying to reassure her.

'What steps can you take meantime?' she asked him, her voice sharp with tiredness.

'We can check at the other ports to see if anyone answering to your friend's description went through. You don't think that Mrs Charles . . . it's a pity you don't know her married name . . . would go back to the hotel where you stayed, assuming she missed the two boats for some reason?'

'She's not a fool,' Karin said. 'Wouldn't she have telephoned the port authorities, or even here, if something had happened?' She steadied her voice.

'That's so,' he agreed. 'Or the police in Dieppe would have taken care of that . . . if something had gone wrong.'

'It's possible she could have had an accident, isn't it?'

'Yes, but the same would apply. The hospital authorities would get in touch with the police.'

'Unless she was unable to tell them anything?'

'We don't want to take too gloomy a view, do we?' She had to say it. 'She might have been . . . molested'

'In daylight? Anything's possible nowadays, but wouldn't people have seen it happening? And they or she reported it? I think you'll find she's been delayed in some way. I know it's worrying for you. Where was your friend going when you parted company?'

'That at least I can tell you.' She felt more cheerful. 'She was going to buy earrings . . . I know where the shop was, but I'm afraid I can't tell you the address' She had a thought. 'I could identify it on the map.'

'Mabel,' he turned to a stout girl in uniform at a desk behind him, 'get us a map of Dieppe, if you don't mind.'

'Yes, Sir.'

Karin's map-reading had always impressed Gerald. It seemed to impress the sergeant too as she quickly found the location of the shop.

'Now we're getting somewhere.' He wrote down the name of the little square behind the Rue de la Barre. 'I'll pass on this information to the French authorities. I think you'll find she's done something simple like twisting her ankle . . . unless,' he fixed Karin with a worldly look, 'she had no intention of coming back with you in the first place?'

'But she had, she had every intention!' She stifled her anger. 'It was I who suggested splitting up because we both had shopping to do.' No one liked the idea of having been conned, she thought. But there had been Barbara's evasiveness, her reticence . . .

'Had she any relatives in France?'

'Her mother was French, but she's dead. She talked about her grandparents, but they're dead too.' Her paternal grandmother? But that had all been vague, a pink carpet, a pink clove smell . . . 'I know her grandfather was killed in the Normandy landings,' she said, thinking, how totally irrelevant that is. I must be tired.

'Any boy friends?'

'I don't think so.' I don't know, she confessed to herself. 'Not there anyhow. But she told me about the man she lived with in Surbiton.'

'Have you got his address?' he asked, pencil poised.

'I don't know that either, nor his name.' She saw him looking at her. 'We didn't know much about each other. We were at school together but we hadn't met for eight years and then she phoned me out of the blue to say she'd like to meet me because she was in London. The Dieppe weekend grew out of that. I don't know who really suggested it; it seemed like a good idea.'

'Phoned you out of the blue, did she?'
'Yes.'
'And speaks French well, I suppose, since she had a French mother?'
'Yes.'
'You didn't think you were . . .' he twirled his pencil on his notebook so that it stood upright like a ballet dancer, 'not to put too fine a point on it . . .'
'Yes?' She knew where he was leading.
' . . . being used?'
'But that's ridiculous! The fact that she speaks French well, is at home in France, she told me that herself, makes it all the more unnecessary to need someone to go with.'
'A cover can be useful.' He must be thinking of drugs.
'People do act on impulse, you know, I mean her getting in touch with me. She intended to go to Dieppe in any case; I only joined up with her.'
'Well, that makes a difference, certainly.'
'No, it was purely for old times' sake. If you'd been at a girls' boarding school,' she saw him flinch at the joke, 'you'd understand. There's a special kind of bond.'
'Well, I wouldn't know about that.' Maybe she should inspire him with a little confidence in her.
'I should tell you I'm a solicitor.'
He raised his eyebrows, nodded. 'You'll have the legal mind, then. My advice to you is to go into the waiting room and I'll get Officer Cartwright to bring you a cup of coffee and a sandwich while I get on the blower. My guess is it'll be something or nothing. And if there's nothing to worry about, there's nothing to prevent your friend phoning the Sealink offices and leaving a message for you, or here for that matter. Is there?'
She had to give round one to him. She did what he asked, and chatted with the policewoman from the office who brought her a tray with coffee and ham sandwiches. 'I didn't want to eat at first. Now I'm starving,' she confessed. 'Thanks.'
'It'll do you good,' the young woman said. 'Worrying,

isn't it, when things go wrong on an outing.'

'Yes, when you least expect it.' She took a sip. 'Lovely coffee.'

'Try a sandwich; they're fresh.' She looked as if she'd been buttoned firmly into her uniform with a button-hook. She had stout legs in sheer black stockings and flat shoes. 'You'd be surprised how many missing people turn up after a few hours with a perfectly good story. It's usually their friends,' her eyes rested briefly on Karin, 'who've got it wrong at the beginning.' Karin took a bite from her sandwich. She suddenly and acutely wanted Gerald.

At the end of an hour the sergeant came back and asked her to come into his room again. He had completed most of his enquiries. The only matter outstanding was that of the junk shop. The French police had sent an officer to see the owner. They'd be ringing any minute. As if on cue they rang. The sergeant lifted the receiver, she saw him nod, nod again, and again, heard him change to 'Mmm, mmm,' then a final 'thank you.' The receiver clicked into place.

'They've seen the man,' he said. 'He remembers a young lady answering to your description coming in and buying a pair of ivory earrings. She said they were for a friend.' Karin was touched in the midst of her anxiety. That was the real Barbara, surely.

'Did he say how she looked?'

'There was nothing unusual or the police would have got it out of him.'

'And when was she there?'

'Just after twelve, he thinks. He shuts for lunch at one and doesn't open till three.'

'Then she'd plenty of time to get back to the boat.'

'That's it, Mrs Armstrong. And they say it's a pretty busy route back too, so no problems from mugging *there*.' He drew a line under his notes, clasped his hands on top of them. 'We've drawn a blank everywhere else. She didn't go back to the hotel, and she hasn't phoned either the shipping office or here. And she hasn't been admitted to the hospital nor has any accident been reported.' There was the look again. 'You're sure she didn't mention anyone she knew there with whom she might have stayed?'

'Not in Dieppe. Her grandmother used to live on the Normandy coast, but she said she'd decided not to go back there. It was all in the past. But if she'd had any other plans I'm sure she would have told me. It was simply a weekend trip. We were going back together; it was all arranged.' And feeling she was protesting too much she still went on talking. 'Besides, she isn't *like* that. She wouldn't cause me any anxiety.' But she had.

'You said you didn't know her very well.'

'We were at school together, that's all. But there's a certain loyalty . . .' I'll be bursting into the school song, next . . . 'Do you want me to wait on here in Newhaven?' She didn't relish the idea: coast towns in winter were ghost towns. All she wanted was to be back in the security of her own flat.

'No need.' The sergeant looked at his watch. 'You've missed the last train. Have you a car?'

'No.'

'Would you like to phone your husband and ask him to come and pick you up? You'll be tired.'

She longed to do that, to be ushered away in his sheltering arms . . . but wishful thinking got you nowhere. He was more likely to gloat at the mess she was in . . . no, that was unfair. She was tired, couldn't think straight. 'He's a busy doctor: I doubt if he could come.'

'Not to worry. We'll run you to Brighton. You'll catch a train there all right. All we need from you for the moment are a few particulars.'

'All right.'

'We've got your name and address. Your business address and telephone number, if you don't mind. Ah, yes, Saithe and Saithe.' Her stock was going steadily upwards. 'And you've already given me a description of the missing young lady. Barbara Charles isn't her married name, you say?'

'No, but since she's divorced she may still use it.'

'You didn't mention her father. Is he still alive?'

'No, he died when she was eight.' Everyone connected with Barbara seemed to be dead. Hadn't she mentioned an aunt? Leave it, she told herself, it's too vague.

'And her own address? No, you said you didn't know that either.' He smoothed out his face.

'It was Surbiton. She told me she lived with a man there, in a house, not a flat.'

'But you don't know his name or address either?'

'No, I'm afraid not.' She didn't meet his look.

'Pity we haven't his address; he'll be wanting to know why she hasn't come home before long. Maybe a quarrel there.' He chewed his lip. 'Yes, it's a pity . . .'

'I know. I'm sorry.' She knew only too well how it all sounded. 'I told you we'd met after a long time. You see, in my job, as in yours, I have to ask a lot of questions; in private life I have to watch I don't carry it over.'

He accepted that. 'But she didn't give much away, did she?'

Karin felt protective. 'She wasn't a talkative girl. Perhaps a little . . . reticent.'

'Reticent, was she?' She could almost see his ears go up.

'She was like that at school. It's . . . how she is.' But she hadn't been distrait then, or apprehensive, or fearful.

'Did anything, let's say, worrying, occur when you were with her, something that would give you an indicator? We have to bear in mind loss of memory. It doesn't happen as often as it does in books, but we have to bear it in mind.'

She immediately thought of last night, when she'd heard Barbara being sick. That had been worrying, she admitted it now. She remembered worrying half the night in that bedroom, and how at five in the morning when the mewing of the seagulls stopped and the dawn chorus began, she'd opened the windows on to the balcony and looked about her. How alien the tall French houses opposite had seemed, their decorated mansards . . .

And there was that strange humming noise Barbara had made. Why had such an ordinarily happy sound sent a shiver of fear through her? Barbara wasn't *crazy*, was she? She hadn't . . . *injured* someone, (you're thinking of 'murdered', aren't you?); had she in her twisted mind thought what a good cover-up it would be to have a seemingly blameless weekend with an old schoolfriend . . . she saw the sergeant looking at her. She was tired, not thinking straight.

'Anything at all?' He was waiting.

'No, nothing.' She was good at looking people straight in the eye. Young Mr Saithe, Reginald of the kinky hair, called it 'Karin's blue beam' and said it was worth a fortune to the firm because it established their credibility. 'Your loss of memory idea might be right, though. I could give you the name of the school we went to; they'd be able to put you in touch with her guardian.' She should have mentioned that before.

'She had one?'

'Yes, I've just remembered. Her mother stopped visiting when Barbara was older. I suppose she was ill, or abroad. He used to come and take some of us to tea with Barbara. Mr Keble, he was called, a bachelor.'

'Thanks very much, Mrs Armstrong. I'll act on your advice.' He got up. 'We'll keep in touch.'

She slept all the way in the train up to Victoria. She hadn't realized how exhausted questioning made you. She must remember that when she was dealing with her next client.

She thought of phoning Gerald when she got into the flat, but she couldn't keep her eyes open. Besides, hadn't she said on that last night when they'd quarrelled so bitterly that she could manage without him? She undressed slowly, dizzy with tiredness. It didn't look like she was managing very well.

CHAPTER FOUR

It was a relief next morning to get into office dress: her navy suit, her high-heeled court shoes. As she was fixing gold hoops in her ears at the mirror, she thought of the ivory earrings which she now knew Barbara had gone to buy for her. Her fears about the girl's sanity seemed nonsense in the light of day. Surely her only motive when she phoned was to ask for advice, especially as she knew Karin was a solicitor.

What, then, had made her miss the boat, two boats? There had been a bizarre, mysterious quality about the whole weekend. She remembered how in spite of her anxiety there had been no real surprise when Barbara had failed to turn up. And as she thought of the girl's sad, pale face, the creeping sense of unease came back again, the fear. Some people didn't seek out unhappiness; they drew it towards them.

Barbara had been . . . why was she putting it in the past tense . . . a girl who lived in the past, who looked haunted by it. Her description of long-ago holidays on the Normandy coast had been so real that listening to her you could almost feel the sun and the sea-wind on your face. But she hadn't wanted to go back. 'It hurts,' she'd said. 'It's better just to remember.' I wonder, Karin thought now, if she lived in the past because she was afraid of the present. There was something she was running away from, which gave her bad dreams . . . she remembered with a shiver the sound of Barbara humming, that queer, lilting sound, other-worldly . . .

The gold hoops gleamed in the mirror as she shook her head impatiently. She mustn't allow herself to become too imaginative. She set about making up her eyes as a form of therapy, squinted at the result. 'My bug-eyed monster' Gerald had sometimes called her. He liked her made up, saying it was a relief after seeing so many pale people lying supine. There was a small core of bitterness when she thought of him; it ate into her heart like acid on metal. Was it aggravated by the fact that he hadn't bombarded her with telephone calls, pleaded with her? She breathed deeply, straightened the collar of her silk shirt on the lapels of her suit, picked up her briefcase and left the flat.

Hampstead was breezy as she drove down the hill into the pit, her name for the City on her off-days, and as usual it was seething as if it had been stirred by a giant stick. The streets were packed with solid blocks of people, slanted forward, shades of Lowry, in their effort to hurry; black slanting strokes occasionally topped by the mushroom of an umbrella. The sky oozed rain rather than threw it down, everything was in monochrome, a typical February day. Taxis darted in and out between cars with cheeky agility, irate drivers hooted at them; the morning race was on.

If I were a fey sort of person, she thought, I could convince myself that the weekend in Dieppe never happened at all, or that I'd had a three days amnesia. Or was the sergeant right and it was *Barbara* who'd lost her memory? It fitted. She could be imagined wandering, lost . . . but wouldn't someone have found her, taken her to hospital? It depended who found her. The deep unease, familiar now, was back again. She heard a car's horn loud in her ear and looked sideways to see a man gesticulating at her, red-faced with anger. She gave him an airy wave and bent her mind on the traffic, but before long it was back on Barbara again.

Barbara . . . *Rappelle-toi* . . . A pale-faced girl with pale hair, pointed face and narrow hands . . . you couldn't imagine her in an ordinary work situation like this, driving to a city office, or going to her job in the Surbiton estate agents . . . estate agents! She grimaced at the wheel, annoyed at her own stupidity: she'd forgotten to tell the sergeant that. She prided herself on her memory when dealing with clients, but, then, she wasn't emotionally involved.

I shan't have a moment's peace until I know where she is, she thought, as she parked her car in the mews which was totally occupied by Saithe and Saithe's office. But when I hear she's all right I'll make sure I don't repeat the experiment. I shouldn't have gone in the first place if I hadn't been missing Gerald so much . . .

She went straight to her room and rang for Bella, her secretary. She came in with her quick little steps, her blonde hair tied back with a brown chiffon scarf, and wearing a jersey and skirt in the camel colour she favoured. She always reminded Karin of a palomino pony.

'Mrs Smithers is waiting, Karin,' she said.

'I know. I told her nine o'clock. Give her a cup of coffee while you do something for me, if you would. I want you to get in touch with all the estate agents in Surbiton, and when you find the one who employed Barbara Charles . . .' she waited while Bella scribbled in her notebook . . . 'put them through. If there's a lot, use a pin. You're always lucky with the office draw.'

'Right. Do *you* want a cup?'

'No, I'll look over the Smithers file while you're busy.'

'I'll get on with those calls then.'

'Thanks. If it takes you longer than ten minutes, scrap it for the time being. I don't want to keep Mrs Smithers waiting too long.'

In five minutes her desk telephone rang. 'I'm putting them through,' Bella said. 'Jaikes and Belham. Got them on the second go.'

'You've the luck of the gods. Thanks.' She waited, heard a girl's voice.

'Jaikes and Belham here. Can I help you?'

'May I speak to Mr Jaikes, please?'

'There isn't a Mr Jaikes. Nor a Mr Balham for that matter.' She sounded pert.

'The head clerk then, please. It's Saithe and Saithe here,

solicitors, Ludgate Hill.'

'I'll get him,' she said quickly. 'It's Mr Perfect.' In a minute or two she heard a man's booming voice in her ear, the one which convinced clients they'd found their dream house, she thought. 'Mr Perfect here,' he said.

'Good-morning, Mr Per*fect*.' He'd emphasized the second syllable. 'This is Karin Armstrong. I wonder if you could help me with a personal matter.'

'Certainly.' She could hear the caginess.

'I'm trying to trace a friend of mine, Barbara Charles, who worked with you in a temporary capacity, I believe.'

'Barbara Charles?' he repeated doubtfully; then, 'Oh, yes, Barbara *Charles*, a thin girl, big eyes, greyish hair. Yes, I remember. She worked here over Christmas. Very competent; quiet. Wish we could get more like her. Didn't want to rush away at five o'clock like the rest of them. When we needed extra help a few weeks later we got in touch with her again, but she said she wasn't available.'

'Could you give me her addres, Mr Perfect?'

'Is it a legal matter?' He was cagey again.

'No, no. I was at school with her. I just want to get in touch. Old Girls' Reunion sort of thing.' In a way.

'Just a minute, Ms Armstrong –

He was back in a second. 'I've got it. Miss Barbara Charles, 7, Easton Grove, Surbiton. If you see her, tell her she'll always get a job with Jaikes and Balham. We don't get many of her kind nowadays: industrious, anxious to please, quiet . . .'

'Yes, that's Barbara. Thank you very much for your help.' She hung up and immediately dialled the Newhaven Police Station. She was lucky to get through right away. 'This is Karin Armstrong. May I speak to the officer who interviewed me yesterday?'

'Speaking, Mrs Armstrong.'

'Oh, good morning, Sergeant. Have you any news of my friend?'

'Nothing, I'm afraid. But I think you can take it that no news is good news.'

She didn't see why. 'I remembered afterwards that she said she'd worked in an estate agent's office in Surbiton, and I phoned them this morning and got her address. I hope you don't mind me jumping the gun.'

'Not at all. It would be better if I rang the station there. Can I have the young lady's address?'

She repeated it to him. 'Would you ring me here if you get any information?' she asked. 'I'm very anxious.'

'I can understand that, but it'll sort itself out. My guess is there's been a complete misunderstanding and we'll find her safe and sound in her own home.'

'I hope so. Thank you for all the trouble you've gone to.'

She hung up and dialled Bella. 'Send in Mrs Smithers right away, please.'

Ruby Smithers had looked very put upon when she first called to see Karin, and it was the same today. She'd taken umbrage. Karin smiled at her. 'Have a seat, Mrs Smithers. I'm sorry to have kept you waiting.'

'It's all right,' she said, looking more put upon than ever. 'I was here at half-past eight, only bus I could get. The cleaners were still at it . . .' All the lines of her face turned downwards; the curve of her mouth echoed the sad curve of her lank hair.

'I'm so sorry. Now, on your last visit I asked you to go over carefully in your mind all that has happened between you and your husband, with dates if you could remember them: that is, the incidents which led you to seek for a divorce. Have you managed to do that?'

'Yes,' Mrs Smithers said confidently, surprising Karin. 'I kept a diary, you see, and I got into the habit of writing it up every night. I had plenty of time, him always out enjoying himself. It was a miserable life, Mrs Armstrong, the lies he told about working late and then me finding out about that woman . . .' That woman, Karin thought. How many times have I heard that phrase? She had no worries on that score. Or had she?

'Thanks, Mrs Smithers.' She took the neatly-clipped foolscap pages. 'Your diary must have been very useful.'

The statement was beautifully typed, properly tabulated under the various dates. 'You've made a good job of this.'

'Well, it's easy for me, you see. I'm a typist, like your one outside; properly trained. And I've got a nice electric typewriter. That's what I often said to Freddie. "I don't spend my money on frivolities," I said. The only expensive thing I ever bought was my typewriter, and that was on H.P. out of my housekeeping. I've turned the little bedroom over the door into my office and I take in work. You can get plenty around our district . . . reps, little businesses who can't afford fulltime help.' Her eyes lit up. 'I could set myself up with a nice little business myself if I could keep the house, maybe expand into duplicating and photo-copying and that kind of thing . . . I love office equipment, hardware it's called now, maybe take on an assistant.' She sat back triumphantly. She sounded fonder of her typewriter than her husband.

'Right, Mrs Smithers. We'll start at the beginning and work through this, item by item. Then from it I'll make out your legal petition.' She began to read.

'On the 20th March 1980, I was sitting up in bed reading when I heard my husband's car, a Toyota Corolla. I looked at my battery-operated bedside alarm. It was twenty to one. When he came into the bedroom he was the worse for drink and he said, "Why the hell aren't you sleeping at this time of night?" It was morning, really.

"I've been waiting for you," I said. "You know I can't sleep until you come in." He swore at me. The words were, "Bloody bitch. Nothing bloody well to come in for . . ."

'I didn't like writing that,' Mrs Smithers said, looking self-righteous, 'but you have to tell the truth. It's all there in my diary.'

So it seemed. Karin worked through the statement with her, marvelling at the detail. Mrs Smithers seemed to have two valuable attributes: an accurate bedside alarm and complete recall.

'You've certainly left nothing out,' Karin said, looking up at her.

The woman looked pleased. 'I have a good memory. You have to have in office work, a trained memory. I never missed one night writing up my diary. And then I don't need much sleep,' she smiled coyly, 'as long as I have an occasional cuppa from my tea-maker.' Karin hid a smile.

The picture which emerged was common enough, the worm turning, the husband finding another woman. But was it? The picture, or indeed proof that the other woman existed, was extremely vague. Could Mrs Smithers be a pathological liar? 'Never go by appearances,' was one of old Reggie's dictums. 'Remember Crippen.' She looked at her watch, and stood up, smiling warmly.

'Everything seems most satisfactory. I'll get the petition off to you as soon as possible. You've made my job comparatively easy, Mrs Smithers.'

'It's my office training, you see.' She sniffed as she gathered up her handbag and gloves. Her back was depressing as she went out of the room. She had no bottom, or at least no curves showed beneath her coat. And her hair was pillow-flattened at the back. Her attention to detail didn't apply to her appearance.

The day passed quickly and Karin was glad of it. Routine was good discipline for an unquiet mind. She had a business lunch with another solicitor, then she saw three more clients on her afternoon schedule. Was the whole world seeking divorce? Young Reginald had said he'd take her off it if she ever felt she'd had a basinful, but neither conveyancing nor crime appealed to her; one was dull and the other sleazy. Besides she was no Portia, she told young Reginald, who was in fact forty, so-called to distinguish him from his father, old Reginald, who was sixty-two.

But like a grey shadow, the thought of Barbara had been there while she worked. She remembered the soft touch of her hand when she'd said at the bar, 'Can I help?', how all sign of maturity disappeared from her face when she giggled, which was disarming. But above all she remembered the aura of sadness which had surrounded her. She had a leaping sense of relief when Bella put through an outside call to her. 'Newhaven Police, Karin.'

'Hello, Mrs Armstrong.' She heard the sergeant's voice. 'I hoped I'd catch you before you left your office.'

'Any news?'

'The Surbition station located your friend's place all right: a block of flats . . .'

'A block of flats!' She interrupted him. 'But she told me . . . I understood she lived in a house, a house with a garden . . .'

'Someone's got it wrong.' He sounded ever so slightly amused which she didn't like. 'Well, we'll give Mrs Charles the benefit of the doubt. The officer made enquiries at the address you gave us and she's known there. She exists all right.' He gave a little snort as if this was the first proof he'd had of Barbara's identity.

'Did he actually see her flat?'

'He saw one which had her name under the bell, but no one was at home. He spoke to an elderly lady living in the flat below. She knew your friend, said she was a quiet pleasant girl of an aloof disposition and that she hadn't seen her about for a few days.'

'Where do we go from there, Sergeant?' The fear was back. She could feel the squeezing pain beneath her ribs.

'It's over to the French for the time being. They're continuing their enquiries, and the officer at Surbiton will make routine calls at the flat in the hope of finding her there. She hasn't done anything wrong, Mrs Armstrong, except in a manner of speaking, to you, by letting you down. If there's been any foul play in Dieppe, rest assured they'll let us know.'

'There's no way of checking if she did come back, through the purser, for instance?'

'We've asked them to look out, of course, but so far, no luck. From your description she wasn't a young woman who exactly drew attention to herself; quiet, of an aloof disposition, the lady at her Surbiton address said . . .'

'Yes. I said I'd give you my home telephone number.'

She repeated it to him 'Don't worry what time you call me, even if it's very late.'

'We'll keep the file open, of course.'

But she wasn't satisfied. She drove home to her flat turning over the problem like worry beads. *Where was Barbara?* People went missing every day of the week, often from choice. But surely not in the way she'd done it?

Are you annoyed that you may have been used? she asked herself, but if she were, it was a very small part of how she felt. She was haunted by the thought of the girl wandering about, nameless, homeless.

Had she lied? Was she ever married? She had only Barbara's word for it . . . just as she had only Mrs Smithers' word; her diaries could have been sheer fabrication. But Barbara hadn't been a liar at school. Schoolgirls were a discerning lot, unreliability showed through in so many ways: in games, in dormitories, reputations were made and unmade by one's conduct, closely observed in a small, contained world.

I miss Gerald, she thought, letting herself into the empty flat. I miss him as an ear, if nothing else, right at this minute. There were signs of him all around, medical books on the shelves, his African head plaques he'd put up on the wall . . . the intelligent man's flying ducks, she'd told him . . . the scatter cushions he'd bought for the divan. He was a homemaker. He'd put up all the shelves, cut the rattan blinds to size and hung them, taken the door off its hinges and shaved it to let it open over their new shag-pile carpet. He'd make a good house-person. I should have said, 'You stay at home studying and I'll go out to work.' She enjoyed picturing his face, and with that came a longing for him, rising like a tide.

He was such a good lover. He said it was because he was medical; he knew all her erogenous zones, unusual ones like the sole of her left foot. He had to creep down the bed to stroke it softly with a forefinger, slide slowly down her naked length which was the really erotic bit, not the sole-stroking of her left foot. He probably knew that too. Gerald, so knowledgeable, and yet so ingenuous; his belief that a miracle would happen every time they made love and it did, nearly . . . 'I want you . . .' she said it aloud, screwing her eyes tightly shut because they were spurting with sudden tears.

She went to the telephone and dialled the hospital number. He often worked late and sometimes slept there. What little time he had left was spent in the flat of a Cambridge friend in Battersea. 'Gerald,' she said when she heard him, 'How are you?'

'Very well.' She had forgotten the effect that cracked bell note in his voice had on her. 'Missing you like hell. I tried to get you over the weekend.'

'I've been to Dieppe. That's why I'm phoning you.'

'Really?' It was cracked ice now.

'It was with a girl, an old schoolfriend. You'll never believe this. She just disappeared when we were there!'

'What are you talking about?' This was the expression of his which she disliked most, so autocratic, so unbearably chauvinistic. She'd told him so, often.

'What do you mean, what am I talking about? You're not deaf, are you? Or moronic? It's a fact, a *fait accompli* since it happened in France. She didn't meet me at the boat coming back as arranged. I waited and waited. I reported it to the police who've moved heaven and earth. She's not in her Surbiton flat.'

'It's obvious the girl had no intention of coming back. She just used you.' She wished that by yanking the cord she could have garrotted him. She thought with satisfaction of his swollen purple tongue lolling out. Where did he get this capacity to infuriate her? 'Wait for a few days,' he was saying. 'There will be a perfectly ordinary explanation. There always is.' This approximated so closely to the sergeant's opinion that she fairly quivered with rage.

'I was going to give you more details but if you can't even listen . . .'

'I'd hoped you were phoning to suggest we met. Look, Karin, we were both tired . . .'

'I wasn't tired. I can cope with my job very adequately, thank you.'

'Right, *I* was tired. We want to take things more slowly, examine the situation, see where we went wrong. I miss you.'

'I'm not in the mood.' She ignored the ache in her heart. 'Can't you tell I'm worried? Something traumatic has happened to me because of Barbara, I've never felt this kind of fear before. It's a kind of . . . transmitted fear. I phoned you mistakenly, I now see, for advice, medical advice, to see if you thought she might have lost her memory, wandered away . . .'

'The world's full of nutters,' he said. 'You want to steer clear of them.' That, Gerald Armstrong, is the biggest clanger you've made to date.

'So I've noticed.' The ache was in her throat now, making it difficult to speak. 'But how can I keep away from nutters if *you* keep asking to see me?'

'Hey, that's a bit steep. Hold on . . .'

She didn't. She hung up.

She flung herself down amongst the scatter of cushions in a turmoil of anger and disappointment. They were completely incompatible; that is what she would tell any couple who came to her who were remotely like themselves. He pounced before anything hit him, he was short-tempered and impossible. Other doctors worked long hours, got little sleep but didn't snap their wives' heads off.

She went into the kitchen and began to prepare her supper, clashing and rattling dishes to work off steam. The telephone rang again and she flew to answer it. It was Gerald again, a different Gerald.

'Karin, I'm sorry as hell. I jumped at you, the thing I swore not to do. I was so bloody disappointed. I thought you were phoning to hold out a hand of friendship.'

'I was. Doesn't one usually go to friends for help? It's time you grew up, Gerald, for your own good. It's only children who get disappointed when things don't turn out the way they want.'

'I know, I know, I know . . . I'm short-tempered, overworked, underslept, I need a wife's loving care . . .'

'You want to be tucked up in bed at night like a little boy.'

'Not quite like a little boy. Look, darling, I'm busy. This isn't a wheeze,' his habit of sometimes using Boys' Own words almost made her weaken. 'Could I come round tonight, it would have to be late, and I'll promise to listen about your friend?'

'It doesn't matter now.'

'Come on, Ka . . .'

'I said no. It was stupid of me to phone you at all.' You're as bad as he is, she told herself. *Someone's* got to give in.

She had the sensation of an avalanche of words being held back, and then he said quietly, in his rusty voice, 'Would you please meet me for dinner and we can talk like two sensible people?'

'We're never sensible when we're together. We only function independently; together we're bad news.'

'A dialogue. I'm only asking for a dialogue.' What she fundamentally liked about Gerald was that at his most objectionable you felt it wasn't really him; that underneath was the true man, a shining knight of a man. She gave in because she wanted to.

'All right. Tomorrow.'

'No can do. On duty.'

'Thursday.'

'Ditto.'

'This is your last chance, Friday.'

He didn't answer, then, 'Yes. I'll call for you at eight' He would be swapping with someone else.

'I'll pick you up at the hospital, if you like.'

'No, I'll come for you. Must go, darling. Thank you.' The 'thank you', she thought, was the real Gerald, the courteous one.

CHAPTER FIVE

I was so happy walking back by the plage . . . I had time to go that way. The old man had been charming, and he seemed to feel as I did, without having seen her, that the earrings were just right for Karin. I had them tucked securely in one of the lining pockets of my duffle. I patted them for reassurance. I thought of how later, when we were sitting in the bar lounge of the boat, I would be frank and truthful and ask her for help. I saw her bright face, the glow of health which is mental as well as physical, the steady eyes, the shining black hair, the well-cared-for capable hands.

So like her mother, the richness, the encompassing quality, the sureness. 'Tomorrow will be a fine day,' Mrs Elliot would say, as if she had ordered it from God and he would deliver in good time. Such a happy home, compared with my cold, loveless one; James, Karin's brother, so accepting of me; the quiet, quizzical father, and the dogs which grinned as they romped about, as if they felt the happiness too. I had the feeling that if Karin had walked in with an orang-utang instead of me no one would have shown any surprise, and her mother would have said, 'Come along and have tea.'

No wonder Karin has that aura of rightness, of complete adjustment. It's strange she has so little insight. I know she'll go back to Gerald. She's a giving person. She doesn't see that they're both strong characters, and they will always argue a lot, but the loving will be worth it. When they get older they'll learn how to avoid rows, or at least one of them will, and that is all you need. I think you have to come from an unhappy home to have insight. A happy background makes you *expect* happiness, as your right.

She ought to have children, although she doesn't realize that either. She is made for it, like her mother, and looks as if she were made for it, in spite of her pride in herself as a career woman. Surely she could have both? But in any event she'll make a home like her mother's home where friendliness will be like a perpetual Christmas tree in the window.

I've decided. I shan't fear her shining intelligence, as if it were a rapier. I'll ask her for help. I feel tremendously relieved. Not to feel alone any more, to say, 'This is what happened, Karin, could you help me, please?'

Suddenly in the midst of this happiness, a seagull flew low over my head, squawking loudly. I put my hands to my face in fear, the pleasure of decision dribbling from me like water going down a drain. It swooped again . . . I could see its cruel beak clearly . . . and behind me I heard someone laugh. I looked round, startled, and saw a young man a few yards away, face pale, a big bare forehead but lank hair on either side of the face, eyes sunken, hands stuck in the pockets of his short denim blouse so that his elbows jutted out.

My mind skidded about. He might be harmless, but his appearance belied it. And there was something . . . no, that was stupid; he was a stranger. My breath came quickly, I looked around me, The plage wasn't quite deserted . . . I could see a few people in the distance . . . but the bitter wind had kept away those who might have come out for a stroll before lunch.

He was watching me, laughing, shouting something, and although I couldn't make out the words, their tone made me decide. I changed direction and quickly crossing the wide stretch of grass . . . without seeming to run . . . I climbed the low wall and went down on the shore. I had to find somewhere to hide from him. Go right down to the edge of the sea, I told myself. The humped whaleback of the pebbly shore will conceal you like the trenches in the war, grandfather's war . . . why did I think that?

Immediately I knew I'd made a terrible mistake. I should have run along the edge of the sea towards the quay; or stayed on the plage in the first place. Too late. My legs were trembling badly and I sat down on the shingle. I tried to reassure myself, looking at my watch. There was plenty of time before I was due to meet Karin. Now that I was here I could stay quietly out of sight until the man had passed; I'd be all right. Keep calm, I told myself. Fix your eyes steadily on that cold grey slab of sea undulating towards you, coming closer and closer in long smooth thrusts. See how clear every wave is, every wavelet, every turnover of the wave where it becomes spume, every movement, every wrinkle . . .

I strained my ears, could hear no sound but the regular slap of the sea on the shingle. He hadn't followed me, and with the thought, a warmth filled me, and I felt my concentration slipping in relief. The sea became grey silk, a bolt of grey silk in a shop long ago in Gloucester Road. Mother's voice was in my ears with its French inflection, its deep-throatedness. 'Three yards, please, for lining.' See how the assistant measures and pulls, measures and pulls, so that the material billows in waves, so that it comes alive like the sea . . .

I sank my head between my shoulders, pulled my knees up, made myself smaller. *Stay here until you're quite sure he's gone. You have plenty of time. Karin won't be there yet.* I put my head down on my knees, making a ball of my body, and my mind, as if it had had enough of fear, went back to Tamaris. The sea-rain is dashing against the window, but I'm safe inside *grand-mère's* drawing room peering into the camera obscura which is a treat reserved for days such as this. The tall church spire of St. Ouen flickers at the end of the tube, and then a cobbled street, a long stone wall with a wooden door set in it. Beside the door I see the windows of the little *chaumière* where Pierre and his wife live. Rouen.

'It's a gingerbread house,' I say, turning the handle carefully so that I am now on the other side of the wall and in that courtyard with the great tubs of flowers spilling everywhere, wisteria, starred clematis, Grecian urns full of tumbling pelargoniums. *Grand-mère* has taught me the names. I pass under the stone of arch into the inner garden; I call it the magic garden.

I want to stay there, to walk down the paths with their green walls of box guarding the flowers from spilling across the path: columbines, marigold, delphiniums, peonies and occasional strong spikes of Canna lilies. But I have turned the handle too quickly and the inner garden has gone. I am inside the church with the spire.

'Don't be taken in by it,' a voice says to me, a haughty aristocratic voice, 'Monsieur Violette-le-Duc was a peasant. It is sham Gothic.' I know who it is: Aunt Berthe. She never helped her sister, my mother, she was a typical Malle. The Malles are never taken in by anyone or anything, so rigid, so hard, so proud . . . why am I thinking of Aunt Berthe? Is it because she is quite near at Rouen? But I'm going back with Karin. She is going to help me; I have decided to confide in her.

I felt in my pocket and took out the last of the marzipan apples I'd bought in the *confiserie* in Dieppe and shared with Karin. Terror had made me hungry. Dare I go now? Had he gone? I looked around, fearfully, but the hump back of the beach prevented me from seeing. I made a pact with myself. I'd eat this and start off. Perhaps I'd be lucky and meet some other people quite soon, even children would do . . .

The sweet taste is familiar. I licked my teeth with my tongue to dislodge the grainy particles. *Grand-mère* used to pop one of those same sweets into my mouth from her Limoges box on the side table. As a bribe. I knew she was going to talk to me of grandfather, of his good looks, his fineness of character, 'more handsome than your father, although I grant you they were both fair.' I knew she was going to tell me of sexual things which would make my ears burn.

'And they say Englishmen are cold!' I remember the pink lipsticked mouth and the long yellow teeth of old age.

'Of course he was lucky marrying into the Malle family, but all the same, he looked like Richard Coeur de Lion, tall golden-haired, a knight of armour. So passionate. On my wedding night I was truly innocent, *ma petite*, I swooned . . .'

I heard the sound plainly not in my mind, but here, on this lonely beach behind me, the crunch of pebbles, the slithering sound of pebbles running down the slope of the whaleback, and as I turned fearfully, I saw the pallid face, bare-browed, the side hair leaping from it as he jumped. Self-reproach at my stupidity blotted out my terror for a second; but only for a second. A greater terror succeeded it . . . *I knew the face.*

Bella came in with her notebook. 'What happened to your usual bright shining morning face?' she asked, sitting down. She was wearing a different ensemble today, but still camel-coloured, a polo-necked jumper with a matching skirt, and she wore an amber pendant. She believed in tonal dressing.

'It must have slipped.' Karin had learned as a solicitor to keep her own council. It was, or had been, she reminded herself with a pang, her usual practice to confide only in Gerald. At least he'd taken the Hippocratic Oath, sometimes she imagined he'd written it. 'Am I full up with appointments this week?'

'Let's see. Today's busy. Two in the morning, lunch with that dishy Mr Rowbottom from Reid, Simpson and Parfitt . . . I'll go in your place if you'd like . . . and oh, yes, a meeting with Mr Old and Mr Young all afternoon. It's the monthly resumé of cases.'

'Tomorrow?'

'You've three in the morning. Is everyone in the world wanting a divorce, do you think?'

'We're prejudiced. Do you ever think of it, Bella?'

'Me? No, thank you. Me and my old man are as snug as two bugs in one rug. We're both orphans. We found a raft together early on, and nobody's pushing anyone to get off it.'

'Do you ever think of children?'

'I thought of it and dismissed it . . . in case being orphans might be hereditary; I wouldn't wish that state on anyone. No, we'll stay on our little raft and share the rowing.'

I haven't even that as an excuse. 'What about tomorrow afternoon?'

'I thought we might get down to petitions.'

'Oh, God, yes, especially for Mrs Smithers. She'll have her computer at the ready to check it. Would you get a move on with them today and have them ready to sign tomorrow at five? I'll go off after lunch but I'll be back in time. I've got something I want to do.'

'Right.'

'Thanks. Send in the first of the walking wounded.'

The day raced by. She made the evening race also by having a bite of food in town and going to see a Woody Allen film she'd missed; then went home, washed her hair, had a bath and went to bed, all without stopping. Ceaseless activity seemed to be the only answer for her present state of mind, a nagging longing for Gerald, a nagging fear about Barbara.

What had she been hiding? The girl's words came back to her, and the look of terror on her pale face. '*You see, there was this one thing he couldn't stand about me, just couldn't stand . . .*' Was it her reaction to losing the baby? '*I got upset,*' she'd said. But wasn't that natural, and shouldn't they at least have been 'upset' together? Had he been unsympathetic, treated her badly, even violently, and she had retaliated in the same way? Even to the extent of . . . murder. No, no, she'd dismissed that idea: it was too fanciful.

Oh, give it up, she told herself. You're becoming melodramatic again. The whole thing is a mass of contradictions. She was beginning to feel sleepy. This was the dangerous time, dangerous thoughts. If only Gerald were here, the warmth of him, the comfort of his body . . . he had a warm, dry skin, smooth . . . her arms crossed over her breasts, her fingers pushed slowly up her neck into her hair. A sybarite existence, give up the partnership, devote your life to Gerald . . . no, no, that was only one part of her. She straightened the curve of her body, concentrated on her plans for tomorrow. After lunch she'd drive to 7, Easton Grove and see with her own eyes where Barbara had lived. She was suddenly asleep.

She found the flat easily, a quiet cul-de-sac off Easton Avenue in Surbiton. The two blocks of flats were not particularly opulent-looking, but probably suitable for business people who wanted something quiet, or retired people who'd grown tired of gardening.

She stood and looked at No. 7, saw the cheap blue-coloured slabs of shiny tiling round the entrance, walked up the short flight of steps to the row of bells. *Flat 27, Mrs B. Charles.* There it was, written neatly on a card.

She rang the bell with deliberate force, rang it again, and waited. What a relief it would be if she heard Barbara's voice on the intercom! she could imagine running up the two flights of stairs, ignoring the lift even if there were one, finding the door open, seeing the pale face with the same-coloured hair, and saying, 'Barbara! Where did you get to? *Rappelle-toi, Barbara. N'oublie pas . . .*' She found herself mouthing the French words as she stood there, felt her eyes fill with tears. She opened the flap of her shoulder bag, took out a tissue and blew her nose. Looking up she saw an elderly woman sitting at the ground-floor window. She was beckoning to her.

She zipped up her bag, walked up the steps and leant against the heavy glass door to push it open. At the end of a long corridor she could see the woman standing at an open door. She was beckoning again. Karin hurried towards her.

'I'm sorry to be rude,' she said as Karin reached her. She had a lined face but brown lively eyes. She leant heavily on two sticks. 'All that cloak and dagger stuff, beckoning. Are you looking for Mrs Charles?'

'Yes, I am.' She smiled.

'Come in, won't you? Karin hesitated. 'I don't bite. It's just that standing is painful for me.'

'I'm sorry.' She followed slowly behind the woman, noticing that the sticks had a steel extension which gripped her arms. The room they went into was well-furnished but the pieces were dull for want of polishing, and the curtains looked dusty. Perhaps she'd noticed Karin's glance.

'It's impossible to get help now. I have a woman who comes once a week, but I keep her busy stocking my fridge, helping me into the bath and so on. Must keep body and soul together, and I'd rather have a clean skin than clean furniture. I'm on my last bottle of perfume. Attar of Roses. Do you like it?'

'Nice.' If cloying.

'Sit down, please.' The woman leant her sticks against her own chair. 'I'm what's known as an indigent gentlewoman. Being phased out soon. My furniture's the same, old and tatty.'

'I think your room's charming.' Karin looked around. Double bookcases made of mahogany, a desk, tables, two sofas . . . there was enough to furnish a much bigger flat.

'You've got a blue beam in your eye. There are some people who never miss a trick. You're that kind.'

'I'm a solicitor. Maybe I'm beginning to look beaky.' She laughed. 'My name's Karin Armstrong.'

'I'm Madge Cornthwaithe. Has Mrs Charles been tangling with the law? I shouldn't have thought so.'

'No, far from it. We got in touch recently and had a weekend in Dieppe together.'

'That was original. Dieppe in summer's nothing at all, but in winter, that's different. And you haven't seen her since?'

'She . . . stayed on.' The woman's eyes were like a robin's on her. 'I called on the off-chance that she might be home now. Something I had to discuss . . .'

'I see.' She shook her head. 'No, I haven't seen her and I spend my days sitting at the window. A quiet girl, but helpful. We spoke to each other when I was taking in my milk and she offered to do some shopping for me. I said I'd bear it in mind, although I do have a dear grocer who delivers for me, dear in more ways than one I may say.' The eyes were darting to Karin's face again. 'You look a little anxious about her.'

'Well . . .'

'I'm not surprised. She was a girl surrounded by mystery; a lot going on behind that face. No friends. I'd like to offer you a cup of tea . . . is it Mrs or Miss?'

'Mrs.'

'I'm Miss. But I'm a comic spectacle when I move around. You can get all kinds of aids from the National Health but I know a woman who fractured her femur falling over her steel claw . . .'

'Could I make some tea for you?'

'No, thanks. I'd much rather talk. Is being a solicitor nice for you?'

'Interesting.'

'And your husband? Is he in the same profession?'

'No, he's a doctor.'

'That's wearisome: you won't see much of each other. But at least you know there's someone to go home to. That's the best thing in life . . . I had Mother, once. It's the empty room. I worked too, once. I was a pioneer, a lady typist. But what's the use of boring you when you've come looking for your friend. Your face is too honest for a solicitor; I can see you want to get away.'

'Not at all, but I'm rather busy. I'm glad to have met you, Miss Cornthwaite, glad you know Barbara.'

'Not to say, know. There were several layers there. Still, I'm glad nothing's harmed her. I always thought she had the look of a victim. There are two kinds of people, victims and aggressors.'

'Yes . . .' This was going to go on all day. 'Perhaps you'll mention I called, if you see her.'

'I shan't see her,' Miss Cornthwaite said surprisingly, 'not unless she comes back soon. I made a mistake renting this flat. It's too quiet. I'm moving to one nearer the town centre and the station. I'll be able to watch people coming home from work; people are what interest me . . .'

Karin got up. 'I'm glad. It should be brighter for you. I really must go . . .'

'We've hardly . . .'

'I must be back in my office to sign mail. I'll let myself out. Thank you for telling me about Barbara.'

'It's I who should thank you.' The woman looked up into Karin's face, disappointed. 'How different you are from the other one, chalk and cheese!'

'Well . . . good-bye.' Karin retreated from the room, closing the door behind her.

She drove the car round the corner and stopped beside a little park to collect her wits. Barbara wasn't back, but No. 7 Easton Grove was certainly not a house with a garden. She felt the unease again, a miserable but now familiar sensation. They'd been getting on well together; she'd won Barbara's confidence; she felt sure the homeward journey would have given her the opportunity to unburden herself. The unease was mixed with a new impatience. This mystery about Barbara was becoming altogether too time consuming. She should be thinking about her own affairs, about Gerald. However much they quarrelled, he was fundamental to her happiness. They would have to sit down quietly together and talk, and talk. Loving shouldn't be a substitute for real communication.

She gazed out through the windscreen, feeling unusually dispirited. Some young women were walking towards her with their children. She saw the happiness on their faces, and felt excluded. It was your own choice, remember, she told herself. 'Timothy!' one of them called, then another, 'Daren!' Despite all the sexist talk you couldn't deny it was the Timothys and Darens who trailed their blazers behind them. As if to prove the point two little girls went past clinging to each other, simpering and giggling. If she had children, how would she face up to this routine of fetch and carry which took up so much of one's time but only a small part of one's mind? And *that's* a superior attitude, she thought.

She got out, locked the car and walked aimlessly down the road which ran beside the park. In the distance she could see a cluster of houses, and she thought she would head for them and then turn back. There was no time for introspection. She was one of the busy partners of Saithe and Saithe. The knowledge left her cold.

There were three houses together, all of a kind and vaguely cottagey in appearance. They must have been built, perhaps at the beginning of the century, perhaps by the same builder. They had privet hedges, deep-pitched roofs and small windows. The one on the corner with more garden than the rest had a stone plinth suspended by chains above the door . . . she walked past it, seeing that the garden was well-kept, that there was a winter planting of wallflowers in all the beds; she guessed that the front would be a picture in summer because of the neatly-pruned roses, and turning the corner, stopped beside the high hedge.

A stone plinth suspended by chains . . . Barbara's voice came back to her, tentative, a spatter of words, a pause, '. . . and I'm always afraid to go in that way in case it falls on my head . . . I have a jinx about it.' She found she was holding her breath as if there was a presence near her . . .

She stood irresolutely, telling herself to buck up; there would be an explanation, and then she turned back, walking very slowly this time so that she would be able to look even more carefully. She came level with the gate, saw the stone plinth again, that the windows were casements, that a cobbled path ran round them . . . a man was working in the centre bed, snipping at rose-bushes. He turned and looked at Karin, pipe in mouth, and she said loudly, clearly, 'May I speak to you for a moment, please?'

He came towards her, secateurs in hand, reminding her of a hero from a John Buchan novel, hair neatly cropped, a square face but a small mouth, especially compared with the size of the pipe. 'Yes?' He had reached Karin. They stood with the wicket gate between them.

'Excuse me,' she said, 'I'm a friend of Barbara's. I just wondered if she'd come home yet?'

He took the pipe out of his mouth and she saw that it *was* small but with square teeth. 'Barbara? Barbara who?'

'Barbara Charles. We spent the weekend together in Dieppe. She didn't come back with me although we agreed to meet at the boat . . .'

'Excuse me,' he looked mystified, 'I haven't a clue who you're talking about. You must have got the wrong person . . .'

'But she lived in Surbiton and I recognized her description of the house just now, even to the, the . . . *Araucaria araucana*', her eyes swung over the garden and there it was, to the right of the door, a handsome monkey puzzle tree . . . 'to that tree.' She pointed.

'I'm afraid there's been a mistake.' He was positive. 'I never knew any Barbara; I've never had a woman living here. My garden occupies my leisure time when I'm not busy in my shop. My name's William Merriman; I'm an antique dealer.'

She felt blood rushing to her face. She scrabbled in her handbag and produced a card. 'Just to let you see I'm not completely round the bend.' She smiled nervously. 'I did spend a weekend with Barbara Charles whom I knew at school; she did describe your house minutely, or a house exactly like yours . . .'

'I take your word for it, Miss Armstrong.'

'Mrs.'

'Mrs. But you must take mine too. I've never had a girl living here by the name of Barbara or any other name. It can be proved if necessary. This girl has seen my house . . . perfectly possible since you say she lived in Surbiton, and described it to you. If you don't mind me saying so, it looks as if she's been pulling the wool over your eyes for whatever reason I shouldn't like to guess. It's your affair.'

She gave in. 'I'm terribly sorry to have interrupted you, Mr Merriman. I'm not off my head. I was with this girl and she didn't catch the same boat back as I did. It's been worrying me . . .' She stopped. She was doing what she never did with clients, letting him think she was emotionally involved. He looked peevish, and the small mouth was sucking almost frantically at the pipe as if there was some soothing drug there.

'Shouldn't you have told the police?'

'I did, right away. I'm afraid you're right. She's been fantasizing about your house . . . I can't thing why.' She said brightly. 'Perhaps because the garden is so lovely.'

'You should have seen it last summer.' He permitted himself a small smile from one corner of the small mouth.

She smiled to show she'd got the joke. 'I'm sorry to have troubled you. Good-bye, Mr Merriman.' He nodded and turned away, walked briskly back to his rose-beds. She made her way back to the car, feeling foolish, but strangely enough, not angry with Barbara. And yet, if she had told lies about Mr Merriman, didn't it point to her complete unreliability, and was the story about her husband and child a pack of lies too? She had certainly shown irresponsibility in not turning up at the boat. And yet, true or false, the girl had been terror-stricken, and surely she had been running away from something?

She drove back to town, deeply disquieted.

CHAPTER SIX

Karin was ready and waiting for Gerald long before he arrived. She longed to see him, a mixture of wanting to see him for his own sake and a need to talk to anyone about Barbara. Husbands were for confiding in, for sharing one's troubles with. How rational she could be about him when he wasn't there, and weren't they always rational enough when they were discussing anything outside themselves. That, she told herself, is a failure of communication, a temperament clash.

She looked at her watch, saw it was half-past eight. *Come quickly, Gerald, I need you, to hell with rationalizations . . .* She went to her desk and rummaged through the pigeon-holes until she found what she was looking for, an envelope of school photographs. She'd show them to him when he arrived, as proof that Barbara was not a figment of her imagination.

She sat down on the floor beside the divan, emptied out the envelope, spreading the photographs in front of her. Here was a class group, 1968, Beatlemania, letters written to John via his Aunt Mimi, 'Please *please* send me a photograph of him . . .'; there was that coarse girl, Gillian Gort, who'd said that Karin's breasts were made for feeding babies. It occurred to her that if the girls at school hadn't teased her about being a milk factory, she might not have been so ambitious to have a career.

There was the Jersey Lily herself, the Milk Queen, the dark girl with large eyes; the photo had come out as black as her hair, the box-pleats of her gym tunic swelling over that much-discussed bust. She was smiling merrily as if she hadn't a care in the world, my automatic response to a camera, and to life. Or it used to be.

She ran her forefinger along the rows looking for Barbara, remote, difficult to find, just as she was today. Ah, there she was, half-hidden behind big Mabel Butterworth . . . like a shy doe peering round a huge tree trunk. She looked as if someone was going to eat her up . . . the door bell rang imperiously and she flew to answer it, her heart pounding. It was Gerald, with a bunch of wilted flowers and an air of bonhomie to cover the fact that he knew he was late.

'Sorry, Karin,' he gave her a husbandly peck, forgetting his role of being estranged, 'a case at the last minute. Jackson came up to me and said, "you're wanted in Coronary Care," and I said, "but you know Gray's standing in for me, it's in the duty book . . ."' He took a deep breath. 'Honestly, it would have been quicker to have gone and seen the patient than explained it to that numbskull . . . you can talk and talk to Jackson but it goes in one bloody big ear and out the other like a steel rod . . .'

'Come in before you let the cold in. How delicate of you not to use your key, Gerald. Don't worry, you haven't beaten your record for lateness. There was that famous birthday celebration in the Greek restaurant where the waiter took pity on me and we were dancing the Balalaika when you arrived . . .' Old habits died hard. She could have cut out her tongue.

'Oh, well, if you're going to go over old scores.' He'd taken her remarks lightly, fortunately. He held out the flowers to her. 'I'm afraid they need a kiss of life, but I bought them this morning. There's a man with a pitch outside the hospital, and I thought better now than never . . .'

'Where have they been since then?'

'In the boot.'

She looked at them. 'My diagnosis is heat exhaustion or hypothermia. Thanks, all the same.' This time his face was grim, and had she imagined that he winced? He looked washed-out and tired and there were bags under his eyes which gave him a new owlish look. She put her arms round his neck, loving him. 'You're working too hard. Couldn't you let up for a bit?' He didn't answer. Instead he kissed her as if he were drinking from a fountain.

'That was good,' he said. 'Don't tempt me further. I said I'd take you out to dinner.'

She smiled at him. 'Sit down and I'll get you a drink.'

'Are we eating Greek?'

'I thought Chinese. It doesn't matter if their food is reheated.' She went into the kitchen, surprised to find that her arms trembled when she reached for the bottle. 'It's still Scotch, isn't it?' she called.

'Yes, but very little. I'm going off drink. I'm having trouble with my stomach.'

'You're always having trouble with it. You're the doctor, but I've told you before; go and have a check-up.'

'I haven't time even to eat. The Membership's coming up again soon; I'll be fine after it's over.'

She came back into the room. 'I've a proposition to make, pro tem. Take some leave from the hospital, even if it's unpaid. I earn enough to keep us.' She saw his face stiffen. 'Give yourself time to study.' She knew it was no use.

'It's out of the question. You should know better than even to suggest it.'

'Okay.' She poured a little whisky, added soda. I have no skill in handling this man, she thought. The emotional involvement is too great. 'Don't say I didn't warn you. You're only twenty-eight. You'll soon be red-nosed with a tummy that gurgles when you bend over your patients.' She wished he didn't look so drawn about the mouth.

'I can be more embarrassing than that, but leave my insides out of it. Thanks, Ka.' He took the glass from her, lay back amongst the cushions on the divan. 'Lovely to be back.'

'You're not back, you're just visiting.'

He took a sip, raised his glass to her. 'To our trial period. How's life with you? How's young Mr and old Mr?'

'Doing very nicely. Young Reginald thinks I have a way with people.'

'God! Send him to me; I'll soon disillusion him.'

'There's no need to be rude.' She fixed him with a look and then remembered this was his usual behaviour when he came from the hospital, firing nervy gratuitous insults sometimes so wildly off the mark that she had to laugh, and then quietening down after a while and becoming the real Gerald. Perhaps her sharpness of tongue had developed as a retaliation, become a habit. 'I was looking at this photograph before you came in.' She picked up the 1968 group photo. 'Look, there's me . . .' She pointed and he took it out of her hand, peered.

'Big for your age. How old were you?'

'Thirteen. Not overly, I should say.'

'Well-developed anyhow. But then you always were, up there . . . where's the girl you were telling me about?'

'Barbara Charles.' She leant over him and pointed. He looked closely.

'Her face and hair sort of run into each other. It must be her colouring. She looks shy, the way her head's down.'

'Yes, she was. Remote. Could someone have a short lapse of memory, Gerald? Say, when she was making her way back to meet me at the boat?'

'It's possible, a kind of fugue, but hardly likely. I'd have to know her history.' He put down the photograph and took a sip of whisky. 'I don't believe it's that, somehow. I think it's much simpler. She just changed her mind. Some girls are like that, thoughtless . . .'

'If you'd met her . . .'

'Appearances can be deceptive.'

She watched him as he leafed through the other photographs, head bent downwards. He was badly in need of a haircut. The hair grew in two long points at the back of his neck, but in between the skin looked young and vulnerable. Tenderness welled up in her, a feeling of responsibility for his well-being. And between his shoulder blades there seemed to be the beginnings of what her father called an academic hump. He was driving himself into the ground. He needed . . . his own words echoed in her mind . . . a wife's loving care.

He looked up suddenly, caught her looking at him. 'Were you feasting your eyes on me?'

'Don't be ridiculous. I was only thinking you were due for a haircut.'

'And I thought it was passion. Look, Ka,' he was serious, 'what *do* you know of this girl? I don't like the sound of it. After all, she appeared out of the blue, so to speak.'

'In a way, but I was at school with her, don't forget. She wasn't a girl you got to know well, but I always liked her, felt vaguely sorry for her. There was a sadness . . . France was a second home to her; her grandmother and mother were French. Funnily enough, they were both married to Englishmen. When I remarked on that she said in her distrait way, "Maybe my mother was influenced."'

'By *her* mother, presumably?'

'Yes.'

'And she said her grandfather was killed in the Normandy landings. I remember his name because it was unusual, Norman Sanctuary.'

'Robust.'

She nodded. It was coming back to her now. 'I suggested we make a trip to see the landing beaches but she didn't like the idea at all. Then it dawned on me her grandmother's house had been near one of the beaches. "It's better just to remember," she said. You had the feeling there was some great sadness in her background which had coloured her life. I felt so lucky, I've been so untrammelled . . .'

'Till you met me.' His voice was bitter.

'Don't say that, Gerald. We'll get it right. We've got to sit down and talk, be our own marriage counsellors . . . I wish this thing hadn't come up . . .'

He looked grey, older than his twenty-eight years, and she wanted to put her arms around him, to comfort him. Could it be that perhaps through Barbara they'd gain the necessary detachment, be involved in caring? You'd get that if you had children, she thought. Was she using the girl as a surrogate child? 'Bits are coming back to me of that weekend,' she said. 'Her father died when she was eight, and she said it was the same for both of them, meaning her mother's father had died when she had also been eight.'

'Where is she?'

'She'd died too. She obviously felt that deeply. Perhaps her death was fairly recent. And there were the earrings. She offered to buy me ivory earrings we saw in a little shop off the Rue de la Barre. I refused, of course.'

'You're not good at accepting, are you?'

'What do you mean?'

'I gave you my love and it wasn't enough.'

'Because you made conditions. I have to fit into your pattern; I'm not allowed to have one of my own.'

'You've always got your back to the wall.'

She breathed deeply. 'Let's stick to Barbara. Perhaps if we solve her problem we'll solve our own.'

'I don't know what you mean.'

'I don't think I know myself.' She smiled at him, tentatively, and he gave her a long look, then shrugged.

'All right. Do you think she has a man there, in France?'

'She hasn't one in England as far as I know, so it could be.' She told him about going to Easton Grove and how she'd come across William Merriman's house. 'She lied about that.'

'Fantasy, or wishful thinking.'

'I thought of that.' They looked at each other. 'She's divorced, Gerald. There was something her husband couldn't stand about her, those were her very words. I think she's hiding from him, or from . . . something she's done.' She saw his look. 'I'm not fanciful as a rule.'

'I'll give you that. Logic's your strong point.'

'I think she's in trouble, grave trouble. It . . . perturbs me. Once I thought she was going to confide in me and then she made a complete *volte face* and pretended it was Merriman she was worried about, whether she should marry him or not.'

'Did she tell you anything about her marriage?'

'A little. She said she lost their child and got "upset", that was her word. There were terrible scenes. I wonder if he was battering her?'

'Anything's possible. If you could only find someone who knew her. You're sure Merriman wasn't having you on?'

'Positive, and it was the same house as she described, even to the plinth on chains above the door and the monkey puzzle tree.'

'No other relatives mentioned?'

She shook her head. 'No . . . let me see, though. Yes, you're right. She did mention her Aunt Berthe. That would be her mother's sister.'

'Does she live in France?'

'I think so. But how on earth could I find out her address? I couldn't just go around looking for Aunt Berthe. Unless I go back to the police. But I'm sure they'd rather I kept out of it. They don't want speculations, just facts.' She got up, wandered about the room, lifting some magazines which were on the floor, feeling restless and unhappy. 'Would you like another drink?'

'No, thanks. I've had enough. Come and sit down beside me instead of moseying about. It's been ages.'

She turned to look at him. 'No funny business?'

He raised his eyes ceilingwards, then started. 'Good God, there's a great cobweb there! It's time I went round with the feather duster. Funny business, she says. My dear girl, I want to eat. I haven't had a thing all day. The insides of my stomach are clapping together like the front row of the Proms.'

She laughed and sat down beside him, feeling the old tenderness. This was her husband who was close beside her, who was tired and needed caring for. This business of Barbara was a distraction. 'I wonder,' she said 'why Barbara lied to me about Merriman. Was it that she didn't want me to know she lived alone? That she was lonely?'

'Living alone can be hell. Pete's in Arizona just now; the

flat's like a morgue. I just go back in time to tumble into bed.' He had on his must lugubrious expression. The bags under his eyes made it worse.

'You're breaking my heart.' She wanted to put her arms round him, have him lay his head on her breast. 'Let's keep to Barbara, as we agreed, not someone who comes home so crazed for sleep that he wouldn't know if it was Strangeways, far less a flat. She's crying out for help. It hovered in the air between us. She was going to confide in me on the way back if she hadn't been . . . prevented.' The tug of fear was there again.

'Prevented?' He looked round at her in surprise. 'You've no grounds for saying that.'

'Only intuition. She bothers me. I can't concentrate on my own affairs until . . . Something's happened to her. I feel it in my bones. I wonder if we could get hold of the aunt's address . . . say at the French equivalent of Somerset House . . .' She stopped speaking. Gerald said it for her.

'Hopeless. But there must be *someone* who knows more about her than you do. Since it wasn't Merriman, and since her mother is dead, it could only be her husband, even if they *are* divorced.'

'You're right, of course.' Her spirits lifted, her mind became acute again. 'Now, let's see. She was married in 1974, that I do know.'

'How?'

'We both left in seventy-three, and I read the announcement of her wedding quite soon afterwards in the school magazine. She . . .' she looked at him. 'Are you thinking what I'm thinking? Our loft at home . . . piles of school magazines, James's and mine.'

'I remember stacks of them beside that old rocking-horse . . .'

'Black Beauty.' She sighed.

'It had the mange. If you can find the appropriate issue you could get her husband's name and possibly where they lived to start with. Then you could get in touch with him and ask about Barbara, or what the aunt's address is. Married couples always know about each others' relatives. They're asked to the wedding for a start.'

'It might have been a registry office.'

'It might not. Besides, girls usually take their men to meet the relatives. Look at that old Uncle somebody or other you had who grew vines.'

'Uncle Ben.'

'That's it. And how he used to pat me on the shoulder and say, "My boy, you'll go far." ' The gaiety went from his face. 'Sometimes I wonder.'

'Why do you wonder?' Her mind was still full of Barbara.

'Because I've lost my belief in myself. Because it's no good without you. I need to be working for you, not myself. I miss you.'

'Oh, don't feel so sorry for yourself.' It slipped out. He turned and caught her by the shoulders, not at all gently.

'God, you can be cruel at times. You don't know the power of your tongue; it's like a whiplash. But it isn't really cruelty, otherwise I'd be out of that door in a flash. It's your form of resistance. You see marriage as a trap. Why did you ever agree to marry me in the first place? Don't you realize that if you gave yourself completely you'd find yourself? It's much more than enjoying ourselves in bed . . .' Hadn't Barbara said something like that . . . His voice had dropped, become gentle. 'What do I have to do to prove my love?'

'What . . . ?' The nearness of his body was making her head swim. He smelled of antiseptic but it was as potent as an aphrodisiac. The need for him was back, overpowering her. During the working day it wasn't a problem, at her desk, 'Bring in the walking wounded . . .' Was it such a joke? Everyone was more or less in that category. They either needed support or they needed to give it . . .

'What do I have to do to prove my love?' he said again. She lay back amongst the scatter cushions, feeling soft and vulnerable, in the centre of *now*, no thoughts of Barbara, or the office. Or anything. It was subtle at first, the feeling as if she was lying in shallow water which flowed softly over her. She didn't want to hurry it. But each time the small waves receded they came back, less small and still less small until they were breaking strongly over her with a steady, pulling rhythm. She knew he was struggling with his clothes, and she had a stupid desire to say, 'Come on in, the water's fine.' They could lie and feel the strength of the waves together, not to swamp them, breathe quietly during the long recession, prepare themselves for the new onslaught . . .

'You aren't helping, Ka.' His voice was a cracked whisper, 'just lying there with that silly smile on your face. I can't undress you and myself in this position.'

'Oh . . .' she sighed. She rolled luxuriously. The photographs scattered on to the floor.

'I'm surrounded by cushions. Who the hell bought them anyhow?' He punched them vigorously, and his stomach gave a loud protesting gurgle followed by a draining noise as if a plug had been pulled out.

'What you need is a Chinese dinner,' she said.

'I need you. Are you going to make me carry you to the bedroom in my weakened state, or are you going to get up and go there?'

'If you insist.' She lay looking at him, loved him completely as she always did before they made love. There were no problems to think about but loving. A high whine came from his stomach followed by a splash as if someone had dropped a pebble in it.

'I'm sorry,' he was laughing, 'can't do a thing about it.'

'I feel so serious about you and you're making me laugh. It's that left eyebrow of yours. It gets lost in your hair.' She touched his cheek. 'And you have a cleft at the end of your nose. I'd forgotten about that cleft, and your smooth skin.' She felt she was rediscovering him, the thin blue veins in his pale forehead which went with the sandy hair and the fair complexion, the grey eyes which had an amber fleck. There was a delicacy about the contours of his face as of someone whose strength would have to be guarded because of a consuming nervous energy. Had his mother recognized this? Did all mothers know the weaknesses as well as the strengths of their sons, and were they fearful that their sons' wives wouldn't recognize these also?

But the laughter stopped when they were in the bedroom. And his stomach calmed down. Or perhaps she didn't hear it any more.

CHAPTER SEVEN

She spent the weekend alone. She could quite easily have driven down to Kent to see her parents, and even more important, searched through the school magazines in the loft . . . it had been a good idea of Gerald's . . . but she couldn't face it. Her mother was a role setter; Karin wasn't sure if she could now live up to the one which had been assigned to her.

She was the one who always arrived smiling and went away smiling, who said life was a load of fun even when it wasn't. Father could shut himself in his study, James go away for long solitary tramps, but Karin must hover in the kitchen or sitting-room and be outgoing. She sometimes thought the verbal fencing she'd been forced to adopt was the reason she'd decided to become a solicitor.

Instead of going home she rang the school. There would be a skeleton staff on at least, and luckily it was the bursar who was taking calls. 'I'm a former pupil, Mr Gates,' she said. 'Perhaps you remember me, Karin Elliot?' She remembered him, gangling limbs like a stick insect and with a centre parting in his hair which had made the girls swoon with laughter and call him 'Bertie'.

'Indeed I do. Seventy-three, wasn't it? I remember your bright shining face. I heard you'd gone on to a fine career after university.'

She was pleased about the 'bright shining face'. He should see her now. 'I'm a solicitor, Mr Gates. How is your wife?'

He hesitated. 'I'm afraid she died of cancer last summer. This has been a bad year for us, a great loss.' He spoke as if he'd failed to balance the books.

'I'm so sorry.'

'Thank you. We must carry on. Now, I know you don't want to hear about my little worries. What can I do for you?'

'I'm trying to get in touch with Barbara Charles. She was in the same year as me. I think she married a year after she left, that would be in 1974.'

'Barbara Charles? Was she a pale girl? Unusual-looking?'

'Yes, she was. Do you remember her?'

He seemed to hesitate. 'I do.'

'I only wanted her address. Do you think you could arrange to have someone look through the school magazines of that year? The announcement would be in, and sometimes they gave a few details.' She thought he hesitated again.

'I think I could manage that for you. Could I ring you back? Miss English doesn't come in on Saturdays.'

'I should have waited until Monday. Please don't bother, Mr Gates.'

'It's no bother. It will keep me busy; weekends are the worst.'

'I'll be here all day. It's very kind of you.'

'Not at all.' He brightened. 'Why don't you come down and see us one day? Miss Beverley would be delighted; she likes to keep in touch with our girls.'

'I will. Life has been hectic recently.'

'And I daresay you're married into the bargain, Karin, if I may still call you that?'

'Of course . . . yes, I am, into the bargain.' She laughed. 'I can't thank you enough.'

The morning dragged. She gave the flat a good going over which she found therapeutic, paying particular attention to the cobwebs above the radiators which Gerald had spotted. As far as he was concerned, last night hadn't been what she'd planned. She couldn't regret anything so completely enjoyable, but it hadn't solved anything.

Bed wasn't everything, she knew that, but in the words of some sage or other it concentrated the mind wonderfully.

It was out of bed which was the problem. That's superficial thinking, she told herself, what you read in those up-market magazines Bella buys.

What is it that makes two sensible people, a doctor and a solicitor, no less, bicker like children? Take his touchiness for instance when she'd offered to keep him while he studied for his re-sit. Be honest, she told herself now, you knew he wouldn't accept such a proposition. It went against all his principles. And have you ever, with your easily-won success, ever tried to feel with him the mortification, the devastation of his plans, at failing the Membership?

They were so different. Did that mean they were completely incompatible? They say opposites attract, but can they live together? He never looked entirely relaxed, or he hadn't for the last year or so. He was like a highly bred horse, jumpy, irritable, perpetually primed for Becher's Brook. Admit it's difficult for you, you've never had any illness, (never been allowed to have one?), you have a cast-iron gut, (eat it up, Karin, no fads allowed here), really to appreciate his kind of temperament.

She'd been under-protected, deliberately, by her mother, Gerald had been over-protected by his. In her case the end result was a brash, opinionated girl, or was it a cover, really, for her own inadequacies? I've always been the one who chivvies and encourages, who says, 'Chin up!' because the mantle was laid on me in infancy. Wasn't that the reason Barbara had sought her out?

Barbara . . . Gerald had been so helpful about Barbara; a good husband, going through the business with her from start to finish, using his skills. She felt that might be where the solution lay, to be involved together in caring about what had happened to Barbara.

At lunch-time the bell rang. There he was when she opened the door. 'Hello, darling,' he said. 'Can't stop. Just flew over from the hospital to see how you were.' He looked tired and owlish, the bags under his eyes seemed to have become a permanency.

'Did you expect me to go into a post-coital decline?' Too flip. She saw his displeased look, the corners of his mouth turn down. 'Just a joke. Would you like me to rustle up some eggs and bacon? You look shot at.'

'It was that Chinese food last night. Went for the gut. Or maybe I was too hungry to enjoy it.' When they were in the room he put his arms around her and kissed her slowly and satisfyingly, rather like topping up from a fountain this time. 'Thank you for last night. You made a new man of me.'

'Same for me. I loved it.' He looked wary. She was stealing his lines.

'I've got my stuff in the car. I managed some time off by missing lunch but I'm on duty tonight.' She stiffened and came out of his arms.

'We didn't agree to anything last night, Gerald, about ourselves.'

He looked genuinely surprised. 'But I thought that was our reconciliation! I thought you wouldn't have gone to bed with me unless you were willing to patch things up, that it was a way of showing . . .'

'I don't need ways of showing. I can express myself perfectly well in speech when I have to. It doesn't mean anything when I go to bed with you except that I want to go to bed with you. I fancied you. I always have.'

'Yes, but . . .' he looked mystified.

'Look, Gerald, it isn't the answer. What I need you to accept is my need to express myself outside the home. You want, as soon as possible . . . and I know it's kindness and love on your part, to take that load off my shoulders. Can't I get it through to you that for the time being it isn't a load, it's a challenge. And that it doesn't matter if my job, at the moment, happens to be better-paid than yours . . . oh, I've hurt you again. You look like your mother when your face goes like that . . . sorry, sorry. But, honestly, your attitudes are outmoded. It's a kind of Sultan complex. I don't blame you. You've been inured in it since you could crawl, just as I've been inured to think of myself as self-reliant and able to cope even when I was shivering in my Clark's sandals.

'When you get your Membership, maybe we'll move out of London and we'll have a house with a garden, and . . .' As she said 'garden' she thought of William Merriman, and then the pale face of Barbara rose in her mind, like a haunting . . .

'I can't leave London.' His face was set. 'You know it's important for me to stay in Hospital till the right opening comes along. I don't want the provinces at this stage of my career.'

'Fair enough. Then won't you try to see my point of view? We ought to have talked this out ages ago. We're full of cleverness and no commonsense. It's not unusual; solicitors go back to marital troubles at home, doctors never see that their wives are ill . . . we're both at fault. Meantime, let me make you that bacon and eggs; I'd really like to do it.'

'No, thanks.' He looked white and drawn. 'I haven't the time now.'

'Will you ring me?'

'Perhaps.' His face had the thwarted look she knew. His mother would have soothed him, made him put his feet up, blanked herself out in service to him. 'Does it ever occur to you that you don't give me my place because you're so busy insisting on *yours*?'

'No, you've got it wrong . . .'

'Have I?' He put up his hands and released hers. There was a white ridge round his mouth. He kissed her coldly, an insulting kiss, and left her. She heard the door bang.

She went to the window and looked down on to the street. His old Rover was there, and strapped at the back of the boot were his two suitcases. She saw him get in and drive off. The two suitcases disappearing round the corner was the saddest thing she'd seen for a long time. She turned away, castigating herself. Obstinacy, the besetting sin . . .

The telephone bell rang shrilly and she ran to it. It was Mr Gates, pleasant, self-effacing, with the information she wanted.

'Yes, you were quite right, Karin. I found the announcement of Barbara Charles' wedding in the summer issue of the school magazine for 1974. She was married to Mr Donald Sheldon on the 4th July of that year.'

'Mr Donald Sheldon.' She wrote down the name on a pad.

'At Brompton Church, south-west London.'

'Yes, her mother had a flat in Gloucester Road, I remember.' She felt cheered. This was the first step forward. 'Does it by any chance give their address, Mr Gates? "The young couple will take up residence at . . ."?'

'Let's see. Yes, here it is. No. 3 Brevitt Gardens, Chiswick. Of course, that's six years ago. I don't know if they'll still be there.'

'It's possible.' It was better not to tell him of the divorce. 'Thank you very much; it was so good of you to go to all that trouble.'

'It was no trouble, I assure you.' Again he hesitated, and then, 'Karin, I may be stepping out of line, but I hope there's nothing wrong?'

'Wrong?' She pretended surprise. 'Why?'

'You see . . . a police officer telephoned last week to ask for the address of Barbara Charles' guardian. I just wondered . . .'

'No, that was quite in order. It's some legal hassle.'

'Mr Keble died three years ago.'

'Did he? I'm sorry.'

'It's a good thing she's got her husband now. That's the most important thing, marriage, the welding of two souls . . . but I mustn't bore you. Do come and see us when you're next in Kent.'

'Thank you again, Mr Gates. I will.'

She went into the kitchen to make some coffee, and to think. When she was concentrating on Barbara, at least she wasn't thinking of Gerald, of his white face. 'A welding of two souls,' Mr Gates had said, and she and Gerald were still operating independently. Was marriage as the Gates had known it a thing of the past? Neither was right, surely, but how much easier it must have been for Mrs Gates who had been satisfied with her home life than for someone like herself. She remembered the dumpy little woman who had waved indiscriminately to all the girls and had 'helped out' Miss Beverley when there was a school function.

It's the partnership in Saithe and Saithe's, she thought, which is at the crux of the matter. It came at the wrong time for Gerald, when he was down.

She poured boiling water on the instant coffee in the cup, stirred it, added milk. I miss him so much. How are we going to become tolerant of each other? Unsought, Barbara's pale face seemed to float before her. Here at least was someone who needed her, who had sought her help. If she's still alive . . . and with the thought her dread came back.

She lifted her cup and carried it back to the room, sat down beside the telephone. She looked at the name and address scribbled on the pad. Would it perhaps be better to call first? No, ring. She found the entry in the telephone book which was heartening. Donald Sheldon became flesh and blood, not a phantom. She dialled the number, heard the ringing-out signal, listened to it for a long time. There was no one there. She tried at intervals of half an hour, but there was no doubt about it: the house was empty. She imagined it stripped of furniture, bare boards, letters behind the door. He became a phantom again.

It was impossible to visualize him, to clothe him with a personality. Barbara had looked unmarried, unattached. Nothing about her gave that completeness which one usually associates with marriage . . . only if it's happy, she reminded herself.

She sat irresolute by the telephone for a few minutes. What to do? The day stretched ahead bleakly. She had never been a girl with a lot of friends, nor had she ever felt the need to confide in those she had. She'd always been too busy, too sure of where she was going. That was the persona which had been unconsciously nurtured at home. Now it looked as if there would have to be a reappraisal.

She must learn to involve herself in Gerald, think of his health. Illnesses were always thrown off at home; cures were sought in a bracing walk. Tantrums were dealt with by visiting some old man or woman in the village so that she would 'count her blessings'.

Habit dies hard, she thought, as she got ready to call on Ruth Stanhope. She had somehow to banish from her memory the sadness of Gerald's mouth, white-ridged, the pathos of the two suitcases disappearing round the corner, as if it had been her marriage disappearing.

She bought toys for the Stanhope children and fruit for Ronald who was an invalid. An hour later she was pushing a pram with a sleeping child round the quiet backwaters of Hampstead. Ruth, in her usual muddle, had welcomed her with open arms.

'Ronald's poorly today, and I'd like it to be quiet for him. It's so good of you to think of us. You can keep Jonathan away for as long as you like; he adores being pushed.' Why was it that the tired face of her friend and the noisy romping children had made her envious. Was it because she imagined Ruth to be living at a more profound level? Was there something hidden in her own problem with Gerald which she wasn't even prepared to acknowledge?

She had imagined that she would be tormented by thoughts of him, but instead it was the pale hovering face of Barbara which haunted her on her walk. 'Help me, help me . . .' She imagined the words. The unease was there, worse than ever. People slid past her as if in a dream; she saw into other dreamlike worlds through the windows of houses; everything was at one remove from her, she thought, in the Saturday afternoon stillness. I'm afraid for her, she thought, afraid . . .

CHAPTER EIGHT

She felt she had lived through a life-time when she got back to the office on Monday morning. How tidy and secure office life was, a microcosm, certainly, but so well-ordered, with her own desk and chair, and in front of her the neatly-typed petition headed *Smithers v. Smithers*. She rang and Bella came in, dressed in a pinafore of camel colour, a brown blouse underneath, her pony tail tied with a brown ribbon. All was right with the world, or nearly.

'Good weekend, Bella?'

'Yes, thanks. We were Do-it-Yourself-ing. I like painting and John enjoys hanging wallpaper, so we had a lovely time. We had fish and chips and beer sitting on the floor like a couple of kids . . .' She stopped short. 'Maybe that's what we are . . . a couple of kids, immature.'

'What makes you think that?'

'Something John said, that it wasn't Do-it-Yourself-ing but Do-it-for-Yourself-ing. It made me wonder . . .' She shrugged. 'What did you do?'

'Madly exciting.' The thought of Gerald was too painful to mention. 'Pushed Jonathan Stanhope all round Hampstead, was ogled at by three old gentlemen, waved at by two joggers and got into conversation with a collie. Jonathan didn't even open one eye. Ronald says he's going to be a high-powered diplomat who sleeps his time away on jets.'

'How is he?'

'Worse. M.S. is terrible. It kicks you back just when you're doing fine. They're both so brave . . . is our friend, Mrs Smithers, here?'

'Yes, she was waiting at the door when I arrived.'

'Give me ten minutes to read this, and then send her in.

And by the way, Bella, this number . . .' she produced the scrap of paper, 'I'm trying to get hold of Mr Sheldon. Would you have a go from time to time?'

'Yes.' She took the note. 'I'll leave you to get on with it.'

How satisfying our relationship is, Karin thought, a tidy feminine arrangement with staked fences. 'Do not proceed beyond this point.' But you couldn't count on anything. Bella was free to give up work if she wanted to; John might move out of London . . . he wanted a house with a garden too. Did he want more? A child, perhaps? She thought of his remark, 'Do-it-Yourself-ing'. One tended to forget that a man's urge to have a child could be as strong as a woman's more accepted biological urge. Gerald had wanted children . . .

No, you couldn't count on anything. Barbara, for instance. Here one day, gone the next, like somone dying . . . the fear was like a sickness rising in her throat. She forced down her panic and tried to concentrate on reading the petition.

'Mrs Smithers, Mrs Armstrong.' Bella had shown in the woman.

One thing you *could* count on was people like Mrs Smithers and their consistency, she thought, feeling calmer. Her face today was even less attractive, surrounded by a new perm with tight unnatural-looking curls which had an element of frizz in them. She looked with her sharp nose like a field-mouse peeping out of its hole.

'Hello, Mrs Smithers. Sit down, please.' She did, her lips pulled tight, ready for anything. 'The petition for your divorce is ready now.' Smile to set her at ease. 'If it's in order it will go to the court today and be put on the waiting list.'

'He'll probably deny everything,' the woman said, pushing up her hair at the back with her hand, and thereby making her face appear smaller than ever. 'He never admitted there was another woman although I taxed him with it every night he came home late.'

'Your husband will present his own petition through his

solicitor. If there are too many discrepancies they will be queried. In any case, adultery doesn't have to be proved nowadays.'

'You mean they don't set detectives on him to catch him sitting up in bed with her and take their photograph?' She looked disappointed.

'No, that's all gone, worse luck.' Karin smiled. 'All we need is proof of the irretrievable breakdown of the marriage. I have to ask you this, Mrs Smithers. You don't think, even at this late date, you could come together?' He should take his chance and run a hundred miles . . .

'No, thanks,' Mrs Smithers said. 'We never did see eye to eye right from the start. We should have had more talks; dialogues, they call them now. We don't agree on one single thing, even politics. He's Conservative, I'm Labour. Constant argy-bargy all the time. Then he started this caper of staying out later and later. Once when I taxed him, he said it was for peace. Can you imagine it? Sitting in rowdy bars for peace when he had a nice home.'

Peace of the soul, Mrs Smithers, but how could you understand? 'Yes, well, I admit it's difficult to understand. Here's a copy for you. We'll go over the petition again. I think you've got enough here unless your husband refutes it.'

'Refutes?' She looked puzzled. If you're going to run a typewriting agency, Mrs Smithers, you'll have to invest in a good dictionary.

'Proves that your statement is in error. If he says, for instance, that as far as he was concerned there were no disagreements; if he doesn't corroborate the incidents you told me about . . .'

'It doesn't matter whether he corroborates them or not, does it? I've got them all down in my diary.'

'But if the entries in your diary . . .' Give it up. Who wouldn't want to get away from a tartar like this, permed or unpermed, with absolutely no insight . . . who else do you know like that, who wants to run her marriage on her own terms only? That was too near the bone. 'Thank you for coming, Mrs Smithers.'

The woman had just gone when Bella rang through. 'I've got a reply to that number you gave me. It's a Miss Boscombe who's answered. I'll put her on.'

'Thanks.' She waited, heard a slightly cockney voice. 'Hello, who's speaking?'

'This is Karin Armstrong.'

'They said Saithe and Saithe . . .'

'Yes, we're solicitors. I wanted to speak to Mr Sheldon, if it's possible. Does he still live there?'

'Don? 'Course he does. It's his house.' She sounded good-natured.

'Is there any chance of making an appointment to see him, do you think?' She sensed the hesitation. 'I'd better explain. I'm a friend of his divorced wife, Barbara, and I just wanted a few particulars . . .' The thought struck her. 'Are you Mrs Sheldon?'

'Not on your life. I'm Chloe Boscombe. I just live here. Don'll be home around five. Could you phone then?'

'I'd rather like to see him if I may. Would it be a terrible imposition if I came to your house about five? I promise I won't take up much of his time.'

'Don't you worry about that. If it's a legal matter you'll want to get it squared up. Do you know the way here?'

'I know Chiswick. Is it far from Turnham Green?'

'No distance if you're driving. Go down Dukes Avenue and it's off there.'

'I'll find it easily. Thank you very much. I'll be there about five.'

'Right. See you.'

She hung up, glad that at last she could take some action to relieve the nagging anxiety about Barbara, and her feeling of disappointment in herself. The belief that she had failed both Gerald and Barbara was still with her. Had she been too brash with the girl so that in the end she had felt unable to confide in her, just as she had turned away Gerald when he'd come back full of hope the next morning? Those suitcases . . . she took a tissue from the box in her drawer and blew her nose, then sat straight, hands clasped, eyes burning, to take a straight look at herself.

Perhaps she hadn't been doing enough of that. Success had come too easily for her; failure was the better teacher. Perhaps it was her failure to find Barbara which was opening her eyes to her own personal relationship with Gerald. But as always, with the thought of the girl, fear rose in her throat, choking her, a fear which had nothing to do with logic, a dread . . .

She rang for Bella. 'I'm going to work like a demon till four o'clock,' she said when she came in, 'then I'm going off early.'

The girl who opened the door to her had a frizzy perm like Mrs Smithers, but it looked right on her. She wore dangling earrings, a tight tee-shirt and jeans, sabots on her bare feet, and a lot of makeup on a face which was pretty but not vapid.

'Hello,' Karin said. 'I phoned you earlier.' The girl's smile was wide, pink-gummed.

'Hello. Come in. I thought you'd be a dry-as-dust lawyer, or something. Don's not back yet. I forgot he sometimes stops off at the pub for a quickie. Well, you know men; they like to unwind. Don't know how they stand it, going out day after day, women too for that matter. It would drive me round the bend.' She led the way, still chattering, into a pleasant sittingroom. 'Me, I'm a home person.'

Karin thought she could see some of Barbara still there. The walls and curtains were a quiet green. So were the chairs and the sofa, as if quietness had been important. But superimposed on its quietness was a lot of colour which might well be Miss Boscombe's choice; some screaming pseudo-abstract paintings framed too expensively for their worth, and what her mother called do-das: little tables, two stuffed dogs, one of inordinate length guarding the door, a herd of blown-glass animals on their own shelves, a pouffe covered in bright leather patchwork.

'I've got a spot of coffee ready. Park yourself anywhere you like.' The coffee was on a plastic tray reminiscent of a rampaging herbaceous border, and the pot was spattered like a daisy field in summer. She poured out the coffee and handed it to Karin in a blue ceramic mug. 'Sugar, cream?'

'A little cream, please. This is very welcome after a hard day.' She smiled, looked around. 'What a pleasant room this is, and such a nice view of the garden! It must be marvellous in summer with that patio.' She felt she was being fulsome, but Miss Boscombe evidently liked superlatives.

'Yes, it's super, isn't it? Don works a lot in the garden; he's very proud of it. I laughed at you thinking we were married, but I couldn't blame you.'

'I thought . . .'

'Don't apologize. As a matter of fact, we let people assume it around here. It's quite a classy neighbourhood. But I don't believe in marriage, you see, Miss Armstrong.'

'Mrs.'

'You evidently do.' She had a short, high-pitched giggle. 'Sorry.'

'Sometimes I wonder.' Karin laughed too, then sipped her coffee.

'I prefer an ongoing relationship,' Miss Boscombe said seriously. 'When they stop being that I move on. Nothing will persuade me into marriage again. I had a disastrous first one.' She rolled her eyes. 'Well, I expect you've heard it all, being a solicitor.'

'Most of it.'

'Of course, I like the relationship to be stable, nothing riff-raffish, and I must have a decent house with it and a garden or a patio. As long as I can get the sun. I'm a sun worshipper. You'd be surprised how much sun you get if you strip at the slightest opportunity, even in England. I can't stand my body to be white. Ugh!' She gave a realistic shiver. 'Have you ever been to Majorca?'

'No unfortunately.'

'I love it. Relationship or not, I'm off there when the

summer comes or what we call the summer here. As a matter of fact I've met one or two nice chaps there. Not Don, though, he's the exception. I met him in a taxi queue. I stepped out of line there, in more ways than one.' Her laughter shrieked, was bottled up again. 'Maybe it won't be successful. Still, you can but try. I'm easy to live with, a real home-lover, except when I'm in Majorca.' Karin heard the noise of the door shutting above the girl's high-pitched giggle. 'Here he is. He hasn't kept you waiting too long after all.'

Karin looked up with interest as the man came in, smiling, said, 'Ah,' when he saw her, 'I noticed the car . . .' He had a quizzical, self-conscious handsomeness, fair eyebrows raised, as if he had a set of expressions to suit each circumstance. He was dressed with careful attention to detail, his light grey suit, beige shirt, and the grey, beige and white striped tie were clever.

'This is Mrs Armstrong, Don,' Chloe Boscombe said. 'I think she wants to speak to you about Barbara.' She saw his eyes flicker; then he was playing his role again, if it were one: genial, a quirky smile, as if it was important to him to be liked. The kind of man, Karin thought, who would attract a girl of eighteen with his surface sophistication, or someone like Chloe Boscombe who would like a 'good-looker'.

'Hello, Mrs Armstrong.' His handclasp was firm.

'I'll go and make some fresh coffee, sweetie,' the girl said. 'This will be cold. Mrs Armstrong and I have been having ever such a nice chat.' She lifted the daisy-spattered coffee pot and clattered away on her sabots.

'I hope you don't mind me coming to your house like this,' Karin said.

'Not at all.' He strode to the windows and peered at nothing in the garden. He was suddenly tense. 'What is it you want to know about Barbara?'

'I'm not prying, please believe me, nor am I acting in any legal capacity.' He turned to face her, hands in pockets, nonchalant, one eyebrow raised. 'Barbara phoned me recently out of the blue and we spent a weekend together at Dieppe. She didn't turn up at the boat going back as we'd arranged.' A flicker of fear appeared in his eyes, was quickly dowsed.

'Did you report it to the police?'

'I did. They're . . . investigating it.'

'So, what's worrying you, Mrs Armstrong?'

'Just that . . . she had every intention of coming back with me.' He looked at her, his eyes flat. 'She mentioned she had an Aunt Berthe . . .' Barbara's words came back to her, 'Some people, like my Aunt Berthe, say they like it inland . . .' 'Do you know where she lives?'

'I didn't know her; she didn't come to our wedding. I think it was Rouen . . .' 'like it inland . . .' Her heart lifted.

'Can you remember her address?'

'No,' he was brusque, impatient, 'given time I might recall it. I don't know . . .' Chloe Boscombe pushed open the door with one of her sabots and came in with the coffee pot.

'Well,' she said, 'have you two sorted everything out?' He looked coldly at her, as if she'd said the wrong thing.

'We're trying to,' Karin said. 'I hope it's not too distressing for Mr Sheldon.'

'Where angels fear to tread?' The giggle ran up and down the scale. 'Better to get it straight, that's my opinion, but a divorced wife is a delicate subject. Isn't it, poppet?' He looked past her.

'Did you ever meet Barbara?' Karin asked her.

'No, I came on the scene before the divorce . . . well, just before. I wasn't the root cause, maybe a tiny little trigger. But I've seen pictures of her, haven't I, darling? Pretty. What my mother used to call "retiring". She used to wish I was a bloody bit more retiring.' She strangled the giggle, straightened her face. 'Got to watch what you say, Chloe, Don doesn't like it. Has anything happened to her?'

'I hope not,' Karin said. 'I feel anxious about her, that's all.'

'Mrs Armstrong spent a weekend in Dieppe with her but

Barbara stayed on.' Sheldon spoke shortly.

'She *intended* to come back with me,' Karin said. 'We made arrangements to meet at the boat.'

'Oh, yes?' For a girl who seemed lively she showed little interest. She poured out some coffee, handed the cup to Don Shelton. 'There you are, ducky. Nice and strong, the way you like it.' She said, as he took it from her, 'Did you tell her about the accident?'

'What accident?' Karin looked at the man. He was stirring his coffee, his head bent downwards.

'You shouldn't keep it back,' the girl said.

'I'm not keeping anything back.' He raised his face and Karin saw the pettishness. 'We hadn't got round to it. Anyhow, it's past history.' He looked at Karin. 'I'll tell you if you like.'

'Not if it distresses you.' She was sympathetic.

'It was Barbara it distressed.' He gave a short laugh. 'It was nothing much, icy roads, a slight skid when we were in the car. The shock. It affected Barbara.'

'She told me about losing the baby,' Karin said gently. 'Was it then?' She heard a noise. The girl was drumming her painted fingernails on the window-pane.

'It could have happened at home, see?' He appealed to Karin. 'I mean, any little thing could have made it happen. It was just unfortunate . . . stop that noise, Chloe!' His voice was suddenly sharp. The girl sat back, clasped her hands. 'Well, you can imagine. She blamed me. Things went from bad to worse. I felt terrible about it. I tried very hard, but I just couldn't stand it . . .' his eyes went to the girl again. She was looking out of the window, ' . . . the way she . . .' he drew his hand over his face then looked beyond Karin as if at some frightening memory, ' . . . the way she became. I tried hard to be patient, but it was no good. We began to drift apart, and then around that time I met Chloe . . .'

'Just as well!' She almost flounced round to look at them both. 'And not before time. He was down to skin and bone, worrying, Mrs Armstrong, and that's not exaggerating, but

I said, well, if you can't stand it, give it up. Not everybody's cup of tea *that*, I said, not for a sensitive, well-brought-up man. So I whipped him off to Majorca. No good torturing yourself, is there?'

'When I came back we agreed on the divorce,' Don Sheldon said. 'Put it like this, I didn't know her any more.' Karin saw something in his eyes for a second, like a remembered terror. 'She was a different girl from the one I'd married.'

'It's very good of you to tell me all this,' she said. 'It must be painful for you.'

'You have no idea,' he said flatly, 'what I went through.'

What about Barbara? Karin thought. 'I'm sorry to have revived unhappy memories. It . . . explains things about Barbara for me.'

'What do you mean?' He looked suspicious.

'I gathered she'd been through some trauma. Indeed, I wondered if there had been any . . .' no, she wouldn't say 'violence', ' . . . trouble. I see it now. The accident, and losing the baby. If I've distressed you, I'm sorry. I shouldn't have barged in like this. You see, Barbara, coming out of the past as she did . . . I hadn't seen her for eight years . . . made an impression on me. I felt she wanted my help. I wouldn't like to think she was still wanting it, waiting for it.'

'Barbara's deep,' he said. 'You'll never get to the bottom of her.' There's still something he hasn't told me, Karin thought. There was an uneasy pause which Chloe Boscombe broke.

'Well, that's the way of the world,' she said gaily. 'We've all got our private faces and our public faces. I bet you're quite different at home with your husband, Mrs Armstrong, than you are in the office.'

'You've no idea,' Karin said, and was rewarded, if that was the word, by another high-pitched giggle.

Don Sheldon saw her to the door. His truculence had gone. Now he seemed to want to win her approval. 'You'll understand, being a solicitor,' he said. 'You'll come across all kinds of cases, all kinds of . . . variations. Some couples just can't get on together. When something happens to one of them, they often don't share the burden; they get wrapped up in themselves, become very private, the way Barbara did. Doctor Brightley said she needed support, and believe me, I tried; my God, I tried. I wept often.' He made the peculiar gesture again, drawing his hand over his face as if to smooth out its expression. Karin saw the flicker of fear again in his eyes. 'You can't go on blaming yourself.' He lowered his voice. 'You can see, Chloe's different, easy-going, you know what I mean, but not . . .' he shrugged his shoulders. Did he mean, 'not in the same class'?

'I understand,' she said diplomatically. 'And I appreciate your taking me into your confidence . . .'

'But I haven't,' he interrupted her impatiently, 'that's just the point. I haven't *nearly* told you the whole truth. But who's to say what the truth *is*. It's too difficult for me. The words won't . . .' His voice changed, became consciously charming again. 'If I come across that address I'll give you a buzz. Like to please the ladies. Have you your telephone number?'

'Yes.' She gave him a card. 'I should have let you see that earlier.'

'You've an honest face.' She responded to the charm of his smile.

'Thanks. And if you hear from her, please let me know. It's a strange thing,' she said, looking at him, 'how Barbara occupies my mind.'

He nodded, his mouth grim. 'She's never out of mine.'

CHAPTER NINE

It is about a week ago since it happened, and I haven't reached my destination yet. When I got as far as Rouen I felt so ill that I had to stay in this little hotel. Luckily I remembered I still had an account in the bank here, and so I'm not short of money. But I haven't wanted food. I've lain here like a sick animal going over and over that terrible episode on the beach at Dieppe.

I lay there doubled up with the pain in my heart and my body. Which was worse, I ask now, the pain of humiliation, of degradation to the point of death, or pain from the bruises, inside and out, which were inflicted on me? But I remember that despite the terrible physical assault my mind struggled with something even more terrible, always lying in wait to confront me.

It was so cold and dark. The sky which stretched over me was starless, the pebbles rolled slowly as the waves receded. Apart from that sound there was a quietness on the deserted beach. The man had gone, slithering over the pebbles as he had come. And I knew by the darkness that the boat had gone with Karin in it, and with it my salvation. Desolation filled me. I wanted to die. And I remember I pulled my duffle coat closely round me, trying to find some comfort in looking back over my past.

Chiswick was nice, and being married to Don was good at first. I thought him so handsome, especially when he got ready for bed and was in his striped pyjamas, his fair hair tousled by pulling his clothes over his head. He taught me how to make love, how to excite him and how to hold on to my excitement. I hadn't realized it was a game with rules which made it better if you knew them.

We spent a lot of time showing our love to each other; we did stupid childish things like hiding from each other and chasing each other about the house and having mock fights on the floor, but always ending up in bed where we did secret things and talked a secret language.

It was such a different life for me from the one I'd led with my mother in the flat at Gloucester Road. She believed in self-control at all times, a stiff-backed formality which didn't admit of spontaneity. I used to hate coming home from the college and finding her sitting there, at the window, waiting for me. The table would be elegantly set for four o'clock tea, the Limoges china and the lace napkins would be in their precise places, silently reproaching me for being late.

'Don't you *know* anyone, Mother?' I once said to her, cruelly. I had refused an invitation to go home with a friend on her account. 'You could ask that nice woman from downstairs to tea. She said to me she'd like to know you better.'

'Why should I need to ask any woman downstairs when I have you?' she said. 'I allowed you to go to boarding school because it was your father's wish. You never gave a thought to my being alone for all those years . . .' But I did, Mother, and if I hadn't, you kept reminding me in all your letters, endlessly . . .

Perhaps it was her Frenchness which made her feel apart from others. Sometimes I wished I could have joined some of the societies or gone on the outings arranged at the college, but it didn't greatly matter to me. I wasn't gregarious either, but the sight of her always waiting for me in the flat depressed me. We lived too closely; we got on each other's nerves.

I suppose subconsciously I was looking for Don. But it was so easy, as it happened, so simple and natural. He lived in a flat in the same block, and we used to travel down in the lift together most mornings. He was very handsome with an Englishness which appealed to me, fair skin and hair, broad-shouldered, perfect manners. He was an accountant.

In no time at all I was head-over-heels in love with him, a tremulous, not-to-be-denied first love. He told me he had a house in Chiswick which had been left to him by his parents, and I longed to live in it with him. It seemed like freedom to me.

When he said that the people who rented it were leaving, and should we get married, I could hardly wait. Perhaps I wouldn't have been in such a hurry if mother hadn't opposed it so much. She thought the idea was absurd, that I was far too young. She wanted me to go to Rouen and stay with Aunt Berthe, and I thought she must be desperate to suggest that. Ever since *grand-mère* had died and left Tamaris to us, my mother and my aunt had hardly been on speaking terms. How I dream about Tamaris . . . But it's Don I'm thinking about just now. How scrupulously polite my mother was to him when he called, but how her English faltered after a time, which was a sure sign she was upset. She always spoke to him in a stilted fashion, and pretended to be at a loss for a phrase.

She had a bad migraine when I said I was going to marry him. I was terrified. She lay in her bedroom for three days, and at night I once or twice heard her being violently sick. I said to Don I was going to call it off, but he said, no, I mustn't give in. He was twenty-five, had a good job, and unlike most young men, he had a house of his own. Most mothers, (he could look like a little boy when he was aggrieved), would be glad to see their daughters marrying a decent man. In fact in many ways they were alike; they both liked conformity.

On the third day she emerged from her bedroom when I was sitting at the table doing my homework. I had examinations that week, and I felt I ought to have some kind of certificate to prove I had completed a year's course. I never knew when I might need it.

'You're still going to marry this man?' she asked me, sitting down at her chair by the window. I thought she sat there so that she wouldn't have to meet my eyes. I was shocked by her appearance. She must have lost half a stone, and her face was chalk white, her black hair dull. I had been prompted by Don, and young girls in love can be cruel.

'You mustn't make a grand drama out of it, Mother,' I said. 'You've done this all my life. It isn't a grand drama. I'm marrying Don because I love him. We have a house. You'll always be welcome to visit us or come to stay.' And then I broke down. 'Mother,' I said, 'you're making my life miserable. Grand-mère Malle married an Englishman, so did you. I thought you'd have been glad.'

She gave me a bitter look. 'And what happened? Your grandfather was killed at Sword Beach by the Boche, your own father died when you were eight. Was there any joy in that, any happiness?'

'But that's nothing to do with Don, or being English!' I burst out.

'Isn't it? I've spent my time in England so that there would be a place for you to come to. I've lived alone in my misery. I sent you away to school because your father wished it, because I promised him. I've squandered my life for you in this wretched country, knowing the only place I could have been happy in was Tamaris, my real home.'

'Well, why not go back?' I said. 'You'd be much happier there, and after all, it belongs to you. Don and I could visit you.'

She suddenly started screaming. The sound pierced my eardrums. I wanted to hide away. 'That's it. Pack me away when you don't need me any longer. After all I've done for you, to please your father. It all began with him. He persuaded me, begged me . . .'

'Begged you to send me away to school?' I was confused.

'No, long before that. When you . . .' She seemed to bite the words back. 'Well, forget about me. I'm not surprised. But I'll tell you something. This *bêtise* of yours won't succeed. No good ever comes out of cruelty, out of devotion to self . . .'

I'd had enough. I couldn't understand her. I went running out of the flat and upstairs to Don's. I was afraid of her; can you imagine being afraid of one's own mother? He comforted me, and said I had called her bluff, but that seemed to me a singularly English way of putting it. It was a far deeper thing than any kind of game. There was something there, buried deep, which belonged to the past.

She came round, as hysterics always do. I discovered this living with her. They put on smooth faces to outsiders, and no one knows the misery they have caused. She gave us a beautiful wedding arranged with all her French elegance; she invited the right people, she sent an announcement to the school for the magazine. I felt like a stiff white doll in my Valenciennes lace dress with *grand-mère's* veil. I felt there was a Malle curse on me. That sounds as hysterical as my mother.

The first two years of being married to Don were like entering a new world of lightness and gaiety which I'd never known. We were idyllically happy, playing house and making love. I was ravished, transported with delight. I was a virgin when Don married me; there had been no opportunities, and I had been unwilling to make them. I wondered afterwards if that was why he'd married me, that I had a virginal appeal for him.

But he was a sweet lover, playful and gentle even in his passion. He teased me about my eagerness. I became a different person. In the morning I was a young housewife who walked out to do the shopping, who had a coffee at one of the many Chiswick coffee shops, who read incessantly, (I had made out a list of books I intended to study), who went walking again in the afternoon along by the river, and who then bathed and put on a fresh dress for her husband coming home. It was a doll's house world, unreal. He at least was experiencing reality every day in his office; I lived in a blissful state of suspension from reality.

The only worry was my mother. She had gone back to France, to live in Tamaris, and so her presence had been removed, but not my anxiety about her. She had begun to write strange letters. Sometimes she talked as if my grandfather were still in the house, but when I thought of Tamaris I remembered how redolent it was of him, and I understood. Once she wrote, 'I go often to Sword Beach. That is where he came out of the sea . . .'

I showed them to Don but he only said she was going 'nicely gaga' through living alone, and not to worry. Eccentrics are acceptable to the English; sometimes their lack of sensitivity disturbs me, or their pretence of that lack. The only person I've known in my life who seemed to listen to me, to be concerned about me, was Karin. But not any longer. I didn't keep my promise to her, I let her down. What an English remark that is, and how important it is to them! If a friend 'lets them down', it is worse than a crime.

But most of the time I didn't worry overmuch about my mother. I was too busy being married and in love. And we were both excited at the thought of the coming baby, the way children would be if they'd been promised a special toy for Christmas. Now our Chiswick doll's house would have another occupant. We decorated the spare room in pale colours; we put up gauzy curtains at the windows which were always open to keep the room sweet.

We decided to celebrate my three months' pregnancy by driving to Buckinghamshire to a pub Don knew, 'one of the few where the food is better than the beer,' he said. We were happy that dark winter night spinning along through Berkhampstead and Tring; I said how pretty it was in the headlights; perhaps we'd sell up and come to live in the country. The air would be better for the baby, there was a good train service, and each morning I'd drive Don to the station. See how I behaved, a dream world . . .

Looking back I had a kind of premonition, the Malle curse. No, that's ridiculous, too fanciful altogether. But the menu was in French, and the dishes we chose, *potage soubise brune, sole à la blanchaille, crème caramel*, reminded me of my mother's cooking which had been exquisite. I was aware of her presence throughout the meal; I could almost feel her bending over me, see her sharp profile, her smooth dark hair, those large restless eyes . . . We didn't drink a lot, a bottle of *Pouilly Fouisse* between us and no liqueurs. Don was driving; he was respectful of the law. 'Chaps have their duty to do,' he said of policemen with breathalyzers.

It was foggy going back and the temperature had dropped suddenly. I think they get a lot of fog in Bucks. We had driven from town through rain, and now we could see that the road was like a skating rink in parts; when we *could* see, that is. The windscreen kept misting up. 'Drive carefully,' I said to Don, and he said, 'You know I always do.' Which was true enough. And he already thought of himself as a prospective father. He talked of cricket bats and schools, English things . . . in no way can he be blamed for what happened. I keep reminding myself of that, keep reminding myself . . .

One minute we were going along at a steady thirty-five, the next minute we had skidded across the road and banged into a tree. It happened so quickly that I knew no terror, only pain as the belt tightened and cut into my abdomen. With the thud of my head against the windscreen I lost consciousness. It must have been momentary because almost immediately, it seemed, I heard Don saying, 'You aren't hurt, say you aren't hurt, Baba.'

There was no broken glass. I felt my head, it wasn't cut, and there was no blood, just a dull soreness. 'Good thing I was wearing my seat-belt.' His face was so white in the darkness that I wanted to reassure him. 'No, I don't think I'm hurt at all. How about you?' And then I realized I was hurt inside. There was a sticky wetness between my thighs.

'I'm okay,' he was saying, 'but the car's taken an awful bashing. Luckily there was no one else on the road. Must get out and see what damage . . .' I wasn't worried about the car. 'Get a doctor!' I screamed at him.

The Tring doctor was very good. He had us both taken to the hospital at Aylesbury for the night, and we were discharged the next day. I sat in the lounge of a hotel in the Market Square for what seemed hours while Don made arrangements about the car being towed in and mended. I couldn't hold my coffee cup; my hands were shaking badly;

I had lost the baby.

We had to hire a car to drive back to Chiswick because Don wouldn't hear of me travelling by train, and when I got home I went to bed and stayed there for two days. I didn't want to move or speak. I didn't weep. Don got Dr Brightley to come in and he was as cheerful as his name and said not to worry; I was young enough to have plenty more.

Don sat at my bedside, looking miserable. He kept on justifying himself to me. 'I was being careful. It was that damned road.' I tried to comfort him. There would be a next time, quite soon, the doctor had said so. My head ached. The dull soreness was still there. A bit of concussion, Dr Brightley had said.

On the second day the ache seemed to have expanded, filling my whole head with its steady throbbing. Don wearied me beyond words with his incessant rumination. Leave it, I wanted to say. It's finished, over. I had been watching the top of his fair head as he knelt at my bedside, and I saw how, close to the roots there was a darkness as if he bleached it, which I knew wasn't so. My vision seemed to be sharpened, and the clarity seemed to make my headache worse. I could see every strand, every hair; some looked as if they had tiny beads of gilt along their entire length. I couldn't bear the clarity and the brightness, I couldn't bear his moaning any longer. I screamed at him, screamed; his face came up, startled; I saw the pores on his nose, how the wings of his nostrils had whitened, and then I don't know what happened. I can't remember. No, that's not true, I don't care to remember. It's too distressing. It tears my heart out even yet, because that was when it all started . . .

CHAPTER TEN

The next morning Karin decided that she had to put personal considerations aside for the time being and concentrate on her work. She had a reputation for reliability to live up to, and Bella had said young Reginald had been looking for her yesterday. 'That's the second time Karin has hopped off early,' she reported him having said. He was like his father: he never missed a trick.

There were letters and documents to sign, and the weekly meeting when old Reginald got himself up-to-date with what was going on and gave some avuncular advice when he thought it necessary.

'Smithers v. Smithers,' he said to Karin. 'I've never read such a tight petition in all my experience. But you know, all those dates and times are no use if they can't be corroborated.'

'I know, Mr Reginald. She kept a diary of every movement.'

'God help us,' he said, 'the ploys some women get up to. If it weren't for men everything in the garden would be lovely, wouldn't it?'

'I like them around.' She smiled at him, wondering if news had leaked to him that she and Gerald were living apart. Although he lived a blameless and harmonious life with his elderly wife, he liked to pretend he was a gay blade, a harmless enough pretence.

She telephoned Carr and Beckett, Mr Smithers' solicitors, explained the reason for her call, and was put through to Mr Netherton. 'Hello,' she said, 'just to let you know my petition in the Smithers v. Smithers case has gone to court.'

'Mine too. Look, I'll be around your way tomorrow

afternoon. Could I pop in and see you?'
'What time?'
'Two-thirty?'
'Fine. I can fit you in between clients.'

Mr Netherton was a stocky, brusque little man, as she'd imagined from his Geordie accent, although there was no logical reason to suppose so. Gerald was tall and sinewy, she reminded herself, and somewhere along the line he'd lost the broad vowels of his childhood. The solicitor sat down at Karin's desk and opened his brief case. He wasted no time. 'Mr Smithers refutes everything his wife has said,' he told her.

'I'm not surprised.' The case was becoming as puzzling as Barbara's, although she could scarcely call that a 'case' as yet. But a mystery. She'd heard nothing further from the Newhaven Police. She said, 'If he's implying my client is lying, he's still got grounds for saying he can't be expected to live with her.'

'The odd thing is, he's wavering now. He says they've been married twenty years and he's fond of her. He's prepared to believe it might be her time of life, as he puts it.'

'Is he, now?' Karin sat back to smile. 'Life's full of surprises, isn't it?'

'That's what I like. No matter how dull your own life is, there's plenty of drama in your work.' He grinned back at her. 'Although a pretty girl like you will have plenty of drama.' He got up. 'Just thought I'd put you in the picture. We can sit back and watch, I think.' He gave her a fatherly smile. 'I hear very good reports of you. Been made a partner, haven't you?'

'Yes. It's generous of you to pass on the good reports.'

'You don't find jealousy in the legal profession. Women have a genius for detail which we sometimes lack.'

'You've made my day, Mr Netherton.' She got up to show him out, unaccountably cheered.

The following morning Gerald rang her. 'Would you

believe it?' he said, voice cracking, 'I've got today off.'

'Have you?' She was wary, although the sound of his voice shook her.

'I wondered . . .'

'I had plans for today, Gerald . . .' She'd thought of driving down to Newhaven Police Station. Barbara was still very much on her mind.

'I thought we might have a walk together. The sun's shining.'

She'd barely had time to notice. It was a rare gift of a day for March; even in the city you could feel the stirrings of spring. And the bluetits which she kept supplied with peanuts outside her window seemed to be flirtier than usual. She longed to be in the country, to walk and peer, to look closely at insects, into the eyes of flowers. 'All right,' she said. She'd scrub going to Newhaven. It hadn't been a sensible idea in any case.

She got ready quickly, tremblingly glad to be seeing him. She knew he missed the countryside which had rolled to his back door outside Newcastle, the moors, the great expanse of sky. Some of their happiest times when first married had been spent walking.

They met in Heath Street. She was struck by how white and thin he looked. They kissed because it was natural to both of them. 'You look beautiful,' he said. 'Your cheeks are pink.'

'I was rushing through my shopping.' They started to walk.

'Does that make your eyes blue too?'

'It's the reflection from the sky. I wish I could hand out compliments to you. You look thinner than ever.'

'I've got a new plan in eating. Little and often.'

He worried her. There was a peevish look about his mouth and his cheeks were sunken. 'Doctors are the last people to take advice, I know, but why don't you consult someone?'

'What about solicitors? You deal with marital problems all day and yet you can't see the wood for the trees in our situation.'

She bit back a retort. It took two to start a quarrel. 'Look, this is a nice day. Don't let's spoil it by getting personal.'

'Right,' he said, taking her arm, smiling at her, the peevish look gone. 'It's a boring old subject anyhow.' He looked around. 'I remember this . . .' They were walking down Lower Terrace to Frognal. Years ago, it seemed they'd played a game of house here. How often in their imaginings they'd evicted owners and had moved into their cottages! Why did that make her feel old, and sad? She spoke brightly.

'Don't you love the additions to that one? It's always the afterthoughts, the hidden patios, the unexpected balcony which makes a house appealing.'

'A natural progression, as if it had grown, rather than been built.' They started up the incline of Hollyhill.

'There's another one I like,' she said, stopping. If only it could be like this always, harmonious . . . 'And no front garden. A feeling of mystery. Do you think there's a magical, secret one at the back?'

'Could be. Talking about mystery, how's the one about Barbara faring?'

Her pleasure faded. The anxiety came rushing back. 'I went to see her ex. I got his address by phoning the school. They looked up an old magazine for the announcement of their marriage.'

'Just as I suggested. You really are single-minded about this girl, aren't you?'

'I keep thinking of her. *Barbara, rappelle-toi* . . .' She laughed self-consciously. 'That's from a book of poems she gave me to read in Dieppe. "Do you remember . . ." It isn't curiosity. It's a kind of involvement. You don't get it with many people. It's odd.'

He spoke gently in his husky voice, as if he had a permanent sore throat. 'I know. I've a few patients like that. They . . . inhabit your mind. The least likely ones, shy awkward ones. Not the pretty girls, strangely enough, although they can turn you on in a different way. What was he like?'

'Fair, handsome, not what you'd call a great presence. Maybe that's unfair. He's called Don and he's living with a breezy girl called Chloe. I didn't get much information from him until she reminded him he hadn't told me about the accident.'

'What accident?'

'Remember I told you she'd lost a baby, or that she'd miscarried? Apparently it was caused by a car accident. He was driving, the road was icy, he skidded and banged into a tree. She lost the baby as a result.'

'No other injuries?' His voice was suddenly sharp.

'He didn't say. Anyhow the marriage seemed to deteriorate and I gather he found solace in Chloe.'

'You're sure there were no after-effects, apart from the miscarriage?'

'I expect that was enough. No other physical ones. And yet he seemed to have been considerate enough, understood that she blamed him in a way.' She looked at Gerald. 'I had a feeling he was holding something back. He said as much.'

'He's bound to feel guilty. I suppose she'd seen a doctor?'

'Yes, he mentioned him. Dr . . . Brightley.' She was glad she'd remembered the name.

'Did he look like a wife beater?'

'I thought of that. Do they ever? He was definitely uneasy. But he said he'd give me Barbara's aunt's address if he came across it. He thought it was in Rouen.'

'Did you make that your excuse for calling on him?'

'Yes, and of course I told him about how Barbara had disappeared. That worried him. Then he asked me why I was worrying since the police had it in hand.'

'There's a bad smell about the whole thing.'

'Yes . . .' The fear was with her again. Had Sheldon secretly followed Barbara to Dieppe and waylaid her on her way to the boat? Had he been following them, spying on them? Her head ached. She tried to shake the worry away. 'Let's go along Keats' Grove. I've never been in his house, have you?'

'No . . .' He was distrait. 'I wonder why people can't communicate?'

'Barriers are put up. If you have a role to play, an official one, it's easy . . . oh, personal relationships are hell.'

The sun streamed into Keats' sitting-room and there was an air of gentle melancholy. Maybe communication meant *not* speaking. Maybe there were too many dialogues as Mrs Smithers called them. Occasionally they pulled aside the green curtains over the manuscripts and tried to decipher the handwriting. Gerald was good at it. She listened to him reading in his hoarse voice.

'"How unhappy I am for love of you."' He whispered the words because there was another couple in the room. '"And endeavour as much as I can to entice you to give up your whole heart to me, whose existence hangs upon you . . ."' He turned to look at her, holding her eyes with his. 'Ka . . .' The sunlight caught the amber fleck in his eyes. They were isolated, as if there was no one else in the room. She would have gone into his arms but the couple were coming nearer.

'Your whole existence doesn't depend on me, tell the truth.' She smiled uncertainly. 'You're busy, you're ambitious, your work comes first.'

He turned from her abruptly. 'It's meaningless without you.' He pulled the green curtains together.

Talk faltered between them as they walked to the pub. She stole a look at him. His face was white, his nose pinched-looking. He'd been and still was handsome with his lean fairskinned face and what she'd called in moments of love, his beautiful mouth. It always embarrassed him. He was the least vain of men, 'Penny for them?' she said. He shrugged his shoulders without answering.

They had a half lager each and sandwiches, sitting at the back looking on to the verandah. The sun had gone and it was too cold to sit out. A solitary grey squirrel dive-bombed into the refuse-bin near the window and reappeared with a titbit which it ate daintily between its paws. She looked at Gerald. He was taking small bites from his sandwich, nibbling round the edges in the same way. She felt a rush of affection for him, laughed to hide it. 'You look like that squirrel.'

'Sorry.' He wasn't amused. 'My appetite's gone.'

'After that nice long walk?'

'You know me. I'm not used to eating in the middle of the day.' He brooded over the sandwich.

'You should eat . . . Oh, Gerald.' Impatient love overwhelmed her.

'What do you mean, Oh, Gerald?'

'I don't know. You're broody; you shut me out. It's been good today, hasn't it, being together?'

'More than good.' He looked at her. 'Why don't we give up this separation lark?'

She was sorely tempted, even to say, 'Okay, and I'll give up the partnership, have less responsibility,' but she resisted it. There was *her* life too. She said. 'When we try, it's fine . . . I've thought and thought about it . . . when we're being careful, stepping warily, but it's that terrible, spontaneous bickering I can't take. It undermines me, my confidence in my work.'

He pushed aside the plate with his half-eaten sandwich. 'All right, well, I've got an idea. If you get the address of Barbara's aunt in Rouen I could come and help you to look for her. I'm due a few days off towards the end of the month.'

She brightened. It might be the solution. To get away, to have a common purpose, and to talk . . . 'I'm due for some time off too. Are you really interested in Barbara?'

'More than interested, but we've *got* to have time together. We can't go on like this, neither one thing nor the other. If we can't get together again, properly, we'd better think in terms of divorce.'

A shaft of pain shot through her. She was surprised at its

intensity. 'Is there anyone else?' She steadied her voice.

'Yes, me.'

'What do you mean?'

'Me a doctor, as a healer of sick bodies, as an individual. I don't want me ruined; I value me; I'd rather cut my losses than go on like this.'

'How about *me*?' she wanted to say, but she was afraid, for the first time. Her hand trembled and the lager slopped on to the table. She'd always been sure of him, that ultimately they'd get it right, given time. But what if they'd used it up? 'All right,' she said. 'I've thought, illogically, that if I could get this business of Barbara's sorted out, we'd get ourselves straight too. Does that sound weird?'

'No. In a way it's what I was thinking. And I've got a hunch too that this girl needs help badly.'

'Yes, I've got that feeling, very strongly. Oh, Gerald . . .' She stretched out her hand to him. His clasp was warm.

When they came to his car parked in Heath Street he took her hands and kissed her on the cheek. 'We're a couple of nutters,' he said. His face stayed against hers for a second, then he got into the car and drove away. His pale composed profile slid past her.

CHAPTER ELEVEN

I had known misery, but never like that. At least when I used to lie awake weeping after the accident I was warm. I could lie close to Don and hope I wouldn't disturb him.

But on that hard beach there was nothing to cheer me, or warm me. I tried to get up but the pain was too great, and there was some blood. I felt like a lamb I once saw being born. It tottered to its feet, the birth cord trailing.

But I can dream, and make plans, I remember thinking. There is a tenacity in me somewhere. I think I got it from my father, and his mother, certainly not from the Malles. Theirs was an obsession.

Often, as a child, when I sat in the dunes near *grand-mère's* house, I would think of my grandfather, Norman Sanctuary. Such a reassuring Anglo-Norman name! Hadn't Karin said something like that? If I wished, I could conjure up the scene *grand-mère* had described to me so often . . .

It was as if I were sitting in the stalls of the theatre. One moment there would be the huge emptiness of earth and sky, the next as if a curtain had gone up; the water and sky were made one by the smoke and spray, and the sea erupted and boiled like a cauldron. The present fell away from me as I watched . . .

Out of the chaos comes a great fleet of landing craft. Their bowels seem to open and spill out tanks, great water beasts which begin to lumber ashore. Round those beasts are their familiars, thousands of little figures of men struggling through the sea beside them, some scrambling ashore, some leaping up in agony to float on the waves and be gently laid on the sand.

Still they come. Sometimes the mist is torn apart when a water beast lumbers against one of the many giant hedgehogs which are sticking out of the water. The beast spits a tongue of flame and then becomes an inferno, lighting up the men who still struggle ashore, still leap in death agony, still float on the tide – pieces of men.

The noise is deafening. Big landing ships loom like whales in the sea behind the smaller craft, with soldiers swarming over them: ant-like figures. The German cannons roar behind me, and I turn to look at the beach. It is like a traffic jam at midday in Rouen. A soldier is directing men and vehicles as they come out of the sea with a nonchalance that amazes me.

I strain my eyes to pick him out of the milling men in uniform, Captain Norman Sanctuary of the First South Lancashire Regiment, but the smoke hangs like a heavy pall. Near me lies a young infantryman. His head has rolled a foot away from him; the eyes, still open, stare uncomprehendingly upwards. Out of the mist I see a German prisoner escorted by two soldiers, and I think, lucky prisoner, he at least has kept his head.

It is orderly chaos now. The soldier directing the traffic is making some sense out of it. The men begin to group. In a flash from the Bofors guns I see him, my grandfather. Quite apart from the photographs, *grand-mère* has described him so often, 'So English, *ma petite*, so tall, straight and resolute.' I had thought of him as Perseus on his winged horse, but he is on the beach, running ahead of his small group of men.

The cannons roar like a thousand yawning giants, the sea becomes pink. What looks like driftwood is an arm, a piece of machinery, a canvas haversack. Above the noise I'm sure I hear him shout, 'Come on, chaps!' The way *she* said it, it sounded like a foreign language. He is running, crouched, towards a blockhouse. His arm goes up and over, like bowling a cricket ball, and the square tower bursts into flames. I'm blinded by the explosion.

I can't see for the thick blanket of smoke. It floats over the sea and seems to churn it into a devil's porridge of men, boats and tanks, '*un véritable charnier*,' those are her words. Slowly the smoke clears like a reluctant curtain on a patch of beach where Captain Norman Sanctuary lies spread-eagled in death. An officer, battle-blouse torn, eyes dazed, comes out of the smoke leading a horse, and I hear him say to one of the soldiers standing at my grandfather's body, 'Found this. Damned fine hunter.' I think, how English, and watch him as he wanders away, leaving a trail of blood on the sand.

Now underneath the roaring and the firing and the bursting of shells there is a fainter noise, the sound of my *grand-mère* weeping, a steady wailing seeming to go on for ever . . .

I remember my mother, Marie, telling me *grand-mère* wept constantly for three days. She had no shame in her weeping, took no account of the two daughters hovering around her, needing to be comforted. I can imagine my mother, a girl of eight, afraid, not understanding grief, crouched at her mother's knees weeping in sympathy as children do, weeping loudly and long to please her mother.

And then, just as suddenly, *grand-mère's* weeping stopped. Her face was restored almost in an hour, and she comforted the two girls, telling them that death was not always a tragedy. 'He died for his country, and at least he redeemed himself in his death.' I asked my mother what he had done that he needed to redeem himself, but she said it was the way *grand-mère* talked. My mother and I were closer when I was small, I think. It was only when I met Don that the trouble began.

It seemed to please *grand-mère* that my mother followed her example of marrying an Englishman. 'You at least have missed the misery of war,' she said often, and once directly to me, 'Your mother will never know the agony I went through. It has never left me.' When I looked at her I saw her black eyes were burning with hatred, not filled with sorrow as I had expected. I was shocked. Perhaps war makes one bitter, I thought at the time.

But as I grew up I saw how she made a fetish of that agony she spoke of, setting it on a pedestal and worshipping it in Tamaris which she bought to be close to my grandfather's last resting-place in the British cemetery.

She liked us to worship at the shrine also, and it became our holiday home when father died, mother's and mine. Aunt Berthe was rarely there. She kept to the family home near the church of St Ouen. She hardly ever visited us there. She preferred to be alone. I remember Sophie, the maid, saying that she had *un ami*, but *grand-mère* forbade him the house because he was small, dark and ugly . . . and French! Sophie had raised her hands in mock despair. But although I felt sorry for Aunt Berthe I never liked her, finding her cold. All the same, listening to *grand-mère's* eulogies, I could well understand Berthe's reluctance to come to Tamaris. It was too much, the constant repetition of grandfather's virtues. It was sick.

After I ran away from Don I often thought of Tamaris. In my flat in Surbiton I imagined it shuttered and empty now that my mother was no longer there. I would imagine going through the gate into the garden and sitting on the white seat where I often sat with *grand-mère*. I would think of the French boy who used to come and play . . . his family had a summer house along the beach . . . and how I disliked him. He was called Marcel, and had a smooth pale face and smooth dark hair. It was only when I grew up that I realized he bore a resemblance to the great Marcel Proust who used to come to spend his holidays at the Grand Hotel in nearby Cabourg.

Tamaris is not a pretty house like some of the older Normandy ones with their thatched, deep-set mansards, their flowered balconies tucked under the thatch, their stone walls, their outside stairs. How I admired them when we drove through the little villages in the *Pays d'Auge*, their age-old atmosphere when compared with the relative newness of our own house.

I remember those drives in blossom-time, and I liked one half-timbered manor house because it was surrounded by a moat. One particular day would come back to me because it was so perfect, clear, cold, blue, and there were two manor houses, one a mirror image in the water. The three ducks sailing on it were blue-white, their beaks a singing yellow. I could even remember the beady blackness of their eyes and the fussy purposefulness as they cleaved paths through the image, shattering it.

I suppose Tamaris is vulgar by comparison, so dull and square like most seaside villas, except that it is taller than most of the others, and from the attic windows there is a soaring view of the sea which impelled me to climb up there especially on stormy days. And it is fussy with its *trompe l'oeil* beams, its tower, its painted wooden balconies, its roofed gate, everything overdone in a turn-of-the-century fashion, just as the furniture of that period was over-decorated, fringed, peplumed and covered with silken shawls.

But that could not be said of *grand-mère's* drawing-room where I went once a day to drink lemon tea. The furniture was of the *Belle Epoque*, small and exquisite like *grand-mère* herself: delicate tables bearing treasures which I was allowed to hold if I had first shown that my hands were clean, pearl-encrusted boxes, an ivory fan, card-cases, a music-box which when wound set the old fiddler on top of it sawing away in time to the music. And, of course, the photographs – always the photographs.

Sometimes, as a special reward, I would be allowed to handle her collection of mineral rocks which she kept on a glass shelf near the porthole window. The light made them flash wickedly, I thought. They had a hurting brilliance, especially the lump of amethyst which was her special favourite. 'See,' she said more than once, 'how it fits the hollow of my hand.'

The only photograph I wasn't allowed to touch was the large one on the mantelpiece in its intricate ormolu frame. 'Look only, child,' she would say, 'but look at those eyes, so candid, hiding no secrets . . .' Once when I turned round I thought her eyes darted wicked fire like the amethyst. And that her smile was sly, full of hate . . .

Apart from the daily visit I was allowed to amuse myself. If I were indoors because of the weather . . . and we got some terrible days when the wind blew and flattened still more the ancient tamarisk tree in front of the house . . . I spent my time in the great glassed-in porch at the front of the house which smelt of the sea. My books and dolls were allowed there, but not my bucket and spade, my glass jars of seaweed, my damp bathing suits, my sun hat, my shells.

These were in our bathing cabin which was a short walk across the dunes, double-windowed with shutters and a half-door painted white. Inside there were deck chairs and basket chairs, a table and a stove for making tea in the afternoon, old sunshades, buckets, spades and sand-moulds of fish, dolphins, sea-horses, castles. There were old tennis rackets with the strings broken, beach balls, beach wraps, espadrilles . . . the damp seaweed smell came back to me as I sat in that quiet cul-de-sac in Surbiton . . .

I saw myself on those long hot summer afternoons, those endless afternoons, a small figure in black bathing suit and espadrilles, playing solitary games in the shade of the cabin. I remembered the shimmer of the sea before my eyes if I looked up, and the broad white band of shells left by the tide, inviting me to search for more for my collection. I heard the voices of the other children, the deeper sound of a man's voice, Marcel's father . . . Aunt Berthe's lover. How do I know that now, or is it a fancy because I loved Proust's books when I grew up, especially the second part of *À l'ombre des Jeunes Filles*, with its descriptions of the Grand Hotel at Cabourg?

What is fantasy, what is fact? Fantasy, I think, is to live a coward's life in one's memories, escaping from the fear of the present, a dark ancestral fear. I am glad I have found the solution. How simple, how truly simple my solution seems, like all things which are fundamentally right. How inevitable! It will be so easy, I shall be a child again . . .

why do my eyes fill with tears at the sadness of being safe? I shan't weep for my mother and father, for Don and the baby, for Karin who was going to be my saviour . . . if only that dreadful thing hadn't happened to me on that cold dark beach. I see now it was ordained, the Malle curse . . . does that sound melodramatic, I wonder? But then a pessimist is always melodramatic because she can't face the cold light of truth. Better to go back to my memories.

Tea in the Grand Hotel where *grand-mère* used to take us. As vast as the sea, an underwater sea, its pillars making dark, mysterious caverns. The potted palms were like sea-fronds, the crystal chandeliers hidden sea treasure. I had to wear gloves, and be sure I had a clean handkerchief in my white moiré silk purse with the clasp which shut with a little noise, and a long golden chain to wear over my white dress.

And what a haughty pleasure it was to sit at those huge windows and look at the rows and rows of striped bathing cabins and the half-clad bodies of people sun-bathing or playing on the beach! 'City people,' *grand-mère* would say with a lift of her head, making the word sound like 'riff-raff'. When I think of those days it makes me forget the constant weight in my heart ever since the car accident, the apprehension, the greater dread of horrible half-knowing, wholly-fearing . . . but why am I allowing myself to become agitated? I'd forgotten for a moment. I have the solution, the glorious, simple solution.

Soon, when I'm strong, I can go to Cabourg . . .

I do not know when I first began to hate my grandfather. I do know that as a child I used to admire his photographs, especially the large one on the mantelpiece, and when no one was in the drawing-room at Tamaris I would pull over a chair to climb up and examine it closely. He became for me the archetypal Englishman, the fair hair cropped short above his ears, the high brow, the high cheekbones and the square chin. Why do I no longer remember him as handsome? Why do I think of his face in the rictus of death, the mouth stretched, grinning, horrible, like that one face from which not so long ago I shuddered away on the beach, hands up to my face? The terrible feeling of the past having caught up with me?

Don't think of that. Shut it out, the harsh feel of the denim blouson, denim jeans, the groping hands . . . think of grandfather in his ormolu frame, the broad square shoulders against the background.

Men, I think, go willingly into uniform because they know what becomes them. Some men, that is. The army tailors seem to make a better job of the shoulders of a jacket than the civilian ones. They transform the unexceptional man into a military figure with the clean cut of the lapels, the buttoned-down pockets, the neat tie and shirt, giving a general air of insouciance, of arrogance. I think of the American uniforms I've seen in films of the Korean and Vietnam Wars, and how even the celluloid shows the fineness of the material and the excellence of the cut.

And those peaked caps. How flattering they are to all men! Grandfather wasn't wearing his in the photograph. It lay on his lap, making a foil for his long-fingered hands which rested on it.

Perhaps of all the young men I met when I left school . . . there weren't many . . . it was the fact that Don came closest to him in appearance which made me fall in love with him and get married so young. As well as wanting to get away from my mother. He was better-looking than grandfather, but they were the good looks one quickly tires of because there was no distinctive feature. Everything was in proportion, nothing caught one's attention. But he had grandfather's handsome fairness, the clean-cut set of his head and shoulders, the mouth which lifted in a smile, even in repose.

Don, as far as I know, only succeeded in making one girl unhappy, myself, and that was through ignorance and fear, whereas my grandfather made three women miserable. He was always with us in that drawing-room of *grand-mère's*. The eyes, deeply-socketed eyes I now remember, followed her when she was speaking of him. If I looked and looked away, I could still feel his eyes on me.

It was that eternal adulation. 'There was something about him,' she would say, 'a certain innocent arrogance which you get in no other race.' Don hadn't got that arrogance. And when she got older, those terrible, embarrassing confidences. 'No consideration, you know, *ma petite* . . .' I saw naked sex in her old eyes . . . 'and yet one loved to submit. It wasn't the arrogance of the Boche who glories in his arrogance, it was the innocence which went with it, like a little boy who picks off the wings of a butterfly like the petals of a flower, thinking there is nothing wrong in it.' '*I was fortunate*,' she said more than once, '*that I was his only love, that he died thinking of me* . . .' Why did she sometimes put up her hand to her old mouth as she said that? To hide a smile? To hide the hate in her eyes?

And how often did she tell me the story of his bravery, how although wounded when disembarking he still managed to lead his men up the beach, hiding behind the dead bodies of his comrades as the Germans raked the beach with shell-fire, and how he had miraculously reached the blockhouse to hurl a grenade through one of the slits. 'Their death was his death,' she would say. 'His was glorious, theirs was bloody. Imagine, *chérie*,' she would bend closer, I would smell her faintly-perfumed, dry smell, 'Pieces of concrete, guns, pieces of the enemy, darkening the sky. It was worth dying for. *He died with my name on his lips* . . . ' Why do old people sometimes smile with a kind of wicked irrelevance?

I don't know what age I was, perhaps sixteen, when I began to feel something false in her stories. I don't know how to describe this sensation. Don, or most Englishmen, would have said 'began to smell a rat'.

I tried to analyze this feeling, and slowly began to think it was because there was no dark side to *grand-mère's* anecdotes. They were full of superlatives. Didn't he have any human foibles, like impatience, or untidiness? The natural reaction to a paragon of virtue is distrust, perhaps caused by envy, but still dislike. Why, I asked myself, does *grand-mère* constantly praise him? *Who is she trying to delude?* I never got much further than that because I was in my last year at school. I was going to Tamaris less frequently because of examinations. And then, in my first year after leaving school I met Don, like my father, like my grand-father, a fair-haired Englishman. No wonder Aunt Berthe was bitter!

Sometimes, in that other world of Surbiton, when I had exhausted my memories of Tamaris, I would reach further back, to a time when I could hardly speak, when living was a matter of sensation. It was my other grandmother, my father's mother, I was thinking of. I knew I lived with her at the beginning; she was always there. And from photo-graphs I saw when I was older, I knew she was jolly and fat, a Queen Victoria figure. I have a picture of her in my mind, hair which was resolutely black, and cheeks which were resolutely pink, and a scent of clove perfume.

There was a lot of hugging against a soft breast of different coloured silks, and sometimes ropes of pearls or sparkling brooches to reach for. I remember the sound of her little chuckling laugh when my ear was close against that breast.

And then, quite suddenly, there was a change. The breast I was held against was spare, without curves, the perfume was different, there were no chuckles or tickles in vulnerable places. One day I seemed to open my eyes and see my mother, the smooth dark hair, the pale face which was long where my paternal grandmother's had been plump and creased with laughter lines.

'Say, Mummy.' My mother's lips were shaping the words. I stared at her for a long time, saw the dark eyes melt and swim in water, and then heard my father's deep voice. 'She'll say it in good time, Marie, don't rush her.' I did, but there was always a gap in my child's mind. I had lost something, some comfort, a presence which had wrapped me in love, and my mother couldn't fill the gap. She never did.

I don't have many memories of my mother and father together. He seemed to be away a lot, and we were scarcely ever a threesome, a family. I was glad when I was sent away to school. I wanted to find someone to love like my jolly grandmother, and I think I found a little of her in Karin, although we were never close friends. Already I was 'different'.

Once when I was about seven I overheard voices coming from my parents' bedroom. They must have thought I was asleep. There was weeping and shouting and then my mother's voice with its French inflection. 'I told you it wouldn't work,' I heard her say. 'She hates me.' I couldn't understand it, nor could I understand why she showed so little emotion when my father died.

It happened one evening when we were sitting at table having dinner. It was beautifully set, as always . . . my mother's French elegance came through in everything she did . . . and he was going through the usual formula as he lifted the lids of various dishes. 'Well, I wonder what surprise Mummy has for us tonight?' It was a game we played, and I liked to please her by saying the names in French.

'Is it *Pommes Dauphines*?' I said first of all, because they were my favourites. I can remember even now their golden shells with their light creamy filling. I think it was the contrast in the textures I liked, the delicious surprise when one's teeth broke through the crisp outer coat.

'Right first time,' he said, 'and what else?'

'*Les Espèrges du beurre*?'

He lifted the lid off another silver dish. 'Wrong. *Petits pois*. Now the main one.'

'*Casserole de lapin*.' I said this reluctantly because although it tasted delicious, like all my mother's cooking, I lived in fear of finding some scraps of fur in the sauce.

'Correct. And this?' my father said, looking at me, fair and handsome, like my grandfather, Norman Sanctuary, like Don, my husband, 'This . . .' The word dragged through his lips again, I saw spittle there, the colour drained from his face, his mouth sagged. I watched his fingers slowly release the hold they had on the centre handle of the casserole dish, heard it crash on the table. He sank back in his chair, his eyes staring, clutching at his chest.

'*Va-t-en! Va-t-en!*' I remember my mother screaming at me as she jumped up. She wouldn't let me help her, or be with her; she waved me away. I ran up the staircase, weeping with fright.

I lay on my bed listening to the voices of the Johnsons who lived next door . . . she must have run for them . . . I stood at the window and watched first the doctor's car arrive and then an ambulance. That was the end. My father died that night of coronary thrombosis. Perhaps I would have got over it in a normal way if she had grieved with me, but she shut me out. It was buried, not forgotton, under the new life which began for me: boarding school in Kent, occasional weekends at the flat in Gloucester Road. All our holidays were spent at Tamaris.

Now the four of us, *grand-mère*, Aunt Berthe, my mother and I sat in the drawing-room on wet days while *grand-mère* talked of her husband. While his eyes in the photograph followed every one of us. I found him less handsome, the bones of his face more prominent. 'It is strange, *ma petite*, that you should lose your father at the same age as your mother lost hers.'

'Yes, *grand-mère*.'

'But at least she did not have the agony of war to put up with, like me. Your grandfather died a hero's death.' The last sentence seemed like a refrain.

'Yes, *grand-mère*.'

'Strange,' she looked pensive, innocently pensive, 'that we should both marry Englishmen . . .'

'There is nothing strange about it at all, *Maman*!' Aunt Berthe was suddenly shouting. 'You brought us up to think they were better, superior, to the local French boys. I could have had an ordinary married life with Marcel's father but you poured scorn on him. He was dark, ugly, you said, he hadn't the elegance, the fair colouring . . .'

'Watch your tongue, Berthe,' *grand-mère* said. 'Little pitchers have long ears.'

How I hated those wet days at Tamaris, the bottled-up frustration of the four of us in that room! If my mother had looked at me and smiled, made a little gesture of ridicule, it would have made it all right, but she didn't. Each year she became quieter and quieter, and then she gave up the flat altogether when I married Don and went to live with *grand-mère*. As if to torture herself.

How I hated him, my grandfather! I think he was the cause of everything, my mother's illness, my marrying Don, the loss of my baby. He'd done something wicked to *grand-mère*. There was a secret in that room which perhaps I would find out. Or was Aunt Berthe the only one who saw through the situation?

CHAPTER TWELVE

For the next two days Karin was submerged in work. Young Mr Reginald was having his usual break in Madeira and she had his cases to attend to as well as her own. She dealt with the backlog, promising herself that as soon as she could fix a date for France she would let Gerald know. But she was piqued he hadn't rung her.

Nor had Don Sheldon got in touch to give her Barbara's aunt's address in Rouen, and there was no point in going to France without it. Her mounting tension had to take second place during the day, but at night the jealousy she had felt when Gerald had talked about divorce came back in full force to torment her. In all their differences of opinion there had been one constant factor, that they were faithful to each other. Now she anguished about this new possibility. Was his paleness and withdrawn look because he was keeping something back from her, that there was another girl?

It was quite possible. He was clever, charming. He worked in a London hospital surrounded by nurses and women doctors. She told herself that she hadn't taken this factor into account, that it might now be too late, and she suffered mental agony at her short-sightedness.

As always, when she was perturbed, she worked harder, played harder. She arranged theatre evenings with friends, not caring what she would see, she went to her club where she tried to sweat out her anxiety in strenuous games of squash and sessions in the pool. In the changing-room her partner said to her, 'You nearly bashed that ball to Kingdom Come. Don't overdo it, Karin. You're losing your pretty roundness. You'd just got it right. Femininity without flab.'

'It's the penalty of getting old,' she said brightly, covering her bosom with her towel. Was she beginning to sag, on top of everything else?

'Love life all right?'

'Never better.' Her voice sounded false to her. 'You always get run down a bit at the fag end of winter. And I've got a big work-load.' She rubbed at her hair with a corner of the towel. 'We're hoping to go off to France for a week soon.'

'Feed yourself up, then. And do what the doctor tells you. You're lucky to have one on tap.'

'Yes, I am.' But had she?

She lost the habit of sleeping soundly. Vague, formless dreams troubled her, and the second morning, she woke in the early hours filled with a sense of fear and confusion. Barbara's name was on her lips. She was always there in her subconscious, a teasing, nagging worry. She got up, wrapped herself in a dressing-gown and made some tea, sitting at the kitchen table staring into space.

It's a dual anxiety now, she told herself, sipping the hot liquid. My life has become unstuck. I can control my anxiety and my sexual jealousy during the day but not at night. It was like a cankerous growth within her, slow, insidious. She remembered a phrase she'd once read: 'Cruelty has a human heart, jealousy a human face.' She daren't think further, construct an image.

But bad enough as jealousy was, she had to face something much worse. How could she cope if Gerald were out of her life for good? Of course, there was her job, her interesting, important job, but compared with life without him, was it sufficient? Would it mean as much to her when she came home night after night to an empty flat, cooked a meal for herself, tried to chisel in on other friends' lives? And as for men, there would only be those who were intent on escaping the net, the raffish kind.

Was it the constant undercurrent of anxiety about

Barbara which was making her gloomy, making her exaggerate the situation between Gerald and herself? Shouldn't she leave the problem of her disappearance to the police, once and for all? No, it was too late, she had become too involved. She and Gerald must get off to France together and find out what had happened there, if possible. Their own happiness depended on it.

She stood at the window watching the dawn breaking. The trees in the gardens across the street were touched with its brightness, the promise of a new day, the sky was pearl-pink behind the flat-faced buildings. Another chance, a fresh start. If life was going to have meaning for her, she and Gerald had to stay together. No one else could take his place.

In the morning, heavy-eyed but comparatively light of heart, she rang for Bella. She came in, wearing a blue outfit. She was pale; her eyes were smudged underneath. 'Whatever's happened to you, Bella?' She was alarmed. 'Sit down. You look awful.'

'John's leaving.' Her voice trembled. She sat. 'He told me last night that cosy domesticity with me wasn't enough. There's someone else.'

'Oh, no!' She was appalled. Was everyone in the world having marital problems? 'Not you and John!' She sounded fatuous, even to herself. 'If I counted on any relationship being stable, it was yours.'

'So did I.' Bella mopped at her eyes with her handkerchief. 'He's been changing subtly. I can see it now, looking back. You always get warnings.' That's true enough, Karin thought. When had she first noticed Gerald's irritability? 'Remember what I told you he said when we were decorating? It must have been the last straw. And there were little things, stupid little things. He stopped putting the milk-bottles out, shutting the garage door at night. He gave up making my morning cup of tea; he pretended to drop off to sleep when we went to bed; he didn't kiss me when he left for the office unless I reminded him. Maybe it's the male menopause . . . no, you needn't look like that, it's recognized now, even in the magazines. He's forty-three. Whatever it is, and whoever it is, I'm willing to wait till he gets over it . . .' her voice suddenly wailed.

'If you think he's ill, couldn't you persuade him to see a doctor?' Why not consult someone? Wasn't that what she had said to Gerald?

Bella's tear-stained face emerged from her handkerchief. 'I suggested it, but he said it was nothing to do with his health, that he's been worrying for some time tht life was passing, that he had nothing to show for it. But he *agreed* with me that there should be no children.'

'He could be backtracking. Didn't you ask him?'

'No, I was too stunned. I know who the girl is, you see, a young thing in the office, pert, pretty. I even asked her to supper because he seemed to be talking about her rather a lot. Now I see she was the daughter he didn't have, or she was to begin with. I've been stupid, so stupid. We should have had a family. Maybe it was better when you couldn't make choices . . .'

'When there was a biological imperative?'

'Something like that. It's a great mistake to think that the two of you together will be sufficient. It's selfish. We've been amusing each other, that's all, the way you'd amuse children. Theatre treats, dinner treats, package holidays to this place and that because we liked the brochures. Pretty pictures for children. Even the home decorating was a game. It's like a house of cards I'd carefully built, and now it's collapsed. But it wasn't a real house,' her eyes searched Karin's face. 'it wasn't *real*.'

'Don't blame yourself too much.'

'You don't understand!' Bella looked at her pityingly. 'I love him. I need him. My whole life was built around him.'

'Would you take him back?' How easy it was to solve other people's problems.

'Like a shot.'

'Well, tell him that. It's you against the girl. Has he left yet?'

'I don't know. I left him packing his case. I went tearing out of the house.'

'Phone him up and ask him to meet you for dinner in a restaurant. You'll have to keep your chin up there.' Shades of mother, she thought. 'Tell him what you've told me, and talk it out, calmly, rationally. Take your time, and don't weep. You may have to change your ideas.'

'You mean about children?'

'Everything, I mean about growing up generally, giving up the games. Have a dialogue, in the words of our redoubtable Mrs Smithers. Have a week off; it may take time.'

'Karin, you're far too good to me.'

'Rubbish. In any case I might be going to France. It's better to be off at the same time.' She leant forward to study the calendar on her desk. 'Say the first week of March? Young Mr Reginald will be back then. That's next week.'

'Right. I'm really grateful. I know you have your own troubles. Don't think I haven't noticed, under your cheerfulness. Have you and Gerald got together yet?'

'We're trying . . . I'm trying.' It was the first time she'd been honest with Bella. 'If I get this France thing fixed up . . . I'm waiting for an address in Rouen . . . he'd come with me. He said so. We never get time to talk about ourselves. It would give us that time, away from our usual surroundings, from work . . . and also I want to see if I can find any trace of Barbara Charles.'

'The one who let you down at the boat?'

'I don't think she let me down.' Her office world with her secretary, her happily-married secretary, was dissolving before her eyes. 'I think she was prevented from meeting me. That's quite different.'

'I got the impression she was giving you the brush-off from what you said, that she didn't want you to do anything about it.' The girl was upset, she decided.

'You may be right, but I'm going to find her. I've got a few leads. Well, we'd better get on with the work since we're both having time off.' She saw Bella's wan face. 'Try not to worry too much; I'm sure you and John will get together again.'

'We *have* to.' Her voice trembled. 'I'm not like you, clever, wrapped up in my work to the exclusion of everything else . . . oh, I'm sorry, Karin, that was tactless. Maybe you're more like me than I imagined. All the same, I don't believe any girl likes living alone if she's honest. Oh, I've seen them. They pretend like mad, and they fill their houses with strangers who drink their booze, or they go out a lot, or work late or whatever, but however much you try to avoid it there's always the moment of truth when you have to open the door and go into an empty room. Even the most career conscious girl has to admit this.'

'Thanks for the homily.' She smiled shakily.

'You're softer than you pretend to be. I know you.'

'I think I'm beginning to know myself. Well, this won't pay the bills. Bring in the appointment book, please, and we'll get started.' She watched the blue two-piece disappear out of the door. The quiet reassuring camel-coloured relationship was a thing of the past. Maybe it had been replaced by a deeper one.

On impulse she pulled a sheet of note-paper towards her and began to write.

> Darling Gerald, I've decided to go off to Rouen at the beginning of March, and then to the Normandy landing beaches. I don't think I told you, but Barbara talked of one of them called *Sword*.
>
> It'll do me good to get away from my job here, it's divorces to the left of you, right of you, volleying and thundering . . . Bella's husband is thinking of it. It's made *me* think . . . about a lot of things which I used to be so sure about. Anyhow, I've given her some good advice. I hope it works.
>
> And I keep on thinking of Barbara, as if finding a solution there is essential . . . for us. I go over and over the facts as we know them. She was divorced from Don Sheldon; that at least isn't a lie. But why,

since they lost the baby through an unavoidable accident, didn't they stay together? Which one of them didn't try hard enough? Should I ask myself the same question? And what was it that frightened him? I saw fear in his eyes that evening at Chiswick.

But her loneliness was real enough. She was so lonely that she had to make up a story about living with a man she'd only seen when she was walking past his house. Bella talked of loneliness this morning, about going into an empty room. And you did. It begins to frighten me. It was that kind of loneliness that made Barbara approach me, I'm sure. Loneliness, not solitude. Solitude is when you have something to look forward to . . .

I want to know why she didn't come back with me from Dieppe. It's no longer a question of curiosity; it's a question of caring. I think that applies to us too. Please try and come with me . . .

She and Bella worked hard to get Karin's desk cleared before they should go off in a few days' time. The usual good-humoured banter had gone. Bella hadn't been able to have dinner with John. He'd said he was going on a business trip for a few days, and he would ring her when he got back. She was torn between wanting to believe him and jealousy that he might be taking the girl.

She appeared each day in a different coloured outfit, so that each morning was a small revelation. There was pathos in it. Where are the dear old camel days? Karin thought of saying, but one look at Bella's stiff, suffering face stopped that. She realized that the multi-coloured scarves, exotic costume jewellery and the differing hair styles, were an attempt to hide the identity which had failed to hold John.

But just as worrying, if not more so, was the fact that she hadn't heard from either Gerald or Don Sheldon. Time was running out. As always, she threw herself into work to forget her anxiety. Young Mr Reginald, fit and tanned from his winter break, chestnut hair a shade lighter on the crests of the tight perm, Savile Row striped suiting seemingly a shade lighter also, was forced to remonstrate.

'I say, Karin, old girl, you're setting too much of a target for the others. Got them worried. You'll run out of cases if you go on like this.'

'Not a chance.' She was expected to be light-hearted where young Mr Reginald was concerned. 'If there's one thing that keeps up with me it's divorce; it's as common as the common cold. I've a feeling we're seeing the great transition period.'

'From what to what, dear soul?'

'From legal marriages to relationships unsanctified by church or state. Is marriage as an institution on its last legs, I ask myself, killed by the pill? Will my job as divorce lawyer be as dead as the dodo soon?' She felt her smile was fixed like a grimace.

'Horrors, but it won't last. The medics have rustled up new scares for the poor dears, thrombosis and cancer, not to mention infertility. There will be a great revolt against it. Irate fathers will come back into vogue brandishing shotguns.'

'Or the medics will produce something better, like instant vacuuming.'

'Don't follow you, my dear girl.'

'Use your loaf, Mr Reginald.'

He did, and looked shocked. 'Poor dears,' he said, 'they get it all, don't they?'

'Don't tell me you're a feminist.'

'I've infinite pity for the darlings, and then along comes someone like you who lets me see there's nothing to worry about, Amazonian class.'

She was deeply hurt. Young Mr Reginald scurried away with a wave. First Bella, now him. Mother's at the root of it, she thought, looking for a scapegoat. She wasn't someone you could run home to; mother was invulnerable. Her public persona had conquered her private one.

Her childhood came back to her, not as a tender, learning time, but as a perpetual jollying, a playing down. 'That's not a proper bump, Karin, that's only a tiny bruise. Run along and forget about it.' Never, 'I'll kiss it and make it better,' which she understood inadequate mothers sometimes said to their offspring. Don't be Freudian, she told herself now, self-pity will get you nowhere . . .

'Chin up, old girl,' When she first went away to school. 'Soon be home for the hols.' 'Best foot forward,' if she admitted she found maths difficult. Father, in the background, with his quizzical smile, secretly relieved that the load had been taken off his shoulders. Have I, she asked herself, been taught not to feel tenderness? Was that the basic lack in her marriage? What was really wrong, she saw with clarity, was the change in women's roles. Parents couldn't be blamed. There were millions of girls like herself, bright, capable, imbued with new ways of thought, who ran into trouble in their marriages. There was no rule of thumb; you had to work it out for yourself.

It came perilously near to the end of February and still Gerald hadn't written or telephoned. She didn't ring the hospital since she knew it made him bad-tempered, but she made a point of trying the Battersea flat at fixed intervals. She had no luck. Pete often went abroad for his firm, so that wasn't surprising, but surely Gerald was back sometimes?

She had to face the fact that he was keeping out of her way. Her few remaining nights became even more disturbed in spite of her frenetic gaiety with people who didn't interest her, or sessions at the club which she was sure only made her bosom sag still further.

Perhaps the next approach from Gerald would be a suggestion that they should see their solicitors. She could imagine young Mr Reginald's face, the pale brown eyes widening beneath the pale brows, the two questing front teeth. 'Not you too, old thing?' Don't joke about it, she told herself. Face up to the fact that if Gerald leaves you, what young Mr Reginald or anyone else says or thinks won't matter a damn. You will feel it, right down to the pit of you. You have to imagine that feeling *now*, go through hell, if you want to avoid it happening.

She tried the hospital again. She would welcome his bad temper if she got him. 'Dr Armstrong's name has been taken off the duty roster,' she was informed by a prim voice she didn't recognize. But that was unimportant. He *had* gone away. Her heart was squeezed in the grip of a jealousy more intense than she'd ever felt. That night she didn't sleep.

In the morning she was grim-faced but determined; she would go alone. There was one anxiety at least she could try to settle. Since Don Sheldon hadn't got in touch with her, she'd try Mr Gates again. When she got into the office she lifted her desk telephone and spoke to Bella. 'Could you ring my old school again, please? You have the number.'

'Yes, right away.' Efficiency, but no camaraderie. Was she allowing herself to become paranoid as well?

Mr Gates sounded pleased to hear from her. 'I hope the information I gave you was of some help?'

'Yes, it was, thank you, but Barbara isn't at that address now. They were divorced about three years ago. Her ex-husband isn't in touch with her.' There was no need to mention Chloe Boscombe.

'She isn't missing, is she?' He was no fool. 'I thought that matter was settled now.'

'I don't think so, but anyhow the police have got it in hand. Mr Sheldon told me she had an aunt in Rouen. As it happens I'm going to France soon and I'll be passing near there. I thought I might call, but then couldn't remember the address. It's a long shot, Mr Gates, but I wondered if you have a note of it in your file?'

'Rouen? Do you know, I think I might. When Mr Keble died I have a feeling Barbara's mother was staying there with her sister. I have a file here; I haven't returned it to Miss English yet.' Why had there been any necessity for a guardian? 'Could you hold on?'

'Certainly.' Was Mr Gates wondering that also, or was he beginning to be suspicious of her interest in Barbara? As long as he didn't decide it should be a police matter. I don't want them in on it, she thought. It's something personal and private. I care what has happened to her . . .

'Karin?' Mr Gates interrupted her thoughts. 'I have it here. Mademoiselle Malle,' he spelled the name, 'L'Hermitage, 12, Rue D'Église, Rouen.'

'Thanks very much.' She repeated it. 'It's just occurred to me,' she tried to sound casual, 'why did Barbara have a guardian when her mother was still alive?'

'The reason given was that Mrs Charles was ill, chronically ill. The details weren't given to me.'

'I see. She's dead now. Barbara told me.'

'What a pity! Cancer perhaps.' He was remembering his wife.

'Perhaps. Thank you for all your trouble, Mr Gates. You must think me a dreadful nuisance ringing you like this, but it's a . . . legal matter.'

'Quite. Don't apologize. Do you know, I still think of you girls by your first names. It's a pleasure to get news of you. They come and go here; they come back sometimes with their offspring . . . looking comically like them if I may say so. It's the continuity I like. If they ever decide to close down independent schools they'll be taking away more than the opportunity for good education. People like patterns; if they're deprived of them they get worried.'

Some people, Karin thought. She wouldn't send her children to boarding schools, if she ever had any. What was the use of thinking that now? 'Perhaps I'll come back some day with Barbara and visit you,' she said, 'for old times' sake.'

'I'll look forward to that. Remember, any time I can be of service to you, I'm only too willing.' He laughed. 'For old times' sake.'

CHAPTER THIRTEEN

Now I'm in Cabourg, nearer my destination, the solution to all my fears. The sea here is different, lively, more welcoming. On that Dieppe beach the waves had no spume, as they rolled towards me only a golden oily gleam on their crest as they unfurled. Strangely enough I wasn't cold there, perhaps because the sullen ache in my ribs where that man crushed me against his body took precedence. Those hands, that skull-face above me . . . even yet I want to scream and scream at the thought of what he did to me, at the aching in my body, in the core of it and on the surface, which stayed with me, day after day, in that little room in Rouen. Even now. Perhaps if I think of someone else . . .

Don, for instance. I must try to understand him. It's important to try and get my life straight before I reach my destination . . . that's a good way of putting it. Everyone has to reach their destination sooner or later, the only difference is that I'm going to get to mine sooner.

Besides, thinking of Don keeps my mind off what I now recognize as my total worthlessness . . . wasn't it confirmed by what happened to me at Dieppe? I knew by the look on that man's face before he attacked me that he, too, saw my rottenness, something to be destroyed . . . Don, yes, back to Don, don't think of it.

Although he was six years older than me when we married he was in reality younger, and when something out of the ordinary happened, he was too immature to deal with it. Why he railed at me, was afraid of me, was because of his lack of understanding, his refusal to accept that this thing had happened to both of us, and we ought to share it, not be revolted by it.

He was a small man, except in height. He cared what the neighbours thought; he wanted everything smooth and conventional, his mind was a turmoil of fear and horror in case anyone found out . . . it was reflected in his face. I watched it, we watched each other like cat and mouse. He had no strength to draw on.

He only railed, and the terrible thing was that since he only had a conventional God who wasn't supposed to inflict such hurt on the Don Sheldons of this world, he railed all the more. He couldn't bear to look at me. Once he ran from me, his hands on either side of his face, shouting, 'Why have I to bear this? What have I done?' I thought my heart would crack with misery. It was then, I think, that I acquired this habit of humming . . . strange. Karin probably heard me that night. I would find myself humming, no known tune, simply a panacea for my misery. I think it was to prevent me from screaming.

If he had only comforted me, taken me in his arms and told me not to worry, that he was with me, stroked the side of my head . . . then I should have been able to tell him of my greater worry. All I was able to say was, 'Don't ever tell anyone about my mother, never, never, never.' He should have been able to see the fear that gripped me, (I believe honestly there is no worse fear), guess how my mind would work, a logical progression of thought. But conventionality blindfolded him from the beginning.

That was why, in those lonely days in Surbiton, in between those temporary jobs at the house agents, I began to think of Karin, of her trustworthiness. How she'd looked after the new girls at school, how they ran to her if they were in trouble, how if anything went wrong, everyone said, 'Ask Karin.' You felt her strength, her valour, sensed the kindness in her blue eyes which could dance with fun but could also fix you with a steady understanding beam, as if the whole force of her being was concentrated on you. I used to pray in bed at night that I could be like Karin, who was so sure, and who was able to help others because of that sureness.

I was shaking when I lifted the telephone, afraid she wouldn't remember me, but the reassurance which came from her was immediate. 'Can I come with you?' she said, when I told her I was going to Dieppe. That was typical of her, to take away any feeling I might have of not being wanted.

Here is someone, I thought, who could help me, but it didn't work out like that, not because of Karin. I was gripped by apprehension the whole weekend. Something would happen and I would let her down, I felt sure of it. She would be like Don; she would run from me with her hands on either side of her head. It was no good telling myself that she wasn't like Don. The fear of disappointing her was too great. And besides, she had a good brain, she would immediately see beyond to my greater worry, my dread . . .

We laughed together, two girls remembering their schooldays, those agonizing days of growing up, the elation, the despair, the trapped feeling all adolescents must have, like a chrysalis about to burst, as if one's skin is too tight. Sometimes I would catch her looking at me wryly. Perhaps it had all been easy for her.

We giggled about Liz Cuthbert and her endless anecdotes, 'The Town Crier', Karin called her; we laughed at Miss Beverley who was in love with Miss Porter . . . so Liz said . . . we sipped Pernods. I was careful to put a lot of water in mine. 'This is fun,' she had said, smiling at me. Her blue eyes on me were like a steady lighthouse beam, comforting, reassuring. How foolish Gerald was to quarrel with her, not to see her essential goodness! But then marriages are private affairs.

I'm sorry I lied about the man with the garden in Surbiton. I passed it every day I went out, and I had a picture of it in my mind, and of the house. I didn't want her to pity me, which can be so destructive, and somehow he came into my mind, his fussy pottering . . . I'm sure he hadn't a wife . . . and I appropriated him, pipe and all. I could never have anything to do with a man who smoked a pipe: smells upset me. I could smell Don when he came in late before we split up. I could smell the woman on him, even tell what kind she was, cheap and brash. I knew before he told me.

I wish I hadn't told Karin about losing the baby. I should have kept it light. That is the trouble with me. I become too intense. I've never quite grown up. She looked at me steadily for a second, and I knew she was waiting for details. But how could I tell her about the accident and not weep? If I were to confide in her I wanted to do it calmly, not as a weeping, jelly-like mess. I'm sure that's why I was upset that night in the hotel. 'Upset' is the word I use when I don't want to delve too deeply, a linguistic avoidance of truth.

What started it was that I'd allowed myself to relive being in the car and the sudden jerk of the safety-belt on my stomach as we crashed into the tree. I hardly knew I had struck my head. There was no blood there when I felt it. But I sat and felt the baby dissolving inside me . . .

I see now I should have been frank with Karin instead of bottling it up inside me next morning, making stupid excuses about drink and eating too much. How good it would have been to have confided, to have felt this heavy load taken off my shoulders! I'm tired of bearing it . . .

But the next day, our last day, I had this good idea of buying the earrings.I would give them to her on the boat and say, 'Karin, just a little gift. You've been so kind to me. I'd like to tell you everything, to go back to the beginning . . .'

We got on so well, the old man and I. He told me about how the first carvers came to Dieppe, and showed me some examples of their work. We spoke French together, and I told him I was buying the earrings for my friend. He was *sympathique*. He found me a box with a scrap of blue velvet inside it, the colour of Karin's eyes. I left the shop walking on air . . . until the seagull flew low over my head and I heard that laugh, making me panic and run down to the edge of the sea.

And then . . . well, what's the sense of going over and over it, my stupidity at sitting there on the beach day-dreaming of bygone days in Tamaris instead of running swiftly to where I had to meet Karin. It wouldn't have mattered if I'd been early.

What's the sense of going over it, of suddenly hearing that loud crunching of pebbles, turning to see him coming towards me? Why relive how I reared back, almost flat on the beach, (what a mistake this was!), feeling the pebbles press into my spine, knowing there was no escape?

'*Votre sac*!' My ears were a bell-chamber for his words, '*Votre sac . . . sac . . . sac . . .*' My voice was locked in my throat, strangled by fear. '*Donnez-le-moi!*' This time when he shouted he struck me across the face with the back of his hand. It made me talk, a babble of words, French and English.

'*Je n'en ai pas . . . c'est plus facile* . . . it was my husband's suggest . . . *Regardez!*' Pointing with trembling fingers to the lining of my duffle-coat. How stupid that was, an invitation to help himself!

He did. After he had ripped open the lining, taken my wallet, stuffed it into his blouson, he helped himself as if from a plate of food. My feeble batterings and scratchings must have been like the condiments which are set beside the plate to heighten the taste. He didn't undress me, nor himself . . . it was too cold . . . just enough for his purpose.

I don't remember much about that part . . . more linguistic excuses . . . I only remember the searing pain of the pebbles pressing into my spine because of the weight of his body, taking precedence over the other pain.

I fainted. And as I came to I knew that the bird was there again, hovering as if its mate were being attacked, its slowly beating wings reminding me of that dreadful rhythmic thrusting which had even pierced my semi-consciousness. I know that he dragged himself out of me, arms flailing, swearing . . . awful words. Ugly thoughts in the Tamaris room were covered by polite French.

I must have been lying there for several hours, dreaming and fainting or sleeping, I don't know which, while my body recovered. Once I know I opened my eyes fully. The sea was dark, but far away towards England I could see the lights of a ship. Desolation filled me, less bearable than the physical pain.

But I wakened eventually and in my right mind, or as right as it would ever be. It was cold, so cold. Cold and dark; desolate. I wept weakly as I tidied myself up, staggered to my feet. The pain in my back from the pebbles covered the other pain, but nothing would ever disguise the humiliation, the feeling of worthlessness. I pulled on my duffle coat, pressed the gaping fastening where his hand had been. Down near the foot of the lining I knew there was a folded hundred franc note . . . astute Don. I always followed your advice. I began to make my way slowly to the plage, having to clamber on my hands and knees over the whaleback of the beach.

Even during that terrible time after the car accident I'd never felt at the end of my tether. Something would happen, I would tell myself, to make things all right again, as they'd been in the early days of our loving, Don's and mine. Even when he shouted at me that night at dinner, those words which went round in my brain night and day, I still thought it would come all right.

But nothing would ever make this come all right. It had been my destiny staring at me from that face so like those grimacing ones in Bosch's paintings. Its awful familiarity had been its greater terror, because I knew what it meant, of whom it reminded me. The face was that of my grandfather's, the flesh fallen away from it in death, like a skull.

I knew what I had to do and how I would go about it. It was clear in my mind. I had to tidy myself up in the station waiting-room, then go to Rouen where I would take a room and rest before I went on to Cabourg. I had no wish to see Aunt Berthe. Her house wasn't my destination.

People passed me but in the darkness they paid no attention. I wasn't afraid of them. There was nothing to be afraid of any more. Sometimes I staggered, sometimes I moaned a little. I had only one deep regret, that I had let Karin down, that I should never get the opportunity to speak to her again, to ask her help. *Tant pis*. My hand slid over a little bump inside the lining of my coat which he'd also missed; it was the earrings I'd bought for her.

Karin found the letter on her desk when she went to her office. She tore it open, saw the scrawled handwriting, and had to sit down, her legs suddenly weak.

> I'm so sorry to let you down. It wasn't my fault. Don't try to get in touch with me. It wouldn't be any use. I have to go on . . . to my destination.

It was signed Barbara, and undated. There was no address. She looked at the envelope, saw the Rouen post-mark, then lifted the telephone on her desk. 'Get that number I was phoning at Newhaven, Bella, please. When I've finished speaking, come in.'

'Okay.'

The sergeant didn't sound too surprised when she read out the letter to him. 'I had a feeling it would sort itself out. Sounds a bit mixed-up, but that's not unusual nowadays. Still, all's well that ends well.'

'I'm not so sure. She meant to come back with me; you can see that.'

'Maybe, but doesn't she say not to get in touch with her? The way I see it is she's changed her mind. You could be reading too much into it.'

'You mean you wouldn't do anything more about it?'

'I'd be inclined not to. She isn't missing any longer, is she? She's written to you.'

'Yes . . .' Would she have been suspicious if it had been someone other than Barbara?

'People can be unreliable. I'm sure you've found that in your work. You hadn't seen her for eight years before that weekend, had you?'

'No.' She knew what he was thinking.

'A lot of water has flowed under the bridge for both of you, I daresay.'

'Yes.' She made up her mind. 'If I hear any more, or if I remember something I haven't told you, can I come back to you?'

'By all means. We could pass her name on to the Rouen Police. But for my money it's pretty evident she's giving you the brush-off.' Bella's words. She tried for the last time.

'"I have to go on . . ." she says, "to my destination." What do you think that means, Sergeant?'

'What it says. She knew where she was going. Always did, if you ask me.'

'I'll just have to accept she doesn't want anyone following her.' She tried to keep the hurt out of her voice.

'I would if I were you. Put it down to experience.' And be careful how you choose your friends. He didn't say it, but she imagined the words vibrating in the air. As soon as she had hung up, Bella knocked and came in. She saw the glowing face, tried to lighten her own expression.

'I didn't want to disturb you when you were busy.'

'It's all right?' She hardly had to ask.

'Yes, we met last night and had dinner as you suggested. He really had been away on business. We had a long talk. Oh, Karin, I'm so happy. Things are going to be different from now on.'

'I'm so pleased.' On an impulse she got up and they hugged each other.

'I realize I owe a lot to you.' Bella wiped her eyes. 'Tears of happiness this time.' She laughed. 'I can recommend oysters as an aphrodisiac.'

'I'll remember. There are plenty of them in Normandy.' She wished she felt as happy as Bella.

CHAPTER FOURTEEN

On the day before Karin was due to go off on leave, Mrs Smithers came to see her. She knew at once that something had happened. It was a softer Mrs Smithers, at least if that adjective could be applied to her ferrety little face and gunshot eyes.

When she was seated she said primly, 'I'm not going to beat about the bush, Mrs Armstrong. Freddie and me have decided to give it another try.'

Although Mr Netherton had hinted in that direction, Karin pretended astonishment. 'Really! Have you been meeting him?'

'Yes.' She giggled. 'Made me feel quite naughty. I kept looking over my shoulder for a detective!' She sobered, moved in her seat, leant over her handbag towards Karin. 'He said he came home late because he got the feeling he wasn't wanted. And that he could prove there was no one else. He told me where he had been with dates and times.'

'Did he keep a diary too?' Karin hid a smile.

'No, but he always had a good memory, Freddie.'

'So he denies that there is another woman?'

'That's what he wants me to think, but I wasn't born yesterday. He either got the push from her or he got frightened when I instituted divorce proceedings.' She looked pleased with the phrase. 'We had a nice cup of tea together and I took his advice.'

'What was that?'

'To go and see the doctor. To tell you the truth, I knew there was something going on down below, if you know what I mean, since I'd always been regular. Well, I saw the doctor and told him my symptoms. He said I was in my early menopause.'

'I see.' Karin turned over the papers in her file. Age, forty-two . . .

'"So that's good-bye to children?" I said to him. Well, I'd said good-bye a long time ago, can't say they ever appealed to me. "Take up new interests, Mrs Smithers," he said. "Far too many people get over-jealous in the care of their offspring." ' Zealous, Karin silently corrected as she smiled. '"Don't regard this as the end so much as the beginning." He gave me some pills as well.' The woman laughed, looking coy, 'My goodness, the things they ask you . . .'

'You're obviously much better. I noticed when you came in.'

'Oh, yes. I'm not always wondering what Freddie is up to for a start. I've put in an order for my office hardware. It's quite expensive, but he'll agree to anything; he's had a right scare, I can tell you. He said when it came to it he couldn't bear to break up our home.'

'So you have made up your mind not to proceed with the petition?'

'That's right. You can tear it up. Freddie and me will have a different relationship, an ongoing relationship, if you like, and he's prepared to give up our bedroom for my office. It faces on to the street and it's bigger, what you might call the master bedroom. I don't want to make him eat dirt, but he's got to learn his lesson.'

'Perhaps you've learned something too, Mrs Smithers?'

'Well, in a manner of speaking, but I was never in the wrong, really. All the same, there's no doubt I've got the whiphand now.' She smiled a tight little smile; her eyes were hard.

'Don't wield it too heavily,' Karin said, laughing quickly in case Mrs Smithers accused her of being rude to a client. 'It's always satisfactory to a solicitor if differences can be settled amicably out of court. There will be a charge for my time, of course, but I'll see it isn't too heavy.'

'You send in your bill, Mrs Armstrong. Freddie will see to that. Oh, and there's just one more thing.' She took a card out of her handbag and gave it to her. 'If you want any typing or copy-work done, give us a try at least. You won't be dissatisfied. That's how I intend to build up my business, by personal recommendation.'

'Thank you.' Karin looked at the card. *The Ruby Smithers Typewriting Agency. All forms of office-work undertaken and expertly executed.* 'I'll see that my secretary gets this.' First Bella and now Mrs Smithers, she thought. I never used to look for signs, or auguries.

That night, the last night before she left for France, she tried Gerald's number again. I am the arch-fixer, she told herself. Her hand was trembling as she held the receiver. Surely I can fix up my own marriage? There was no reply.

CHAPTER FIFTEEN

The last time she'd travelled to France she and Barbara had had the stress of getting taxis, so it was at least a relief to put her case in the back with a load of books, to leave from her flat at Hampstead and to drive down the M23 in time to embark at Newhaven.

She whipped up her anger against Gerald to cover her disappointment that he wasn't with her. 'Gerald, darling, please try and come with me,' she'd written. There was no greater insult than the unanswered letter. She tried to console herself by telling herself how independent she felt as she made her way to the bar to celebrate her freedom with a gin and tonic. It was an empty freedom.

Memories flooded back of the last time she'd been here with Barbara, little over a fortnight ago. There had been the pleasure of the outward trip, the renewal of a schoolgirl friendship . . . but then the misery of the return journey without her. In fairness perhaps she shouldn't have expected Gerald to have the same concern about Barbara as she had, but there had been the other reason for coming with her, the opportunity to talk about themselves. It hadn't been important enough for him, but the bitterest pill to swallow was that the reason might be another girl. She lifted her drink and went to sit in a seat by the window; the vast empty greyness of the sea did nothing to cheer her.

Was this how Barbara had seen it from Dieppe as the boat started on its return trip? Had she stood and watched it, deliberately, or had something happened to her, something terrible . . . she shivered, turning up her coat collar. An angry flurry of rain threw itself against the window. *If she hadn't intended to come back with me, why embroil me at all?*

Then, the earrings. She'd gone to the shop; the owner had said she was buying them for a friend. Surely she hadn't been wrong in thinking Barbara meant her? So why buy them at all if she had no intention of meeting me? The police had ignored pointers like these. But then, she reminded herself, there was the letter: she wasn't a missing person. But she is in danger. She shivered again, and it wasn't the cold air from the window that caused it. *I have to get to her before it happens.*

She watched a seagull beating its way to the French coast, its determination as it was pushed back again and again by the wind. I should have shown this same tenacity where Gerald was concerned. I should have been involved from the beginning the way I'm involved with Barbara. I never 'thought' Gerald, the way I'm 'thinking' Barbara. Was that because I thought he could take care of himself, whereas I felt Barbara needed me, needs me, at this moment, to save her . . . Gerald doesn't need me or he'd be here. It was an irrefutable fact. It is also an irrefutable fact that I should have given our marriage the same care and attention I gave to my job.

It all seemed clear enough, sitting there with the drink in her hand, gazing at the sea. The gull had won now; it was acting as courier, keeping just ahead of the ship, looking around occasionally as if to see that it was following. Limbos were comforting; problems ahead, problems left behind, suspended between them.They invoked a philosophical resignation.

Of course, it was obvious. She and Gerald were too alike, both hard-working, both ambitious. He hadn't made allowances for her ambition, because of his conventional background. Did *cherchez-la-femme* mean 'mother' 90 per cent of the time, she wondered. But she should still have put their marriage first, because marriages were there long after careers were gone, if you look after them. Maybe, she thought, with a flash of intuition, marriages need to be nurtured like a baby, and while one was nurturing a baby, one was nurturing the marriage at the same time.

I miss him, she thought. I miss him more than I did at first. Then it was chiefly a physical longing, but now it's different. It's the bond I miss, a belonging, a knowing that I'm part of him and he's part of me. It's the continuous experience I'm missing, and you never miss the water till the well runs dry.

Odd, she thought. If we'd been together all the time I wouldn't be here at this minute. I should probably have turned down Barbara's suggestion that we go to Dieppe together. But we weren't together and I did accept. Something more than determination to find the girl stirred in her, a feeling that she'd been *chosen* to find her. She looked out at the broad grey expanse again, so narrow in reality and yet such a decisive barrier. There was a faint glimmer of white on the horizon: Dieppe.

She drove off the boat just after three o'clock and along the Boulevard Marechal Foch. The sky was a spring blue but the wind was cold, and the seagulls wheeling over the long stretch beyond the *plage* looked as if they were seeking refuge inland. She remembered their sad mewing round the rooftops when she and Barbara had stayed at the hotel. Some children were running about holding up their arms to them as the birds circled. A dog barked at their heels. Soon it would be the holiday-makers who would flock in, and the particular look of a seaside town in its off-season would be lost for another year. She liked it like this. Its Frenchness was more apparent.

She turned off the Boulevard and ahead of her was the old *château* where she and Barbara had seen the ivories. It hung, grey and forbidding, above the town. Sometime she must go back and see them again; they'd been exquisite. When she found a place she parked the car and locked it, then made her way on foot towards the little square where she remembered the junk shop had been.

Yes, she was coming close, here was the Rue de Sygogne.

She remembered asking Barbara if that meant 'little cygnets', and she'd giggled, the pale face becoming pink, and said 'No, you're thinking of "*cigogne*", and that's a stork . . .' They'd got on well together. It had been a good weekend until . . . she turned right, then left, saw the ruined church, and crossed the narrow street.

'*Objets trouvés*', Barbara had said, the windows were crowded with bric-a-brac, old smoothing irons, firebacks, tables, chairs, pieces of brocade, china, glass, oil paintings, silver, ivory. She stood, peering in. She had the feeling that any moment there would be a hand on her sleeve and she would hear that soft shy voice. Her mind was full of her.

There were lots of earrings on the glass shelves close to the window: old silver ones with stones set in them, garnets and zircons, gold ones with seed pearls, ivory ones carved in flower shapes, but none with an intricately-carved little ball suspended on each ivory stalk shaped like a spire. *How could they be there? Barbara had bought them.* When she pushed open the door she had an overwhelming feeling of having done the right thing.

The man who was behind the counter looked older than fifty, less then sixty, with a broad-planed face, leathery, lined, dark-complexioned like a sailor. He gave her a welcoming smile. '*Bonjour, Madame, puis-je vous aider?*'

'*Bonjour*. Um . . . *peut-être*.' She would get nowhere if she had to attempt to speak French. There was the Common Market, wasn't there?

He said, still smiling, 'I speak English, a little. There were many English coming here.'

'Oh, good. Do you remember . . .' why am I raising my voice as if he were deaf . . . 'do you remember a girl who came to buy earrings, ivory earrings?' She saw his eyes become watchful. 'It would be seventeen days ago exactly.' She'd checked her diary.

'You are a friend of hers?'

'Yes, I am.'

'She had hair,' he waved his hands round his head, '*argente* pale . . .'

'That's right.' It was always difficult to describe Barbara's hair. 'Platinum. With the sun on it, it was spun with silver.' Now she was becoming lyrical.

'I should tell you that the police enquired about her just after that; I hope there's nothing wrong?' His eyes were still watchful.

'I don't think so. I've had a letter from her, from Rouen. I just wondered if you remembered how she looked. Silly, I know. I was . . . disappointed when she didn't come back with me. But of course, now that I've had her letter . . .' she wasn't making sense. The man, however, was smiling.

'You'll be her friend for whom she buys the earrings! Such a happy young lady, and her French . . . like a native.'

'Happy?' She echoed the word.

'A radiance. She said she was buying the earrings for a dear friend who'd been kind to her; that she would give them to her on the boat going back to England.'

The dread was there again. She smiled. 'It's a woman's prerogative to change her mind.' She'd known it. Barbara had been prevented from meeting her.

'When I took them out of the window,' the man seemed reassured, 'I laid them on a scrap of blue velvet and she was enchanted. "Like her eyes," she said. Pardon.' He looked closely at Karin. 'She was right. The blue of aquamarine, if you will permit me to say so. When she saw them lying in their little . . .'

'Box?'

'No, no.' He cupped his hands.

'Oh, nest?'

'*D'accord*. Well, it's rarely one sees such happiness, like a child who'd suddenly found the answer, a radiance, *une splendeur*. Don't worry. It's easy to miss a boat.'

'She didn't ask for a glass of water or anything, feel faint?'

'Faint? No, she wasn't robust, you understand . . .'

'Yes, I do. You've been very kind, most helpful.'

'There's no difficulty, I hope?' A leathery fold appeared between his eyebrows. 'The police were here, as I told you . . .'

'No difficulty.' She beamed reasuringly. 'There was his letter . . .'

'Yes, that would make a difference.' He still looked puzzled. 'She did say she had to catch a boat.'

'No cause for worry; we just missed each other. Thank you again. When I've more time I'll come back and look at your beautiful things, perhaps with my friend.'

'I'll be glad to welcome you both.' He bowed over the counter, his eyes not quite clear.

Karin left the shop with all her anxiety refuelled. Everything he'd said pointed to the fact that Barbara had meant to catch the boat. Was there a man involved after all? The police seemed to think so. But if that were the case, wouldn't she have used that as a valid excuse in her letter? And the police had checked the hospitals . . . I've been through all this before, she thought, walking quickly. She's *got* to be in her aunt's house in Rouen.

She started up the car and drove slowly through the town following the signs. It was full of Barbara. *Rappelle-toi*, Barbara . . . Bits of the poem came back to her as if they were written in the sky. *Tu souriais. Et moi, je souriaìs de même.* 'You smiled, and I smiled too . . .' 'A kind of radiance,' the man had said. *Un homme sous un porche . . . et il a crié ton nom* . . . Why was it coming back to her so vividly, as if French were her second language? 'A man under a porch . . . sheltering . . . called out her name . . .' There was a man in it, she was sure. But, then, she asked herself, how do you explain the letter?

She felt a new urgency. Barbara was in terrible danger; she had to be found before anything happened to her. She carried on a distracted conversation with herself as she wove through the traffic. Are you thinking of kidnapping? Murder? You've let this affair obsess you. She's a grown woman, divorced, mistress of her own life. Why should you poke your nose into it? Because she's a victim, victim, victim . . . the rhythm of the engine seemed to score the words into her brain. Fear filled her, as if the car ventilators were drawing in the fear from the Dieppe streets.

From the Rue Gambetti she quickly got on to the D915. 'Rouen, fifty-eight kilometres,' she read on the signpost. No distance at all. There was the *Mammouth*, the hypermarket Barbara had told her about. Driving on the busy road was a relief; the questioning stopped; she had to concentrate, especially with those madmen who came rushing out of side roads. It was good to give it her whole attention, to feel her anxiety lift a little.

Rouen was as busy as she remembered it, no sign of the fifteenth century in the crowded streets. She quickly found her way along by the *quais* . . . Gerald always said she had a compass in her head when it came to cities . . . then along the Rue de République towards l'Église St Ouen, then past the tower on the north side. Wasn't it Joan of Arc who'd been conned there into believing that by abjuring she would go free? She had a desire to stop and go in, but Barbara's aunt came first.

The back of her knees felt weak. The sooner it was over the better. 'Chin up.' She thought she heard her mother's voice in her ear. 'Best foot forward.' There was a bit of Joan of Arc in her mother, she thought, a kind of tunnel vision.

She'd arrived. The street was narrow, cobbled, a fugitive from an earlier age. L'Hermitage, 12, Rue d'Église was hidden behind a high stone wall with a window set in it.

Mademoiselle Malle . . . She turned off the ignition, seeing in her mind's eye a dried-up, aristocratic-looking woman with a black waisted silk dress buttoned up to the chin and flowing down to her feet. She got out, locked the doors, then rang the bell, stiffened her knees, pulling her back straight, getting her smile ready.

An old man, Balzac-like, appeared at the window. Mademoiselle was at home, she gathered. She gave her name, put her card on the wooden shelf to confirm it, saw him lift the telephone and his lips move under his drooping moustache. He slid off his stool, disappeared for a moment to reappear at a small door inset in the large wooden doors. He bowed, stood aside to let her in, then indicated that she was to follow him.

Even in March she could see it was a beautiful courtyard. The stonework of the tall walls of the house was ancient, and the urns of flowers looked the same. There was a stone sundial in the centre and round it more flowers which looked like cyclamens. She bent to touch one as she passed and her thumb slid on a rigid, shiny surface; plastic. She felt unaccountably cheered, as if a pin had been stuck in an impressive looking balloon.

She followed the man into a cold flagged hall, and then up stone stairs, to a broad landing which was carpeted in a soft, thick blue pile. Portraits hung on the walls, their frames gleaming in the light from a wrought iron chandelier. Electric candles, she noticed. He knocked on a heavy panelled door, and Karin waited while he opened it and said in a rough-sounding voice to someone inside, 'Madame Armstrong, Mademoiselle.' There was a flood of unintelligible French from inside, highly-pitched, the man stepped back and she heard the voice say, 'Come in, Madame, if you please.' The door was shut behind Karin.

The woman had yellow hair, bright yellow, a high-bridged nose, aristocratic certainly, but no long flowing black gown. She wore a brown velvet trouser suit with a cream silk shirt, and there were heavy crystal earrings dangling on either side of her much made-up face. She looked about fifty. '*Bonjour, Madame,*' she said. 'Please be seated.' She indicated a tapestried chair with a high back.

'Thank you.' Karin smiled. 'I'm so glad you speak English; my French is hopeless.'

'My sister, Marie, married an Englishman. I've been to London many times.' She smiled thinly. '*Maman* taught us that it was a courtesy to speak the language of our guests.'

'As long as they weren't Serbo-Croats or Chinese.' Karin

saw her attempt at a joke had been a mistake. 'I must explain why I've taken the liberty of barging in on you . . .'

'Barging?' Mademoiselle Malle's eyebrows were a thin, plucked line drawn on her brow; it gave her a fixed, disdainful look.

'Calling without writing, or even ringing you. I happened to be passing through Rouen and I wondered if Barbara was still here?'

'Barbara?' The eyebrows stayed up, one inch from the careful yellow waves. God, Karin thought, I hope it's not going to be another Mr Merriman set-up. 'Barbara, my niece? I haven't seen her for . . .' she shrugged her shoulders . . . 'I don't know for how long.'

The fear was back in full strength. She'd been right; the police had been too easily satisfied. Her legal training told her not to be too frank. 'I'm sorry.' She smiled, hoping there was still some colour in her cheeks. 'I shouldn't have troubled you. We spent a weekend in Dieppe recently and I gathered she was going on to Rouen to see you.'

'You must have misunderstood her. She never comes to see me nowadays.' She spoke with what Karin thought might be called *ennui*. 'If she's anywhere she'll be in Cabourg.'

'Cabourg?' This was even more mysterious. 'I don't think I know . . .'

'It's on the coast near Caen. Fortunately it escaped damage during the *Débarquement*.'

The *Débarquement*? 'Does she go there often?'

'I don't know my niece's movements. Since she became divorced I haven't been in touch with her. If there is anything to be communicated, our family lawyer sees to it.'

'Have you any idea where Barbara would be staying in Cabourg, if she's there?'

It was more than *ennui*. The black eyes were cold. 'None at all. The family home has been shut up ever since . . .' she stopped suddenly. 'Why do you ask?'

'It's simply that I wanted to see her . . .' The woman brushed this aside.

'I wasn't married, you see. I haven't anything to do with it. *Maman* thought everyone should be married . . . to Englishmen.' Karin was used to recognizing inflections in her clients' voices; bitterness was difficult to deal with. She preferred them to get angry and knock the furniture about.

'All mothers think they know best,' she said lightly. 'Of course I knew Barbara went to France on holiday. We used to envy her at school: she spoke French so well. The name of the house . . . it's on the tip of my tongue.' She saw a kind of amused malice in the woman's look. 'I ought to have told you before that Barbara and I were at school together.'

'Were you?' The eyebrows lifted again. 'My sister adopted many English customs. Barbara was always too gauche, that manner of hers . . . she lacked the niceties of the properly brought up French girl, not at all *bien élevée*.' She paused, shrugged. '*Que voulez-vous*? It wasn't in the blood.'

'In the blood.' Karin echoed. 'What do you mean?'

'She wasn't a Malle,' the woman said. She looked at Karin disdainfully. 'My sister adopted her.'

'I didn't know that.'

'Barbara wasn't told. Marie even tried to pretend to me she was her own child; she couldn't admit to being barren. It was easy to accomplish, and my mother was so engrossed in my dead father that she scarcely took it in. But I couldn't be fooled, ignorant spinster that I was supposed to be.'

'Who was her real mother?'

'My brother-in-law's first wife; she died in childbirth. His mother took care of her at the beginning . . .' It came back to Karin: the other grandmother, warmth, the pink carpet, and was it a pink smell? A small child's impressions. 'But when the grandmother died,' the woman was saying, 'John Charles persuaded Marie to adopt her. No wonder we didn't see Barbara until she was four years of age.'

'All's well that ends well.' She smiled.

'If it does. My sister was always patronizing to me.'

'Well, she can't be any more,' Karin said flatly. It was as if she'd struck the woman: she recoiled, eyes wide, then almost immediately seemed to pull herself together. When she spoke her voice was cold.

'I don't know why I tell you these things; perhaps because you said you knew Barbara. May I ask if you are staying long in Rouen?' The inference was plain. Karin got up.

'No, I only stopped on the chance of seeing your niece. I'm sorry to have disturbed you.'

'I am busy, yes. My days are very full. Everyone begs me to do this and that.' She was infinitely patronizing. 'Rouen is a place to pass through nowadays, of course; it is finished. If only they would leave places as they were. It's the same everywhere. Such happy holidays we had long ago . . . if it hadn't been for *Maman's* grief.'

'Grief?'

'She never allowed us to forget it.' She got up abruptly and walked across the room, stood with her back to Karin, looking out of the window. 'The *Débarquement*,' she said again.

'It must have been terrible.' Mademoiselle Malle turned round to face her.

'Yes, it was. It happened not far from our house, although we weren't there at the time. But *Maman* recreated the scene for us, many times. Marie and I used to dream of him at night, struggling out of the sea . . .'

'Your father?'

She nodded. 'Now it's a holiday *plage*, but then there were many signs: ugly concrete, tangled barbed wire, the rusted remains of your amphibious tanks. Signs of war. We weren't allowed to forget, I can tell you . . .'

'You're talking about the British invasion?'

'Naturally.' The woman's look said Karin was an idiot. '"Signs of war," she would say. She would point out the place where your General Rennie landed. She knew it all. *Mon Dieu*, how she knew it!' The woman broke off abruptly. 'I'm afraid I'm talking too much, and we've both got a lot to do. I'm sorry I can't ask you to wait.'

'That's all right. What you've been telling me is so interesting; I might drive along that way; I've some time to spare. Who knows, I might even see Barbara.' She looked at Mademoiselle Malle. Her eyes were dull now, set in a pallid skin which seemed to be stretched tightly across the bones of her face. The absence of wrinkles only made her look older.

'I shouldn't think she'd want that,' she said flatly, 'not Barbara.' At the same time she lifted the receiver of the white telephone on a table beside her. The flood of French was impossible to follow. When she looked up at Karin she was smiling, the same thin smile. 'Now you really must excuse me. Too much talking tires me. Go now, if you please. Pierre will open the door for you.

'If you do see Barbara, will you tell her Karin sends her love?'

Mademoiselle Malle passed her hand over her brow. 'I'm sure I shan't see her. Everything is finished.' The hand she extended was limp. She wore an enormous cabuchon ring. Karin took the tips of the extended fingers.

It was only when she was opening the car door that she realized she'd been deflected from asking the name and address of the house at Cabourg.

CHAPTER SIXTEEN

Since their last meeting when they'd walked in Hampstead, Gerald had waited anxiously to hear from Karin. He'd made it plain enough, he thought, that he'd like to go to France with her, but . . . their relationship was at a delicate stage. He'd thought it better to wait until she got in touch with him. He appreciated her anxiety about Barbara, but chiefly he wanted the few days together so that they'd get a chance to discuss their own problems.

As the days passed he was surprised how dispirited he felt, a pathological lowering of mood. He castigated himself for even having mentioned divorce. There was no one else, never would be. He thought of ringing her to apologize, to tell her that life without her would be meaningless, but a strange kind of apathy had taken hold of him. To get through his day's work took every ounce of energy he had.

He found himself thinking of his father with something like fear: of his recurrent dyspepsia, his periods at home when he'd sat quietly with pale drawn face, like his own; he thought how he'd become churlish and unapproachable latterly. It was cruel even to think so, but the atmosphere of the house had lightened with his death.

His mother had taken up the reins; clever, capable, working part-time when the family were at school; full-time as secretary of a small manufacturing company when they were grown-up. Mr Braddock, the owner, often said she was his right-hand man. And hadn't he proposed marriage, and hadn't she turned him down for the sake of the family? His sisters, Elsie and Grace, had to buckle to and help with the housework, but he, the clever one, and what was more important, the son, had been waited upon hand and foot.

But now it was with tenderness and some guilt that he thought of his father. I ought to have talked to him more, got to know him . . . but his mother had always been the king-pin, the cheerful martyr, he saw now, subtly drawing attention to her ability to cope. How had his father felt, knowing he was a failure in her eyes? Achievers, he thought wryly, had to have a good gut.

Supposing the niggling discomforts he himself suffered from, the headaches and the occasional pain, were the precursors of the same illness, leading to chronic ill-health? A fat lot of use he'd be to Karin then. And as always, when he worried about his failure to build a good relationship with Karin, and especially now that she hadn't got in touch with him, his symptoms appeared to be getting worse.

Jack Carstairs said to him in the canteen one lunch-time, 'You pick at your food like a bloody sparrow.' Hadn't Karin said something like that that it, except that it had been a squirrel? 'Have you got a tumour or has your wife left you?' Carstairs looked how he'd like to look: well-fed, happy, verging on plumpness, which would no doubt become portliness when the mantle of consultancy fell on his broad shoulders.

He laughed, but found himself seeking sympathy. 'No, we're still together . . . just. As a matter of fact, we're hoping to pop off for a week to France, that is, if Karin can fit it in. She's a partner in a firm of solicitors.' He laughed again, he hoped lightly. 'She seems to imagine I resent it . . . the partnership I mean.'

'Well, do you?' Carstairs stuffed a huge piece of pork pie in his mouth. Gerald winced at the sight.

'No, that's the last thing . . .' He managed another laugh, more like a whinny, he thought. 'I envy her paypacket, though. When you think of the coppers they give us here.' He'd said enough. 'Does your wife work?'

'She did, for a year. Now we have a kid. There's no time

for tiffs, I can tell you, nor anything as high-falutin' as careers for women, just who's going to lift Jonathan at night for his pee. It concentrates your mind wonderfully on essentials.'

'Is it worth it?'

'Having a pee?'

'No, fool, kids.'

'In the long term, yes, I think; we're going to have three, but God, what wouldn't I give sometimes for a sterile marriage and a wife who isn't always tired at nights.'

'I'm the one who's tired.' Gerald laughed again. He felt like a death's head.

Carstairs gave him a brief professional look. 'You know, lad, you should have a check-up. No one can be that tired, not when there are two bodies in a bed.'

He'd been forewarned. When he asked Professor Charrington for a week's leave, he said, hardly lifting his eyes from his desk, 'If you don't mind my saying so, you look as if you could do with it.' You shouldn't work us so bloody hard . . .

Towards five o'clock, when he was bending over a patient, he felt a stab of pain, searing in its quality, and for the rest of his round on the ward he held himself stiffly, beating back his apprehension. Don't think of father . . . When he was in the men's cloakroom a couple of hours later he was suddenly and violently sick. He drove home in what he called to himself a reflective frame of mind to an untidy and cold flat reminding him that Pete wasn't there.

The kitchen was a mess, but in any case the thought of food sickened him; the taste of vomit was still in his mouth. He had intended to phone Karin and tell her he'd managed to get a week off, but even that defeated him. Where the pain had been there was a burning sensation, and yet he was cold. He wouldn't let his mind dwell on diagnosis. He'd snuggle up in bed until he was in better shape, then get going.

The first thing would be to ring Karin. He'd say, 'Life's no good without you. Let's get off to France soon and talk, and love . . .' He went to his bedroom and without bothering to undress, got under the duvet and fell asleep instantly.

When he wakened the pain was there again, and this time he didn't disguise from himself what it was. The gnawing, boring ache in his epigastrium was an old friend, but the sword blade which had pierced him this afternoon was new. So was this, by God, he thought, so was this, as he writhed. Everyone had been telling him for ages to get something done. He'd no one but himself to blame, or heredity. Karin had told him, Carstairs, even the chief, but he hadn't reckoned on this agony . . . he had to call it agony. One advantage in being a doctor, he thought, in the clear moments when he could think logically, was to be able to give things a name. Most of the time he was too concerned with the red hot poker which seemed to be sizzling through his guts, making coherent thought impossible.

In between the bad spells he managed to get to the telephone in the hall and dial the hospital number.

'Dr Armstrong here,' he said, 'Registrar on C Block. Look, I'm the patient this time. I think I must have perforated. Could you send an ambulance right away? I'm sorry, but . . .'

'Right away, doctor,' the girl said, as if it were an everyday occurrence to have one of their staff admit himself. 'What's the address?'

The sweat was sticky round his hairline. The poker was now cruelly turning, tearing as it went. If only Pete had been here to drive him to the hospital . . . 'You look a bit shot at,' he'd said the night before last when he was packing. 'Sure you're all right?' And his father had only been fifty when he died of a perforated ulcer. He managed to croak Pete's address into the receiver. It was the last logical piece of thinking he was capable of until he found himself tucked in bed in No. 6, his own ward, with Sister Crowther looking down on him. He'd time to smile sheepishly, then her face wavered, dissolved . . .

For the first few days he was sedated all the time. He knew there was a bit of a rush on, that he was bundled into the operating theatre and given an anaesthetic. When he woke up he was back in bed, but too weak to be curious. He craved sleep like a lover. At times he was conscious enough to know it was a way of avoiding discomfort. He couldn't call it pain after the torture chamber the flat had turned into.

Sometimes, in a half-waking state, he'd realize that people spoke to him. He recognized Carstairs' moon face hanging above him, felt him press his shoulder, say, 'I've been trying to get Karin at her flat.'

'Am I going to die?' he asked. He saw Jack's smile. 'Not even if you tried, old son.' Tears came into his eyes; he was deeply ashamed.

The name Barbara sometimes surfaced in his mind, always bringing with it a sense of foreboding. He must get better quickly, help Karin. She'd been worried about that strange girl ever since she'd come back from Dieppe. He hadn't taken it seriously enough. Once when Carstairs was there again he muttered the two names, Karin and Barbara, and he saw the sly grin. 'How many women have you got, for God's sake?'

In those days of semi-consciousness, pain reduced to mere discomfort by sedation, his mind took off on pathways of its own. Karin was always there, she was part of him, he saw through her eyes. He perceived the source of her anxiety, and understood it.

Two girls go off together to Dieppe; one comes back. Karin had a trained legal mind. She had to find the explanation. Barbara, she'd always insisted, had meant to come back with her. He puzzled, lying there, felt the solution was important to Karin and himself, to their marriage. He thought of drugs; it could account for the lying, the secrecy; he dismissed it.

His mind tussled with the problem, not very successfully, sometimes slipping into a half-dream state because of the sedation. But each time he surfaced the thought was there, the anxiety, Karin's anxiety. Barbara was in some kind of danger. And then there came a greater anxiety: Karin might become involved too.

He was suddenly well and fully conscious, after he'd been in hospital about a week. It took him a day or two to convince Carstairs. Nurse Somerville said she was almost sorry: he'd been such a good patient, just lying there and doing what he was told. He had to let her see he was fully compos mentis.

'There's nothing unusual in my little attack,' he said, 'doctors often succumb to their own speciality. Look at Jones in paediatrics, he jumps around like Peter Pan, and that new orthopod who walks with a limp. And the psychiatrists! Anyone can see they're a bunch of nutters. When can I get up?'

'You can ask Dr Carstairs. He'll be round soon.'

'I'd like to make a few calls.'

'I'll bring the phone to your bedside, doctor. After he's been.' He had to be content with that.

Jack Carstairs soon came breezing in with jacket flying and Sister in full sail behind him. 'Look, Jack,' he tackled him immediately, 'I'm fully recovered. They didn't even operate.'

'Were you looking for my embroidery? No, your extreme youth saved you from the carving knife; just a gastroscopy.'

'I guessed that. What did it show?'

'A small volcano inside your stomach was causing all the damage. Not a pretty sight: swollen, red and oedematous at the edges, base covered with a light slough, the . . .'

'Spare me the rest.'

'Oh, you've no need to worry. Peptic ulcers have a spontaneous tendency to heal.'

'I'd like to get up and out as soon as possible. You know why.'

'Don't rush it, Dr Armstrong,' Sister said kindly. The bow under her chin moved with the smile.

As soon as they'd gone he asked Nurse Somerville to rig

up the bedside telephone. He was surprised how his hands trembled as he held it; even the simple matter of dialling seemed to take a lot of effort. He rang Karin's flat, but there was no reply, lay back for half an hour and tried again. No luck. He dialled Saithe and Saithe and when he asked to speak to Mrs Armstrong, he was told she'd left the day before for a week's leave. He closed his eyes, feeling sick, and hung up.

In a few minutes he rang the hospital operator. 'Has anyone been phoning me while I've been in . . . Maggie, isn't it?'

'Not that I know of, doctor. But I've been off ill. We had a temp. She . . .'

'Never mind. Would you try that number again? The Holborn one.'

'Right away.' He took a little rest while he was waiting. The bell rang. He lifted the receiver.

'I forgot to ask you . . .' It sounded like the same girl . . . 'have you any idea where Mrs Armstrong has gone?'

'I haven't her address, I'm afraid, but I remember her secretary saying she intended to go to France. I'd put her on to you, but she's gone off on leave as well.' Was there a smile behind the voice? 'That isn't Dr Armstrong speaking, is it?'

'Yes, it is.' He hung up.

The next morning he got shakily out of bed and set off for the canteen in slippers and dressing-gown. He tried to keep his quiescent ulcer from palpitating while turning a deaf ear to the ribald comments. 'No, it isn't the psycho from Ward C . . .' and catching sight of Carstairs drinking coffee, 'I'm as fit as a fiddle, Jack. I'd like to discharge myself.'

'You look pretty ropey yet. I'm not so sure.' His look over the raised cup was professional.

'Let the poor chap off the hook,' Bailey said. 'Look at him; he's panting for it.'

'It's the Prof.,' Carstairs said doubtfully. 'He said to

keep an eye on you for a few days more.'

'There are . . . family problems.' Gerald tried to look meaningful. 'I'll take it easy at home, stick to the pap, come in for more tests whenever you say.'

'Will Karin be there to look after you?'

'I expect so.'

'Okay.' His eyes were kind. 'Report back in a fortnight. I'll square it with the chief. But don't go flying all over the place and getting yourself worked up. From now on you'll have to lead the life of a man of fifty.'

Bailey had gone. 'Is the prognosis bad?'

'You're thinking of your father? No, not a bit of it. The treatment is a hundred per cent better now as you know. But you may have to slow down a little. You're not teacher's pet for nothing. Don't think too much of the glittering prizes.'

'I'm thinking of Karin,' he said. 'Thanks, Jack. I'll look after you when you have your first coronary. You ought to watch that flab.'

He was elated to be out of hospital, and light-headed with excitement as he drove to Battersea to pick up his mail. Pete must still be away, otherwise he'd have been in to see him. And perhaps he'd give his mother a ring now that the shouting was over. But first of all, he'd phone round Karin's friends just in case she'd changed her mind about France. He found her letter lying behind the door.

'Darling Gerald, I've decided to go off to Rouen at the end of March . . .'

He took it into the kitchen and sat down on a stool, shaken. It was as bad as he'd thought. She'd presumed he was ignoring her letter and started off on her own. He bent his head to the letter again.

'. . . She was divorced from Don Sheldon. That at least isn't a lie. But why, since they lost the baby through an unavoidable accident, didn't they stay together?'

Accident. The word seemed to leap out of the pages at him. Sometimes people were different after an accident. There was a trauma . . . His skin crawled.

Concentrate. Who was the doctor Karin had mentioned in connection with Barbara? It came to him as he worked through the alphabet as far as B. Brightley; he could look him up. He finished reading the letter.

'I want to know why she didn't come back with me. It's no longer a question of curiosity; it's a question of caring. I think that applies to us too. Gerald, darling, please try and come with me . . .'

She's on to something, he thought. She's a good solicitor. I used to think it made her a less good wife, not realizing it made her a better one because she was fulfilled. Her idea of fulfilment might change, but I have to accept the whole Karin, at each stage of her development, as she is, just as she has to accept me. No one was ever completely grown up. And growing up together was bound to cause problems for people as single-minded in their work as they both were.

He sat there, perched on his kitchen stool, thinking of her, deeply, tenderly, sexually day-dreaming of her, of her shining black hair, her warm smell, her energy, her light-heartedness when making love. Right up to the very end when she became serious, wide-eyed. She wasn't an eye-closer. But afterwards, how beautiful she was, her face on the pillow, the tenderness of her mouth, the moist eyes, the wisps of hair across her brow . . . he shook himself. First things first.

CHAPTER SEVENTEEN

Karin drove into Cabourg the next day in a snow storm, having been forced to spend the night in Caen. Despite the weather she still enjoyed the thrill of an approaching coastline, the memories of childhood holidays, an elemental thing of sea, sand and sky. Barbara had spoken of the same memories.

There appeared to be one main street in Cabourg, lined with shops ending in the distant Grand Hotel. This, its vast bulk seemed to say, is the apogee of existence, your journey's end. Go no further. Did it dominate the people who lived in Cabourg, was it their dream to eat in it some day, to sample its richness? Did future brides plan their receptions in the Grand Hotel to impress their friends?

But were there any friends? Indeed, were there any people? Through the driving snowflakes Cabourg looked like a ghost town. There was no one in the street, most of the shops were shuttered, the town seemed to have gone to sleep waiting to be touched to life by the first warm days of spring. Perhaps the sign of spring was when the Grand Hotel raised its sun blinds.

She stopped at a restaurant with a glass-fronted café protruding into the street. There were the usual red and white gingham covered tables, but no people. Still, there was no *Fermé* sign. She got out of the car and went in; she sat down; nothing happened. There were glass doors leading to the interior and she got up and pushed them open. It was about three o'clock. A family sat at their ease round a littered table, cracking walnuts. They ignored her.

'*Bonjour*,' she said, wondering if she should add, '*tout le monde*,' thinking what a ridiculous language it was anyway.

The world surely didn't consist of a Norman family cracking walnuts. The face of the Frenchwoman turned towards her was like a walnut itself: round, brownish, lined, the features stuck on as an afterthought. '*Je voudrais un café*,' Karin said, considering it a fairly innocuous phrase and not demanding too much of the woman. She added, '*s'il vous plaît*' to drive the message home.

A young girl appeared from a door behind the counter, obviously a daughter of the house by the general resemblance and the same total lack of surprise at Karin's arrival amongst them. The woman glanced at her, cracked another walnut and said, '*Un café pour l'Anglaise*.'

Karin retreated to her seat at the front feeling ousted, but also like a goldfish in a bowl, although no goldfish would willingly have chosen such a dispiriting outlook as a deserted street partly obscured by snowflakes which were now rapidly turning to driving sleet. The daughter, if that was who she was, appeared with a cup and saucer on a tray; and now Karin saw she was a lumpy girl who wore clothes which though unstylish on her, might have been trendy in Chelsea: sleeves gathered bunchily into the armholes of her patterned dress, a low waistline, black stockings and black strapped shoes.

'Thank you,' Karin said. 'Do you speak English?'

The girl smiled as if it was a ridiculous, no, an impossible question. If she had asked where England was, Karin would not have been surprised.

'Hotel?' she said desperately. 'There are some hotels open, *ouvert* . . .' was it feminine? What a language!

The girl adjusted a baby-pink plastic clasp in her straight black hair, then surprisingly stuck her thumb over her left shoulder and said, '*Tout près*.'

Karin's heart lifted. She had the names of several written down, but driving through the sleet to find them didn't seem like a good idea. Once she had found a base, she could start on her search for Barbara. '*Merci bien*,' she said, and then, greatly daring because she was ravenously hungry, 'Sandwich?'

The girl looked horrified, frowned and pursed her mouth to consider this. '*Du pain simplement*,' she said finally. She would grow exactly like her mother in a few years.

'*Bon. Et un calvados, s'il vous plaît.*' She surprised herself, but this time not the girl. This foreigner, this Englishwoman who had arrived in their restaurant in the middle of a snow storm was beginning to show some sense.

Karin had always believed in impulse, and the glass of calvados when it arrived, flanked by two long pieces of unbuttered bread, justified her belief. It was fiery, it clutched at her throat as it went over it, then spread a warm glow all the way down her alimentary canal. The glass-fronted café looked quite cosy after all, very Norman, there was even a frieze of William conquering all round the top of the walls. The snow which had changed to sleet had now disappeared, and one or two people appeared on the street, looking this way and that like survivors from a nuclear holocaust.

Greatly fortified, the glow now in her head, she paid her bill and went out into a cold, almost dry street. In the near distance the Grand Hotel looked whiter, the gardens in front of it more green. For two pins I'd take a room there, she thought. I could dine in style and sit sipping calvados at a window looking out on to the sea.

The hotel next door was without a restaurant, but the room she was shown was at least warm with a vaguely Habitat air because of its white-painted functional furniture and the wallpaper of overblown pink and white roses on a green background. Once established, with her toilet things in the pink bathroom and her dressing-gown on the green counterpane of one of the twin beds, Karin felt she could look out on the quiet street with a degree of satisfaction. She adapted quickly. She would put on her warmest clothes, then make for the tourist information office where they would be more likely to answer her questions. She would have a good meal somewhere tonight, (not with the walnut crackers next door), and tomorrow start on her search for Barbara.

The first thing would be to find the Malle home. Was it Barbara's now? Mademoiselle Malle had seemed bitter about not having inherited it when her sister died. What a strange woman she'd been, and in some way, pathetic. '*Maman's* grief,' she'd referred to. Was it also Barbara's?

She'd talked about her grandfather that weekend at Dieppe, Norman Sanctuary. The kind of name to stick in one's memory. '*Grand-mère* worshipped her husband,' she'd said, and, 'The house was a shrine.' Was it a grief which had been passed from the grandmother to Barbara's mother, and then to Barbara herself? It sounded unhealthy, a blight, like a frost in spring. It must have been an oppressive background for a sensitive child.

She'd spent all her holidays in that house when she was at school. Did that account for her sadness, her withdrawn air, as if she lived in a different world? And had that world been a remote seaside house, gloomy, haunted, where a dead man had been kept alive by his neurotic wife? Would it draw her now, or repel her?

My home is entirely different, Karin thought, pulling on thickly ribbed stockings, then tweed trousers on top. It's a home one leaves, which doesn't draw one back, a springboard for life. There are no ties, no strings. James and I have always been encouraged to strike out on our own, (he's gone far enough, to Australia); we were never urged to go back for comfort. She never remembered her mother writing to ask when she would be coming to see them. She made no demands, and yet if Karin came home, she was treated as if she'd never gone away.

'Oh, there you are, Karin, just get that trug in the garden room and go and cut some flowers for the hall. Tall ones, be sure and bash the stems at the foot, and use the cloisonné vase.' Or, 'Father's in his study. I shouldn't disturb him until lunch-time.' Or again, 'Now that you're here, we might pay a call on the vicar. He keeps asking how you're getting on in London.'

She smiled ruefully. Perhaps it was best. At least there were no neurotic complications, no longings, no wish to creep back for shelter or confidences. She could imagine saying to her mother, 'Gerald and I are still not living together,' and being interrupted before she got to the confessional part. 'Well, you young people know what you're doing. Your father and I never had time for that kind of thing.'

She found a woolly cap at the foot of her case, put on her jacket which Gerald had said made her look like a Michelin man . . . Gerald. She stood. So far she'd managed not to let her mind dwell on him. Now that she was here she longed for him to be with her, to protect her . . .

Her spirits swooped downwards with a sense of foreboding, but immediately she was reminding herself that she'd given him his chance. She'd written, hadn't she, and he hadn't replied. She'd telephoned the hospital but he wasn't there. Perhaps at this moment he was with someone else. Leave it. She shut and locked the door behind her. She would see what she could find out in Cabourg. Barbara was her first priority.

The young girl in the tourist information office was just shutting up shop. Madame Fournier, she said, who was really in charge, had taken a fortnight's holiday in Madeira to prepare herself for the summer influx of visitors. Fortunately this was conveyed to Karin in English. The girl, who was studying languages in Caen University, was 'filling in'.

'You don't live in Cabourg, then?' Karin said, disappointed.

'*Mon Dieu*, no.' She shook her head decisively. '*C'est triste en hiver*, Cabourg. Pardon, I must practise my English.' She repeated it. 'It's sad in winter here.'

'It seems to me to have no soul, do you know what I mean?'

'Oh, yes, I do, no soul. That is right. Now, if you were to go to Dives, which is hardly any distance away, that's different, it's alive. There's some industry, and in the old town there are many things to see, the Hostelerie of

William the Conqueror, for instance. He sailed from there in 1066. Normandy derives its name from "The Men of the North", you know. It was an autonomous province of England, but after the fall of Chateau Gaillard in 1204 it became French for one century. In the Hundred Years War Normandy . . .' Karin interrupted her as politely as she could.

'You know a lot about the history around here.'

'I read it up for coming here.' The girl laughed. 'I'm glad you came in. But, truly, I want to do the job well for Madame Fournier; she's my aunt. Did you know, for instance, that the first syllable of the name "Cabourg" comes from the Norse root, "Cath", meaning a harbour basin . . .'

Karin was firmer this time. 'What I'm really looking for is a house belonging to a family called Malle. I understand it's on the coast not far from here.'

'East or West?'

'Towards the Normandy landing beaches. West.'

'That's right. *Les Plages des Débarquements*. There are quite a few little resorts there.' She produced a brochure with the name 'Calvados' on the front, flicked through it. 'See,' Karin followed her finger, 'there's le Home-sur-Mer, Merville-Franceville, Ouistreham-Riva-Bella, Colville-Montgomery . . .'

It was like trying to stem the Seine. 'Is that one named to celebrate where General Montgomery landed?'

'Yes, it's at the end of Sword Beach . . .' Sword Beach, Karin registered. The girl almanac was still talking. 'There's also Hermanville-Plage, Lion-sur-Mer, pretty little places in summer, what we call *familial*, not like Deauville. I'll give you this map and also one of the landings. It might interest you.'

'Thank you. This house I was talking about . . . I've a feeling it will be near Cabourg, and yet a little isolated. If I drove along the coast . . .'

'The road goes inland near Franceville. There's a stretch of *marais* there. It's fairly deserted . . .'

'Is that far from Sword Beach?'

'It's on this side of the estuary, but I wouldn't say *far*.'

'Are there any houses?'

'The odd few, I think.'

'What about the telephone directory? Could you look it up and see if there's anyone called Malle?' She spelled it out.

'Certainly.' The girl lifted a directory from her side, flicked through it, then ran her pencil down the columns. She looked up at Karin, shaking her head. 'No, I regret. Of course, many of the houses are used only in summer, so it's possible they don't *have* telephones.'

'Yes, I suppose so.'

'You could go to the *Mairie*. They might be able to help you. Or the police.'

'Yes, I could. It's rather late now, isn't it?'

'For the town hall, yes. Not for the police.'

'I might try them.' She felt reluctant to approach any official, particularly the police. She had a feeling Barbara wouldn't want that. She smiled at the girl. 'You've been very helpful. One last thing. Could you tell me a good place to eat here?'

'There are only two open. I'll write them down for you, unless,' she looked up, smiling. 'you wish to dine in the Balbec?'

'What's that?'

'It's the restaurant in the Grand Hotel. Balbec is the name Proust gave to Cabourg in his novel which won the *Prix Goncourt*. We studied it in our first year. So boring.' Her eye-pencil made her eyes look enormous as she widened them.

Karin laughed. 'I don't know how you manage to fill in your time here.'

'I brought my boyfriend along. We keep each other warm, at least.' What naughty French eyes she had! Karin felt envious, not of the eyes.

'You were wise. Thank you so much for your help.'

'It's nothing. How long are you staying?'

'I'm only passing through.'

'How wise.' They laughed together.

It was still light when Karin went out of the tourist office, as if there was a hidden sun behind the clouds on the horizon. The sleet and rain had gone. The Grand Hotel loomed majestically close, and on an impulse she walked towards it, then skirting its massive bulk she found herself on the deserted promenade. There was a woman with two dogs on the beach, and a little way from her a child stood, holding a piece of wood in the air. For a moment the scene looked like a painting, the figures frozen where they stood, even the dogs arrested in mid-bound it seemed; then the next moment it became animated, the dogs darted as the child threw the stick, the woman clapped her hands, laughing.

'*Encore, Madeleine . . .*' The woman's voice floated to Karin, seeming to trail away. Proust. Why did she think of him? Was it because the girl in the tourist office had mentioned him? *À la Recherche du Temps Perdu* . . . In search of lost time. There was something about being here, the loneliness, the unreal figures on the beach, which touched her, seemed to be opening a door.

Perhaps one had to be in a certain frame of mind, to have time to stare, to be out of one's milieu, to experience that extra perception. Here on this deserted beach, with only those distant figures like a frieze, memories and sensations came back to her of the past. She walked slowly, head bent, letting them take possession of her . . .

The day when James went off to school and she'd gone running down the garden to find a favourite corner where she could weep unseen. She remembered the smell of chrysanthemums from the open door of the green-house, the special ones for the village show, huge heads almost frightening in their magnificence, and that overpowering smell they had, especially the white ones with their curled green centres. She had gone back to the house after a long time and mother had a special tea ready for her with Devon splits. 'When you've finished,' she'd said, 'you must go and write a letter to James so that it will be the first one he gets.' Her sadness had begun to go as she bit into the soft scone, savoured the summer taste of the strawberry jam and the yellow sweetness of the cream.

Was it food and smells which were always the triggers? She remembered preparing dinner for Gerald in the flat at Hampstead, the green salad pungent with garlic which she knew he liked, the earthy smell of mushrooms and the rank smell of the liver, the saltiness of the bacon.

They had eaten the avocado she'd prepared . . . what a green bland texture it had, emollient, almost, the savoury liver in its bed of mushrooms, and then she'd said, 'Do you want cheese? I've stilton, and pears, and . . .' And he'd interrupted her the way she'd interrupted the kohl-eyed girl in the tourist office and said, 'No, I want you.'

It had been a special night, a night of nights. Their love had had a quality which made them both tremble. They hadn't laughed or joked as usual. When he slid down her body she thought she'd die of love. His skin on hers contained a thousand delicious shocks. 'It's never been like this, Ka,' he'd said.

Her eyes misted and her legs trembled as she walked. Sexual joy flowed through her, to be followed by the keenest remorse she'd ever experienced. Her heart ached so badly that she had to stop walking and wait until the pain passed. Bitter, bitter regret. The certainty was like a knife thrust. Gerald was the most important thing in her life, his love, their being together. She should have gone to Pete's flat, at least made sure he'd got the letter. She'd dashed away because of hurt pride and that remark of his, 'I feel we'd better think in terms of divorce . . .'

She walked down the steps on to the beach, going in the opposite direction from the woman and child. She felt remote from them, as if she'd seen clearly, felt deeply, for the first time in her life. She wanted to be alone, she needed solitude.

The sand was firm, nearer the sea there was a speckled

band of shells which had been washed up by the tide. She walked towards it. They were mostly fan-shaped scallops and clams with strange, beautiful markings, and from time to time she stooped and lifted one to examine it, putting those she most admired in her pockets. Some day, she thought, when this odd interval in my life is over, I'll come across them, remember this wide cold curve of sky, the deserted beach, the feel of the keen sea-wind on my face, the sadness . . . *tristesse*. The French word was better.

Where was Barbara? Was she near? This place suited her, its remoteness, which had been part of her nature. She remembered the pale face, the thick, pale hair. She felt close, as if Barbara were trying to speak to her, almost heard the words 'Help me.'

She turned and walked back towards the steps again, noticing this time the rows of bathing huts which were probably the property of the hotel. How different it must be when the sun shone, when the beach was lively with people, when the bathing huts were unshuttered. Hadn't Barbara spoken of a bathing cabin at her grandmother's house, or was she imagining it? She passed her hand across her brow.

What was real, what was illusion, on this strange evening in a shuttered town on the Normandy coast? There was the imagined past of Barbara's, and her own, of holidays on the Dorset coast with the same sea-smell, the trails of bladder-wort encrusted with sand, the skin prickle of a drying bathing suit on her warm body . . . the two pasts ran into each other.

Holidays weren't like that any more: Proustian. Families didn't set off together any more . . . perhaps the French family was still inviolate. Those sumptuous villas she'd seen flanking the hotel would be occupied by families from Paris or the industrial towns inland. Every year would be providing memories and remembered smells and sensations, sand, sea and sky, an elemental combination. No one was complete without their memories.

Some lights were twinkling towards Trouville, and she

saw that the woman with the child and dogs had gone. So had her feeling of elation, of clarity of thought. She was merely cold now. The cold crept into her bones and she shivered, pulling her cap over her ears, hunching her shoulders, thrusting her gloved hands into her pockets. Now there was no sense of solitude, only loneliness. She wanted desperately to be back in England, to be with Gerald. In the long windows of the hotel the great chandeliers were glittering. She walked towards them.

On the terrace in front of the hotel she was able to see into the interior, and as she walked she imagined her progress caused a ripple of interest inside. Perhaps they thought she was a guest who'd decided to have a late walk on the beach. Waiters emerged from the shadows and seemed to take up their stations, aware of her and yet appearing not to be aware of her. She saw long corridors. At the end of one a solitary white-coated figure seemed to waver, like a small ghost. She went up the step, pushed open the door into the foyer with its green foliage and hushed atmosphere and went towards the desk where there was a man in black. She took a deep breath as she drew near him. 'Good-evening.' She'd try English.

'Madame?' He bowed. Did they always say 'Madame' to play safe?

'Could you tell me, please, if my friends, the Malles, are staying here?' She was suddenly trembling. She'd phrased it wrongly. She spelled out the name, and then thought, why did I say 'Malle'? It's Barbara I'm looking for. I should have said 'Madame Charles' or 'Madame Sheldon.'

She'd mucked it up. Or perhaps first thoughts, being intuitive, were best. She waited. The man had repeated 'Malle', was now searching, or pretending to search through the book in front of him. Now he spoke gravely.

'I'm sorry, Madame. There is no one of that name here.'

'Thank you.' She must retreat with dignity. 'They must have changed their minds. I intended to leave a message for them.'

She turned away. He could have said no in any case. It

might not be allowed to give information about their guests. The main door swung open and the woman with the child came in. They were talking animatedly in French. The dogs had been spirited away. Their arrival deflected the man's attention. She might be a countess, a *comtesse*. He bowed and said, 'Madame, Mademoiselle,' as they passed through the foyer. They might even be visiting royalty. Karin, retreating under the slight stir caused, saw a notice pointing to the bar and followed it. Was there no French word for bar? Or Salon de Bridge, another one. The calvados had done something for her morale in the café. Now she would try an aperitif. It would make her seem less like some oddity who had come in out of the cold to ask strange questions.

She sat down in one of the many tub chairs, having difficulty in choosing since they were all empty. '*Un Ricard, s'il vous plaît*,' she said to the young waiter who materialized at her side. In mediocre hotels you saw them coming. She couldn't think of anything further to say and she smiled at him instead. He bowed as if accepting a gift he hadn't expected.

Red velvet and gold tassels, crystal chandeliers picked out in torquoise; further away marble pillars, golden velvet and green velvet and foliage and fish swimming in tanks and more crystal chandeliers. Long windows on to the terrace. All so immense, like the beach, so *triste*, so not of this century.

The young waiter brought her Ricard on a silver tray with a glass and a crystal jug, poured until she held up her hand. Not to speak was right: the silence should not be broken. She sat sipping her Ricard, alone in the vastness. She recognized it as an experience. There was an attraction in being alone. Strangely, she felt close to Barbara, who was a solitary person. But with the thought of Barbara her pleasure in the moment went. Her hand went to her throat.

CHAPTER EIGHTEEN

Gerald drove straight back to the hospital, intent on going to the medical library. As he got out of the car he noticed a tenderness in the sky, a fragility in its blueness which made him think of Karin. She was like a child when they were in the country. She got down on her knees like a child. 'Look, it's a tiny fly, iridescent . . .' His heart was suddenly suffused with love.

He was by this time pushing through the swing doors, and he hurried along as usual, head thrust out in front of him, body at a forward slant. You bloody penguin, he thought with new insight, relax for God's sake. But he forgot in a second, and as he drew near the library door his speed quickened again, and he opened it and went through at a trot.

The room was empty. He went to the shelves and took down the directory he wanted, leafed through it until he came to the B's. It wasn't a common name. Brighouse, Bright . . . ah, here it was, James Cross Brightley, MBBS, London, 1958, Clin Asst St Thos. Hosp. General practitioner, Chiswick.

What a stroke of luck! he thought. He could telephone him, say by way of introduction that he too was a Tommy's man. His elation went. It wouldn't matter whose man he was; Dr Brightley wouldn't divulge any details of his patient. Never mind, he cheered himself. There were hundreds of subtle ways in which a lead could be given; that was all he needed.

He was replacing the book on the shelf when his chief came in. His half-glasses were perched on his nose, making him look more professional than usual. He peered over them. 'Ah, Gerald, it's you. Glad to see you up and about again. Feeling all right now, are you?'

'Yes, Sir, although I can't remember much about it.' He felt himself grinning in the sixth form manner all Charrington's men seemed to affect. 'Still, it's a salutary experience to go through the process oneself.' See how the poor sods feel. He stopped that in time.

'I'd say you'd lost a bit of weight, but that's to be expected.' He took off his glasses. 'I'm glad I ran into you. Sit down. I'd like to have a chat with you.' He chose the only comfortable chair, leaving Gerald to perch on a stool. 'Relax,' he said, leaning back, crossing one knee over the other. Gerald leant back about a couple of inches. 'I know what you're thinking. The old fool's going to hold me up. Isn't that it? No, don't bother to deny it. But I'd point out that at sixty-two I'm here, and at the same age I doubt very much whether you'll be.'

'I feel . . .'

'. . . fine? You're like a piece of taut string. You were about to launch yourself off on something when I stopped you, and your acidity's mounting and . . .'

'It wasn't medical, Sir. Just someone I was going to look up.'

He ignored this. 'You're married, aren't you?'

'Yes.' Gerald's heart juddered.

'Everything all right there?'

'Well you know how it is.' He laughed shamefacedly. 'I don't think our generation's very good at it. But I had time to think in bed . . . first chance I'd had.' Now the chief would think he was getting at him.

'I sometimes think if you lot had to sit your finals in marriage as well as medicine you'd make a pretty poor showing. On the other hand you might give it more attention.'

Gerald moved uncomfortably on his stool. 'That's the way of the world just now, I'm afraid.'

'So my daughter keeps on telling me. She's on her third live-in or love-in or whatever it's called. Anyhow, it's her affair and yours. What I wanted to speak to you about was strictly medical. I understand from Carstairs your father died of a perforated ulcer?'

'Yes, he did.'

'At what age?'

'Fifty.' His heart juddered again.

'I bet you resemble him down to the last tic. I want to give you a piece of advice, and I do this reluctantly because I don't get many men of your calibre.' He paused. 'You should think carefully about going on in the hospital game.'

'Oh, I think I've a fair degree of insight.'

'Maybe so. But it's a rat-race. You're all set for it, aren't you?'

'I suppose so.'

'And rooms in the Street? And never seeing your wife, or hardly ever? Let me tell you, there's only about one in a hundred who have the temperament for it. I'm lucky. I'm pyknic. The tall nervous ones soon lose their hair, have lines on either side of their mouths, are tetchy, rude to their nurses, difficult to live with, worry constantly about their virility and head straight for an early death.'

'For God's sake,' Gerald said, half-laughing but wholly alarmed. 'You're coming on a bit strong, aren't you?'

'Sometimes it's necessary. Patterns repeat themselves if you're not careful. I want you to take a long close look at yourself.' Charrington stood up, put on his half-glasses. 'I know you're churning up inside at this minute because I'm holding you back from whatever you were doing . . .'

'No. I'm very grateful.'

Charrington's look seemed to verge on sympathy. 'It's been all go for a long time, hasn't it?'

'No more than for the others.'

'I believe you're having a fortnight off?'

'Yes, I asked Carstairs. I'm having a holiday . . . with my wife.'

'Good.' He looked reflective, the glasses off again, twirling them in his hand. 'I've a brother who has a nice practice in Gloucestershire. None of your single-handed nightmares; it's well-equipped, run on modern lines with three good men. They've worked out a compatible life style for themselves which enables them to get enough job satisfaction without having their kids screaming with fright when they come through the door . . . are you with me?'

'They're looking for another doctor?' Gerald said. His heart was like a lead weight.

'Yes, in the next month or two. But of course it would be a come-down for a rising young consultant.' The words made Gerald's mouth twist. His face went red.

'Anything wrong?' The professor had a keen eye.

'No, nothing, Sir.'

'I see I'm boring you.'

'No, not at all. It's very kind of you. But, you see . . .'

'Think it over.' He strode to one of the shelves, dismissing him.

You can watch the cogs working, he thought, driving away from the hospital, but the bravado did nothing to cheer him up. Branded like a leper now. 'Pep case'. Why were they all so bloody sure? But Gloucestershire! His heart quailed, tonsilectomies, old people's bunions, horsey people . . .

He went into automatic pilot, one part of his mind ready for an emergency on the road, the other on Karin. What had really made her so determined to take the Saithe and Saithe partnership? There was the pleasure in the reward for hard work, which he understood, but wasn't it also because she saw very little in their marriage for her, a perpetually tired, run-down man who gave all his energy to medicine, came home drained?

There was that weekend they'd had in Aldeburgh, a mellow autumnal weekend when they'd walked along that humpbacked stony beach in perfect harmony. And driven along the Suffolk lanes and bought presents for each other at the Maltings, although they'd both agreed they couldn't face the opera. But hadn't he decided they must get back on Sunday morning instead of Sunday evening because there were patients he had to see? And hadn't Karin been annoyed because they'd had a good night and she'd wanted to have a leisurely breakfast in bed in that creaky old place they'd put up at? And since the weekend had been in lieu of their summer holiday, could you blame her?

He was on the Chiswick flyover and had to concentrate on his driving. They had to talk, that was evident. The Gloucestershire practice would have to be considered, or at least discussed. And then, as he started looking out for Brightley's premises, the reason for his journey hit him, to find out more about Barbara. Until he did that he wouldn't be able to find Karin, far less talk to her. The foreboding which he'd felt in hospital came back, that she might be in danger. He had to get to France quickly.

Dr Brightley was holding his surgery which meant hanging around. He told the receptionist he would wait, and endured the agony of sitting in a dark little room on his own for at least twenty minutes with nothing to do. No doubt she thought he was a rep . . . he was pacing about when the receptionist came back with several mugs on a tray.

'Would you like a coffee, Dr Armstrong? I always make some when it's getting near the time for the doctors finishing.'

'That's kind of you. Ah, good, milk. I take plenty of that.' He poured some into the mug he lifted. 'Just what the doctor ordered.'

'Have you an ulcer?' she said, as if she were enquiring if he took sugar.

'Does it show?' He laughed falsely. 'As a matter of fact, I've just been medicated for a fortnight. I'm all right now.'

'Stop rushing and agitating,' she said. She was a bosomy woman in her middle fifties, ulcer-free, no doubt. 'I see them coming in here year after year until they perforate and drop off their perches.' Charming, he thought, sipping his coffee.

'Always agitating, jumping up and down every time the

doctor's bell goes, saying it's their turn . . . it'll be their turn all right before they know it,' she added darkly. 'They won't read a magazine like ordinary folk; there they are, pacing, picking away at their pimples or something or other; you can always tell an ulcer the minute it walks in the door.'

They might as well box me up, Gerald thought, smiling sycophantically at this doom watcher. The door opened and a ginger-haired man in his forties came breezing in.

'Dr Armstrong?' He held out his hand. 'Brightley. Sorry you've had to wait. I see Mrs Crowther has been entertaining you. Seen it all, haven't you, Edith? Come along, doctor, and bring your coffee with you. It's more comfortable in my place.'

'Thanks,' Gerald said. He followed behind the broad back of Dr Brightley into a large sunny consulting-room.

'Take a pew. I assume you're not a patient.' He laughed.

'No, far from it.' He paused, but Dr Brightley wasn't an ulcer spotter like his receptionist. 'I looked you up in the medical directory. I'm a senior registrar at St Thomas's.'

'Hard luck.' The doctor wasn't impressed. 'Are you looking for an opening? We're nicely settled here, I'm afraid. Six in the practice, every second weekend off, a whole day once a week, cars paid for and six weeks' holiday a year. Study leave, of course, seminars, whatever the hell you call them, but at least it's an excuse to take the wife somewhere exotic, like Blackpool.'

'I'm okay where I am,' Gerald said curtly. 'I'll get to the point. My wife was at school with one of your patients, Barbara Sheldon. She was married to a man called Don Sheldon here in Chiswick. She's trying to trace her.'

Dr Brightley was scribbling on some paper on his desk. His hand was huge and knobbly with a flush of ginger hair on the knuckles, a golfer's hand, perhaps. 'You want their address?' He didn't raise his head.

'Do you remember them?'

'Very well.' He rolled the piece of paper into a ball, threw it into his wastepaper basket. 'Very well indeed.' He looked at Gerald. 'You realize, Tommy's or not, I can't divulge any medical information?'

'Yes, of course. I only wondered if the husband had a note of Barbara's address so that I could pass it on to my wife. I know they're divorced.'

'Yes . . .' He pursed his lips. They were full and red for a man. 'I tried to help there. Difficult situation . . . well, I suppose there's no harm in giving you Sheldon's address. He hasn't taken his card away, so he must be still here. Though he hasn't consulted me since his wife left. I'd like to help further, but honestly, you chaps don't realize, cushioned as you are in a teaching hospital, how careful you've to be in general practice with confidential information. Patients can get litigious.'

'I'm only asking for the address.' He made himself relax. There was no point in antagonizing the man. 'It's just that this girl's been quite friendly with Karin, that's my wife. They spent a weekend together in Dieppe and she didn't turn up at the boat. Karin had to come back without her.'

He saw the doctor's eyes sharpen. 'Did your wife notify the police?'

'Yes, when she got back to Newhaven, but then in a few days fortunately she had a letter from Barbara saying she'd decided to stay on in France.'

'That was all right, then.' He looked at his watch. 'She had a French mother, I think. She didn't give much away. Her own worst enemy, you know the type.'

'I think that's how Karin feels. She's in France just now and would have liked to look her up.'

'She has the letter, hasn't she?'

'There was no address on it. Only the Rouen postmark.'

Dr Brightley looked impatient. 'We've all got problems.' He drew a piece of notepaper towards him. 'As it happens, I remember the Chiswick address.' He scribbled something under the heading. 'To tell you the truth, I never got very far with Mr Sheldon, didn't want to talk. You might be luckier.' He handed the paper to Gerald and pushed back his chair. 'Must press on, if you'll excuse me. I've got a big list today.'

'Thanks for your help anyhow.' Gerald stood up too. 'And for this.' Dr Brightley was at the coat stand shrugging himself into a sheepskin jacket. He said with his back to Gerald:

'It wouldn't surprise me if Mrs Sheldon could do with your wife's help, if she finds her. Nice girl.'

'Karin will do her best. She's like that. I'm joining her in France.'

'Good. Having a bit of a holiday?'

'Yes, thank goodness.'

'It must be great to get away from Tommy's, apart from anything else.' He came forward, smiling, hand outstretched. Sometimes, what hadn't been said conveyed more than all the bonhomie in the world.

CHAPTER NINETEEN

I wish I could drive, but all that was put paid to after the accident at Tring. Les Sapins is three miles or so out of Cabourg, and I have been visiting there each day. I still cherish the secret hope that even at this point something will happen, something will be said which will make me feel I am needed, that will restore my faith in myself. Perhaps at heart I am cowardly . . .

Today, after my usual visit . . . they distress me so much and I have to summon up my courage each time, to walk through those gates, up that long drive . . . I decided to walk along the road towards Franceville and look at Tamaris. I say that casually, but ever since I've been here I've known I have to go. I have the need to familiarize myself with it again, since it is my destination, my solution, and yet my dread.

Although I have the keys I've resisted this impulse so far, feeling I have enough to cope with for the moment. Each day is such a strain that I usually go back to the hotel and creep into bed, sometimes getting up for dinner, sometimes not, I'm glad Cabourg is so quiet; it suits me.

Of course, I don't remember Tamaris as it is today, with the cold wind driving. Tamaris . . . what a lovely name it is! I say it softly to myself as I walk, 'Tamaris, Tamaris . . .' It means summer to me, the hot sun on my face, the warm sand under my feet, running down to the sea which always seemed to beckon me, to hold out its arms to me. When its weight slowed me, when I fell on its gently heaving breast, it was like someone's arms round me, making me feel safe from harm. There was only one shadow in Tamaris, those photographs of grandfather, so perfect, always smiling, impossible to live up to.

I remember Aunt Berthe once saying she preferred *Le Pays D'Auge* because the people were nicer than in Cabourg which was *nouveau riche*, and there were trees. I think she was being spiteful. I love the lack of trees, the clear sky, nothing to impede the light. Is there anything like the light of Normandy in the whole world, I wonder? How often I thought of the Normandy light in London and Surbiton where one goes about in winter in perpetual gloom.

But here, walking along this empty road, the sky throws down a cold clear light on me, and I remember those tired soldiers who might have walked as far as this looking for shelter. I never go to Pegasus Bridge but I think of the parachutists dropping like great bats from the night sky at Ranville. They would be glad of the bare landscape because it would make their landing less hazardous. All the same, I heard of one who was discovered by the Boche, (they always call them Boche around here), stiff in death in the high branches of the trees round the church. I shouldn't feel sorry for myself when I think how those men launched themselves into a foreign sky with such courage.

When you have company anything is easier to bear. That's why Karin is like a jewel in my memory. She meets people half-way. She listens while they speak. Only people who are sure of themselves can give their whole attention to others. It's the unsure who look uneasily over their shoulders all the time. It wasn't my fault that her trust in me was spoiled. I'd made up my mind to confide in her on the boat. I'd bought the earrings, I was walking happily along the plage . . .

Don't think of him, that man on the beach. Banish him from your memory. Regard him rather as an agent pointing out the way to you, to Tamaris where it all began, but where you could make it end, without violence. How I hate violence, hated it long before he attacked me on the beach, have hated it all my life!

Here is the footpath across the swamp which only those

who know *grand-mère's* house well could take. I was always warned not to go alone, but in reality it's quite well marked and much shorter than going by the road through Le Home. The full force of the gale catches one here, and yet there is a kind of elation as one battles against it, a cleansing tearing kind of joy which leaves no space for inward-turning thoughts.

I become a soldier, my head to the wind, parachute under my arm, aware that I've landed far from my target, the bridge. I can understand the dread of being separated from my companions, just as I am separated now, miserable, cold, alone. I struggle on until I reach the dunes where I hide from the Boche fire. I pass a dead comrade, lying like a great white bird in the swamp . . . it was a strange place for *grand-mère* to buy a house, near the landing beaches, but rich ground for her grief.

I hear the sea, I begin to glimpse it through the marram grass, and then the house, that tall bulwark of a house which she chose. I long to get close to it, to see the painted beams, the *tourelle* which was my playroom and where there was a telescope which had belonged to the previous owner, the man from Caen who was a retired sea captain. Now I'm going through the dunes and my feet sink into the soft sand, less golden than that on the beach; now I'm going round the front of the house and there's the tamarisk bush, slanted even more by the wind. And there's my second home, the bathing cabin, closely shuttered, the paint peeling off the wood. I walk towards it, turn and lean against its roughened boards to look back at the house.

It seems to speak to me, rearing up with the dunes behind it, the sea in front of it, (it speaks with an air of authority like *grand-mère*), and its wooden balconies, fretted trimmings, wide-mouthed decorated chimneys are in a way like *grand-mère* who was a fussy dresser for a Frenchwoman, with her shawls and scarves and bows and beaded handbags.

The key I have is for the side door into the back hall. The front porch is shuttered against the storms, and the door is bolted from inside. I begin to tremble because I feel my mother's presence so strongly, and I wonder what she would think of this intrusion.

I can hear her voice at this moment. 'Barbara . . .' said with the French emphasis on the last syllable . . . 'Don't sit in corners. Why don't you play with Marcel? Run about on the beach with the other children . . .' And yet if I did so, and if I invited them in, they were made unwelcome by her cold stare and her pale face, and they never came back. Especially Marcel, who lived on the far side of the estuary.

Still, there was always the bathing cabin. There I could pretend it was my own house, and I was a different Barbara. I could play at shops, gather shells to be used as money (graded carefully as to size), make sea-gardens in jam jars with the seaweed I gathered. I could read endlessly, books, which I was allowed to choose from the book-case in *grand-mère's* salon . . . but never from the top shelf.

'You are never to touch the books on the top shelf. Do you hear? Never! They are sacred!' Even Sophie, *grand-mère's* maid, received the same order, and would ceremoniously bring her a feather duster each morning to flick over the shelves. My reading was eclectic, dictated by the limited choice, *Tiler's Natural History of Birds, Beasts and Fishes, The Young Fur Traders, The Arabian Nights* . . . oh, those beautiful illustrations.

The key turns easily, but the door rasps and groans when I push it open. I turn right in the darkness, all the shutters are closed, I remember, walk across the hall and open the second door to the left. The first is a small study. I switch on the light, and there it is as I remember it, *grand-mère's* room, the chairs in a semi-circle round the fireplace, the large photograph in its ormolu frame where a clock might have been . . .

I peer closer. Something is wrong, terribly wrong. I grow cold, as I always do at the thought of violence. The glass covering the photograph is smashed, as if someone had put a foot through it. There is a large ugly crack across my grandfather's face; smaller cracks run from it; his smile is obliterated, his mouth broken by a network of tiny cracks. Only his full, long-lashed eyes are untouched . . . 'So candid . . .' I hear *grand-mère*'s gritty voice, like the sea rolling in the shallows, and now, for the first time, it rings falsely.

How had it happened, the desecration? Or had it simply fallen and been propped up again by whoever tidied the house after *grand-mère's* death, Aunt Berthe, or Sophie? It would be in keeping for Aunt Berthe to hand over the task to Sophie, who although 'simple' (I can hear the disdainful voice of my aunt), was devoted to her mistress. I can see Sophie now: the raw sea-pink colour of her face and hands, the cheeks deeply dimpled, the knuckles also. She had boot-button eyes which expressed no feeling except when she was telling me about a dog she'd once had, called Fifi. 'A commanding presence,' she said. She spoke of it as a lover does.

I turn to look at *grand-mère*'s chair. There it is with the curved, waisted back, no arms, the table beside it on which she kept her lorgnette, her handbag, her box of marzipan apples bought always in a *confiserie* in Cabourg. My hand goes to my mouth, a shudder passes through me. On her beaded footstool, also smashed to pieces, is the small silver-framed photograph of grandfather which always stood beside her on the table. I kneel down and look closely. The features are indistinguishable because of the slivers of broken glass, but the eyes still stare out of the debris, as if in anguish.

I stand up, trembling. I know now. What has been done to the photographs has been done deliberately, selectively. There is no other disorder in the room. The awkward placing of some of the larger broken pieces has been done by Sophie, perhaps, when tidying up.

I'm cold, with a kind of horror, a realization. For some reason, perhaps to escape the sight of the smashed photographs, I remember *grand-mère*'s burial at the little cemetery behind the church, two years ago. Aunt Berthe had sent a telegram to me, and I had crossed the Channel on a windy fretful day, in this same month, March.

Only Aunt Berthe, the *notaire*, and Sophie in a black hat pulled down over her purple-pink face, a shapeless black coat, purple-pink hands hidden in black cotton gloves, were at the graveside, beside myself and the priest. The wind tossed the trees angrily and whipped our clothes about us. Monsieur Claybelle's nose was red and his eyes were watering behind his pince-nez. The priest, who was old, looked grey, as if another burial like this one would finish him. He mumbled through the prayers.

Afterwards, as we huddled inside the porch of the church, Monsieur Claybelle asked for my instructions about the house. Sophie had locked up after Madame Sanctuary's death and given him the keys.

'Perhaps you would like to have them?' I said to Aunt Berthe.

She shook her head, her black eyes unyielding. I wondered how anyone could be so unyielding at their own mother's funeral. 'It's yours now,' she said. 'I never want to see the place again.' She was the antithesis of Sophie, disdainful in a waisted black coat bordered with black fox fur at the hem as well as at the neck and waists, a chic black hat . . . as if she'd gone to a couture house for the outfit, as if in celebration . . .

The *notaire*, who couldn't help overhearing, looked away, wishing to take no part in the discussion. And yet when Aunt Berthe had driven away after conventionally kissing my cold cheeks, he turned to me. 'If you would like accommodation for the night, Madame, my wife would be pleased to welcome you.'

I should have liked to accept his offer, to be part of an ordinary household even for a few hours. I was lonely in Surbiton. I'd found a rented flat there which suited me; it was outside London which I loathed, and far enough from Chiswick. Don never got in touch with me. I expect he was happy with his woman, glad to be rid of me. I was too much for him to bear. I didn't blame him. 'No, thank you, Monsieur,' I said. 'I intend to stay the night at Le Havre so that I can catch the early boat tomorrow morning.'

'Very well.' He looked relieved. 'Allow me to drive you to Cabourg at least.'

In the car he tried to make polite conversation. 'How is your husband, Madame Sheldon?'

'I'm divorced,' I said.

'Tut, tut.' It was a condemnation of contemporary society, and then as if trying to say something which could not be refuted, 'Your grandmother was a reserved woman. She didn't wish to know anyone in the village, or in Cabourg. I think she underestimated their kindness. They would have helped her in her . . . trial.' He skirted delicately what was uppermost in both our minds.

'Yes,' I said, 'perhaps she was wrong.'

'My wife tried, and the priest, Monsieur Bouvier . . .' his voice trailed away, and then, as if seizing at a straw, he launched into details about the will, telling me that the money would be divided equally, apart from a bequest to Mademoiselle Sophie D'Erlanger, and that he'd be in touch with me as soon as *grand-mère*'s affairs were settled.

I thanked him. I was hardly listening. I was watching the road intently. We were coming nearer and nearer the gates of the long drive.

'Your aunt is also reserved,' Monsieur Claybelle said. I thought he might be a gossip, given the chance.

'Yes, she is.' Still nearer . . . those pine trees marching along beside the neat white fencing, It had been someone's estate for a long time. Perhaps they hadn't liked being so near a growing resort like Cabourg and had sold it.

'Your grandmother didn't wish Tamaris to go to your aunt because she'd shown little concern when she was ill. She was grateful to your mother, however, for looking after her as long as she could. But, sadly, Madame Sanctuary was alone at the time of her death. A stroke, the doctor said. A sudden stroke. But they are always sudden, aren't they? One wonders what brought it on, nevertheless . . .' A side glance at me. 'Sophie found her, dead on the floor. Her right hand was cut and had been bleeding. Clenched in it was a piece of mineral rock. The doctor had to prise the fingers from it, he said. Such a grip. There was a post-mortem, of course, but there had been no foul play, and her death had been from natural causes. But . . .' I felt his glance again. He wanted me to question him, I knew. I saw the gates ahead of us. All my attention was focused on them.

'Would you let me out here, Monsieur?' I interrupted him, rudely, but I had enough to think about. 'I have to . . . pay a visit.' My heart was beating sluggishly with fear, making me sick, but it had to be done. I could see quite clearly the stone pillars, the open gate, the beginning of the long, twisting drive . . .

Something was glinting on the shelf to the left of the porthole window. 'A piece of mineral rock,' the *notaire* had said. 'The doctor had to prise the fingers . . .' How clear it was to me now. I walked towards it, lifted the piece of purple quartz, clenched it in my right hand. Her favourite piece, the amethyst. I remembered her telling me the names of the rocks: jasper, onyx, agate, sardonyx, cat's eye, amethyst. 'My favourite, the amethyst. It is hard enough to cut glass,' I remembered her saying. And smash it? The glass in photograph frames is thin. I put it back quickly, as the doctor had put it back, taking it from the dead hand with difficulty. My palm has red marks on it. The amethyst glitters cruelly in the light coming through the porthole window.

Crystal would make a good weapon. The small silver-framed photograph of my grandfather wasn't only broken, it was mutilated, as if she'd struck again and again, and on the large one the blows had been aimed at his mouth. Why his mouth? The mouth which had once kissed her. I began to tremble again, and to calm myself, I turn and walk to the opposite wall on which the great bookcase of his books rests. This at least is unharmed. I run my eyes along the forbidden top row. '*You are never to touch the books on the top shelf, do you hear? Never! They are sacred!*' The husky French voice comes back to me. I couldn't have reached them in any case, then.

But now that I'm grown up and divorced, it's easy. And she's no longer here. I reach up and take out a book at random. *Wetfly Fishing*. Inside on the flyleaf the printed dedication reads 'To the Beloved Memory of Alexander Montgomerie Bell, True Sportsman and Loyal Friend.' So English! There is a picture of the author, a portly gentleman, luxuriously side-whiskered and bearded, and wearing a frock-coat. Perhaps the book had been passed on to my grandfather by *his* father. Mother once said to me that the English were great hoarders. My knees are trembling.

I read some more titles, *The Stellar Heavens, The Weir of Hermiston* (Stevenson liked France), I remember, *Poems of Today, The Wind in the Willows* by Kenneth Grahame. It has always been a strange book to me. I knew it was a favourite with English children (the girls talked of it at school), but my mother thought it bizarre. I lifted it down to look at it and a letter in an envelope (the ragged flap exposes it), drops at my feet. I pick it up and read the address, 'Madame Norman Sanctuary, l'Hermitage, 12, Rue D'Église, Rouen'. It is yellow with age, and unfranked.

My trembling is now uncontrollable. I know he's lying in the war cemetery not far from here, but his presence fills the rooms, I feel the eyes in the smashed photographs are still on me. I know I'm holding two objects which his hands have touched. I'm sure the letter is from him. Nervousness makes me riffle through the book, reading the little notes in the margin, 'ripping', 'jolly good for Toadie' . . . I imagine a fair schoolboy with large eyes. My mother always said I should never deface a book . . .

What was that noise? I wheel round, terrified. A kind of rustling. The room is empty; nothing. My nerves are on edge. I watch my shaking fingers take the letter out of the envelope, unfold it carefully, since it is yellow and thin. I begin to read it.

When you come back from shopping with the girls, I shall have gone. There's no other way. I must go and fight for my country.

All along I've been giving in to you for the sake of peace. Now it's war and I must stand firm. I gave in to you when we were married, making my home in Rouen, giving up my architecture and painting, working in the *Mairie's* office every minute of which I loathed, with those smooth French officials who thought me as odd as I thought them.

I found joy and happiness in our daughters, but that joy was lacking between us because of the stubbornness of your temperament which at first I'd found so wilfully charming. It grew with the years into a terrible rigidity of belief in your rightness which stripped me of my manhood. No wonder I had to find comfort elsewhere.

I might have known what would happen when we heard that the German Army had marched into Poland. You laughed, boasted of your Maginot Line, said that Hitler would never stand a chance against the French. You poured scorn on me when I said it would be a long and bloody affair, said it was ridiculous of me to think of going home to fight. You were always so sure, so unfeminine in your efforts to destroy me.

I wouldn't like to relive this last week of tears and threats. God knows what Berthe and Marie must have thought lying in their beds listening to us. I was ashamed. I thought, they're at a tender age, they'll understand that something is terribly wrong and yet be unable to understand why their parents should be having their own war.

You knew your refusal to come with me to England if I enlisted faced me with an agonizing decision. I would lose my children. You thought I would remain, because I've always conformed except for my furtive coupling with kinder women than you. But what you couldn't understand was that I could never live with myself if I stayed here, that I'm English first and foremost, and it's more important to me than being a husband, even a father. I always had pride in my country, but your refusing to live in it with me had made that pride into a burning desire to fight for it.

It's ironical to think that it was my admiration for France and all things French which drew us together in the first place, and now it's my Englishness which is parting us. I have the feeling that this is the end, that we'll never meet again.

But I know you'll survive the war, and I pray to God our children will also. If you've any influence with them when they grow up, encourage them to marry their own countrymen. Say, if you can, that it's their father's dying wish. I know that to be true.

But now, at this moment, if I'm honest, I wish I'd never seen this country, nor you. Don't let that distress you. It's the final flurry of a weak man who never had the courage to do or say what he thought . . . or so you said. We were wrong for each other from the start. I was bewitched by the glamour of France in you. Perhaps it had nothing to do with our nationalities, and yet nationalities decide temperament. And that is what wars are about, big and small.

Pray for me, and my country, as I'll pray for you and yours . . .

I turn the yellowing pages back to look at the date. Thirteenth September, 1939. Before the holocaust.

My heart seems to be in my throat, a fluttering thing trying to escape. I look round the room again, and see it for what it is, a shrine to hate, not grief. She'd even taken a malevolent delight in reversing my grandfather's last wish . . . 'If you've any influence with them when they grow up, encourage them to marry their own countrymen.'

Everything she'd said had been lies, a smoke screen for her hate, no less dense than the smoke screen which covered the beaches. She was only honest when she smashed the photographs in her last hour, when she managed to take a piece of amethyst in her hand and smashed and smashed and smashed . . .

CHAPTER TWENTY

Karin soon found one of the restaurants the name of which the girl in the tourist office had written down for her, and one look as she went in told her she'd chosen the right place. It was in a side street, the building flat-faced and steep with attic windows, unwelcoming in its exterior, but inside it had that indefinable air of being reliable. It was warm, well-kept, and there were good smells floating from the kitchen. They were obviously expecting clients judging by the huge pile of plates on a side table. It was strange, considering their pride in their cuisine, that the French didn't go in for plate-warming.

She sat down at an unobtrusive table in the corner and looked around. The walls had the usual flock paper, but surprising idea, were covered in carpet up to about three feet. To run a Hoover over one's walls was at least novel. There was a sprinkling of people already there . . . those who'd escaped the holocaust, she told herself . . . and they seemed to be composed of the business fraternity of Cabourg such as it was; everybody knew everybody else, and there was a great deal of good-humoured banter between the tables.

A leisurely-moving girl presented Karin with a well-filled menu. She'd treat herself, she decided, scanning it. After all, one didn't come to the Normandy coast every day of the week. She chose *fruits de mer*, followed by mussels, followed by *colin* with *sauce Normandaise*, and sat back feeling relatively happy for the first time that day.

She had a feeling something good was going to happen, that she'd get a lead soon . . . she looked across the room at an elderly man and woman who were coming in, followed by a small pug-faced dog of a nameless but French-looking breed. Greetings of '*M'sieu, 'dame*' resounded on all sides. The leisurely waitress almost hurried forward to pull out chairs for them at the table next to Karin's. It must be their usual place. The woman settled herself, said a few words to the man, and then smiled at Karin, a friendly smile. '*Quel mauvais temps! Vous vous êtes bien amusée?*' She laughed to show it was a joke, and Karin, catching the drift, laughed with her.

'*Oui, Madame*. I don't understand French very well. I'm English.'

The woman smiled even more broadly. 'What a treat for me! I can practise on you. I have a daughter who lives in 'arrogate, Yorkshire. I visit there many times to see my grandchildren. Where is your home, may I ask?'

'London, Hampstead.'

'Ah, I must tell my husband.' She rapidly translated to the bemused man beside her, then turned again to Karin. 'We live in Paris, but we have a summer house in Cabourg. You will be amused when I tell you that today my husband and I have come to plant roses in our garden!'

Karin looked appropriately surprised. Even allowing for the weather, she hadn't thought the French were great garden lovers.

'And you, you're visiting someone in this area?' She had all the curiosity of the gregarious.

'No,' Karin said, 'just passing through. But I remembered I had a school friend who used to live here and I thought I'd look her up.' The idea came to her as she spoke. This couple had a house, and judging by their age, they might have lived here for a long time. 'I've been unable to locate her. Her grandmother's name was Sanctuary; her husband was English.'

The woman's smile went. She leant forward to speak in French to her husband. He was nodding from time to time, looking grave. Karin waited. They seemed to be prompting each other, little pauses, raised eyebrows. 'Do you happen to know them?' she ventured. The leisurely waitress appeared at her side and placed a heaped plate of shell-fish in front of her.

'*Bon appetit,*' she said, and then went to the French couple's table. Now the two elderly heads were in earnest consultation over the menu while the waitress stood patiently. Karin picked out a prawn on her fork from the miniature mountain in front of her. The couple had lost interest in her. She ate another prawn, and with the salty taste came the memory of the empty beach. Apprehension filled her, spoiling her enjoyment of the food.

'*Madame?*' It was the elderly lady again. The important matter of their dinner had been settled. 'You asked me about Madame Sanctuary. We knew her, or should I say we knew of her. A recluse. My husband remembers there was something in *Ouest France*, that's the local paper, when she died. Suspicious circumstances, you know. There was a little damage done to her house, not much. But it was established by the police that there hadn't been an intruder. She died of a stroke.'

'How long ago was that?'

'About two years, I think.' She turned to her husband and engaged in some rapid French cross-talk. 'Yes, Bernard says it was the spring before last. The house has been shut up since then. There were rumours it was left to the granddaughter, not the daughters . . .'

'What kind of rumours?' She saw the husband touch his wife's arm and whisper something.

The woman's smile was apologetic. 'Bernard says I musn't gossip. He's right; my tongue runs away with me sometimes. But I do remember the girl walking on the beach when she visited from England, tall, slight, peculiar hair . . .'

'That would be Barbara.' She mustn't press the woman or she'd become suspicious. 'Could you tell me where the house is?' She had to ask that.

'Yes, it's on the way to Franceville. There's a stretch of *marais*, how do you say, unclaimed land, swamp, and a path runs across it. If you have a car there's a road down to the beach further on. You can't miss the house. It stands on its own, very tall.'

'Thank you very much.' She was getting somewhere at last. 'My friend might not be there, of course, but at least I can tell her I tried.'

'Yes, you can say you tried.' The woman seemed uneasy. As if to avoid Karin's eyes she spoke to the dog which was sitting on a chair beside her. '*Tu as faim, non? Ne t'inquiète pas . . .*'

Karin interrupted her. 'Excuse me, but you didn't tell me the name of the house.'

She looked up from stroking the dog. 'It's called Tamaris. A lonely house. You can't miss it.' The pug-faced dog growled as if resenting Karin's interruption.

'Thank you,' she said. 'Tamaris. You've been most helpful.' She lifted her knife and fork.

The sea-food had lost its flavour, the mussels had an oily taste, the *colin* had no taste at all, but she washed it down with a half bottle of white wine. She'd look for the house first thing in the morning. There was no point in going when it was dark. She lifted the copy of the newspaper she'd bought, and studied the first page. *Ouest France*. She saw it was published in Rennes. Wasn't that Brittany? If so, it was too far to go. You aren't a detective, she chided herself. Any mystery surrounding the grandmother's death is no concern of yours. It's Barbara you want to find.

The couple seemed to be engrossed in their food. Perhaps *M'sieu* had ticked off his wife. Occasionally she fed scraps to her dog and sometimes Karin could overhear the flood of French as she bent forward to her husband. Don't bother whispering, Karin thought, I can't understand a word.

Tamaris. She repeated the name to herself several times in case she forgot it. Occasionally she heard a petulant growl from the dog as if she were out of favour. It was always awkward when people fell silent after having talked so freely. And she was definitely out of favour with the waitress who looked aggrieved as she carried away the half-eaten food. 'May I have a calvados with my coffee?' Karin asked her. All she wanted was to get back to the room with the pink and green wallpaper, and somehow sleep until the next morning when she could start off on her search. She forced herself to sip the calvados when it came, to drink the coffee slowly. But it was a relief when she called for the bill.

'*Bon retour*,' the Frenchwoman said when Karin got up. There was no warmth in her remark.

'*Bonsoir*.' She doubted if she'd ever come back. She envied the elderly couple their apparent closeness. The man was holding out a piece of food on his fork to the woman, perhaps a peace-offering. I wish Gerald had been with me, she thought, walking out of the restaurant. She drove back quickly to the hotel, and when she was in the green counterpaned bed she wept for him.

The next morning when she wakened there was a thick sea mist, and Madame at the reception desk shrugged her shoulders when Karin pointed through the glass door. '*C'est normal*,' she said, and went back to her writing.

She walked about miserably all morning, afraid to venture out of the town. The thought of a deserted *marais*, a lonely house, shrouded in mist, was too frightening. People swam past her like ghosts, the few cars in the street rolled past her noiselessly. She sat in a café for a couple of hours, ordering an occasional coffee and then a sandwich to keep the owner happy. At two o'clock it was as if a blind had shot up. Through the plate glass window the Grand Hotel at the end of the street sprang into a pristine white prominence, its red sun-blinds coyly half-lowered over its many windows like eyelids. She paid her bill thankfully and set off.

She located Franceville a few kilometres out of the town without difficulty, and was soon bouncing down the unmetalled surface of the side road towards the sea. The rust-coloured swamp stretched all round her, and through her half-open window came an aromatic smell from it, thyme, perhaps, evocative of seaside holidays long past. Everything here made her think of the past.

She had a sudden fancy, unlike her usual practical nature, of life being a see-saw. When you were young, with no past, you remained high, suspended in the present. She'd now reached a stage, perhaps the unusual circumstances had precipitated it, when the past began to have equal meaning. Lost time had to be regained, assimilated into the present. Perhaps if I led a more contemplative life, she thought, I could ponder on this, even try to read Proust. She smiled at herself, but she admitted it was a possibility where before it had been an improbability. I've changed, she thought, since I met Barbara.

The tall structure of the house had been against the skyline for some time although she hadn't acknowledged it to herself. But as she came closer, as it seemed to rear up from the sand dunes, she knew that this house with its back to her, blocking her view of the sea, was Tamaris. The coldness in her heart was there again, like the nagging of a tooth. She tried to forget it as she parked her car, got out and walked around the white stuccoed side which was stained with sea damp.

Tamaris. There the name was, painted on the swinging board which hung above the curved wooden gate, sheltered by the pantiled roof above it. The gate itself was grey with lichen; there were boards missing from it, and those which were left were stripped of paint. The bush growing beside it with its flattened top showed the force of the north-west gale. Such bareness, she thought! No wonder the large front porch was so securely shuttered, as were all the front windows with their wooden balconies and their useless decoration of flutings and whirlings and wide, tiled chimneys. How peculiar to build a house which required so much paintwork in such an exposed position!

She pushed open the gate which was rusting on its hinges and went up the path made of broken shells and pebbles. She knocked loudly on the flaking door and waited, knocked again even more loudly. No sound inside. No footfalls. No voices. 'You didn't expect any, did you?' she muttered to give herself false courage. She bent down and looked through the letterbox, saw a collection of faded deck-chairs, a tattered beach umbrella, decayed plants in ceramic pots. The floor was covered with tiles, wedgwood blue and white.

She stepped back, and taking a deep breath, called 'Barbara! Are you there?' Her voice was dragged from her lips by the wind. She strained her ears. Was that a small rustling sound inside? Did you get mice near the sea? Rats? Rats with webbed feet which swam? She tried to joke with herself, but the sickening fear was there again, far worse than before, working up from her stomach into her throat, choking her.

She gave up, she half-ran out of the gate towards the bathing cabin she'd noticed before, closely shuttered like the house. And as derelict. She leant against it to get her breath back, telling herself not to be stupid. It's an empty house, an empty bathing cabin, no one in their senses would be there in this weather. If you saw it in summer you'd think, what a delightful place . . . she shuddered.

Think what fun bathing huts can be, how you used to like childhood holidays on the Dorset coast. Your own little house, you thought, putting up curtains, sweeping it out. But you weren't so keen to make a home for Gerald, were you? Is that the basic trouble? But he was never there! If he'd slept in a Habitat window he wouldn't have noticed. He came home greyfaced, craving for food, bed, sometimes a brief loving, but most of all, sleep. Ah, but you should have understood, shouldn't you? To become engrossed in *your* work was no solution, and wasn't the final straw your being given the partnership by Saithe and Saithe, especially when he had failed his Membership? What if he *had* been run-down and tired and unable to hide his pique? You should have been more understanding.

She turned and shook the door violently, even pushed against it with her body until she noticed the rusty padlock. No use. No intruders allowed. But who would want to intrude in this deserted place? Even squatters would run away from it. Anyone would sense the atmosphere, the feeling of the past, of . . . unwholesomeness. You're getting fanciful again. Stop it. Go and have a last look, then clear out.

She walked through the dunes again and back to the house, went round the side this time to see if there was another door. Was it her imagination or was there a trace of footsteps in the sand which had silted against the wooden threshold? She might have failed to notice them the first time. But, how could there be? The wind would erase any marks. 'Footsteps in the sands of time . . .' Why did her mind keel about so? She knocked on the door in a sudden burst of fear and anger, banging against it with her fists. Was there a faint sound inside, a moan, no, less than that, the feeling of a presence? But her voice when she shouted 'Barbara!' had no conviction in it, nor carrying power. She gave up, as if her emotional strength had suddenly run out of her . . .

'And smashed and smashed and smashed . . .' the words seem to be ringing in my brain. And yet, over and above it, or beneath it, how can that be, I hear the rustling, louder now, and this time I daren't look round. The book and the letter fall to the floor, grandfather's letter, the yellowing pages spread awry on the carpet.

My hands clutch at the outside of my thighs, I feel the rough denim of my jeans rasping them. After a time they relax, lie flat, and I force myself to listen. Nothing. Silence, except for the soft sough of the sea, a lipping of the small waves at the shore. And yet this time there *is* something else in the room with me. I can hear another heart beating.

Everything around me becomes very clear as if I'm looking through the Caen man's telescope. Far away and very clear. The small boxes on the table beside me have a worrying brilliance, the lorgnette winks, blinding me. A piece of rock crystal near the small window darts viciously, like a chameleon's tongue.

There is a greater rustling, no, more than that, a whirring, the dull noise of rubble falling, and from the fireplace a bird falls at my feet, a young seagull with blackened wings, open beak and pulsating breast. Its round eyes are fixed on me, black and gleaming, and I'm reminded of that seagull on the beach at Dieppe. And of the skull-faced man who leapt on me, covering me with his vile body.

My knees give way, I cower, my hands in front of my eyes. It will peck at them as it tried to peck at *his* eyes. My heart seems to crack with fear, my head suddenly aches, (a familiar ache which has become a warning), and as the room swings round me I go down, falling through coloured lights which madly spin into darkness, a greater darkness, a void, and then a nothingness . . .

I recognize the pattern. The emergence as if from a long sleep, as if from the dark bottom of the sea, feeling slowly towards the light, bottle-green at first, then pale turquoise, then golden. Joy floods through me. I hum softly my little song of release. I'm on the beach, my favourite beach, near Tamaris.

But the joy recedes just as quickly. It's no longer as I remember it. There are soldiers everywhere, crowded as thick as ants where they've crawled out of the sea. Some wave to me and point forwards, and I think, now is my chance at least, if I can find him we can talk. I can tell him that *grand-mère* lied to us about him, that she poisoned the lives of her daughters, and through them, mine. But that I know how to put it right . . .

I go from group to group touching the rough stuff of the tunics. 'Have you seen him?' Some shake me off impatiently, some smile kindly as if I were a child, one man leers at me as he rolls a cigarette. 'Have you seen him?' I ask, but now they can't hear me for the roar of the aeroplanes and the cannons spattering along the dunes. In the distance I see a soldier with his arm raised, and my heart lifts; I recognize him. He seems to be throwing and beckoning in the one gesture, his voice floats towards me. 'Come on, chaps!' The blockhouse in front of him bursts into flames which shoot straight into the air, lighting the figures of men running from it. I must run too, run along the beach which I know so well, the hard ridged sand pressing into my insteps, the cool water running between my toes . . .

I'm tired of running, so tired. The soldiers have gone. All I see on the deserted beach is a helmet covered in netting, lying at the edge of the sea. I know it's his. I see the strap trailing on the wet sand, the shadow in the sand made by the helmet. I know he's dead, and that he found himself in death. As I shall.

Peace fills me, standing alone on that wide beach outside Tamaris. How beautiful, I think, the freedom, the space, the soft wind on my face! I hear its sighing sound. But as I look around, the beach blurs, fades, disappears, and I know I've been dreaming, a waking dream, as I lie . . .

My hands feel on either side of my body, Not hard sand, but the thick woollen pile of carpet. There is no helmet nor shadow of a helmet, the soft light coming through the porthole window glitters on silver and glass, makes the amethyst sparkle. I am in *grand-mère's* room. It must be late afternoon now. It's time I got back to Cabourg.

Nothing has changed, the smashed photographs, the book and letter on the floor where I dropped them. The bird is still there. Its broken wing lies useless, the other one scuffles feebly on the carpet, its breast pulsates.

'Poor bird,' I say, no longer afraid, 'you helped me before at Dieppe.' I kneel beside it, but as I do there is a terrible noise in my ears, of knocking, of fists battering on the side door. He's found me! The man on the beach at Dieppe! My heart contracts with a terrible pain. He's been trailing me all the time, through Rouen, Caen, Cabourg and then here. I can't bear it. I put my hands to my ears, desolation filling me, no, more than desolation, a dissolution of my whole being. I'd wanted peace, had planned for it, and now violence had once more caught up with me. I was wrong to waste time at Les Sapins, wrong to hope . . . I open my mouth to scream, I sink to my knees with a hideous falling fear. *I realize I am making no sound . . .*

The light was beginning to go as Karin bumped slowly along in the car, the desolation she felt was overpowering. What is it in the atmosphere which affects me so badly? she thought. Is it what the woman in the restaurant had said about Barbara's grandmother, the image she'd created? 'A recluse . . .' she'd said, '. . . damage done . . .' 'Died of a stroke . . .' What kind of damage? She tried to imagine the room behind the locked doors, and the fear swept through her again. Someone *had* been there. Hiding. But no cry. If it had been Barbara, wouldn't she have called out? 'Do you remember . . . *Rappelle-toi* . . .' She chided herself. You're being fanciful again. But she was not satisfied, she hadn't done enough. Somehow she should have broken into the house, found . . . what could she have found? It had happened two years ago. She put her foot down on the accelerator. Nothing would induce her to turn back.

At the end of the road she turned right instead of left, and kept driving. She couldn't face Cabourg yet. A church rose in front of her, and she slowed down to read the notice on its grey stone wall. *To the Cimetière Britannique*. She looked at her watch, ten past five; she had time to see it before darkness fell.

She drove in the direction of the arrow. There was no one to ask. She should have made for the shops, the village centre, people. And wasn't the deserted road like a scene from one of Chabrol's films? Menacing? Nonsense, grey winter road, flat, a stunted hedge. It must be the house which had cast a cloud over her. She wanted Gerald very badly.

The cemetery, when she reached it, strangely enough, dispelled her gloom, a tranquil enclosure surrounded by trees. The setting sun gave a warm glow to the white crosses arranged in a rough kind of battle order or semi-circle, and not in the serried ranks she'd expected.

She walked between the curved rows and peace came to her like a benison. She hadn't known death. And now she was walking on the bones of those men who'd died for her and for her generation. Had their loved ones thought that?

Had it sustained them? 'He died that we might live.' She walked lightly, as if she might crush the bones, place her foot on a skull.

A cemetery is the one place where banality ceases to be banality, she thought, as she read the inscriptions on the crosses. They became poetry, since poetry is the expression of one's true thoughts. If one smiled, it was because one feared one might weep. 'We lived in hope, we pray in vain, To see you safely home again.'

She sat in the rest-house, looking over the quiet lawns, feeling ashamed, embarrassed, ungrateful, feeling sorrow, anger, regret. The tears were hot on her cheeks. Everyone under thirty should be made to come, and thinking that embarrassed her even further. Who was she to say what everyone should do? She got up because she couldn't sit still. She'd never known emotion of this depth. She was weeping for the world, a girl of her own generation who'd walked back in time. She didn't know why she was weeping.

It was cold. When her tears had stopped she walked slowly amongst the quiet crosses, knowing the name she was looking for. This was where he would be lying, not far from Tamaris . . .

CHAPTER TWENTY-ONE

I opened my eyes and found myself lying on the floor in *grand-mère*'s room. At first I was confused, and thought I ought surely to be in that high attic bedroom above the Cabourg restaurant where the food was supposed to be so good. Then I remembered my visit to Les Sapins – it seemed so long ago – and how my distress had driven me to take the path across the *marais* and to Tamaris, instead of going back to Cabourg. I staggered to my feet, feeling cold and stiff, saw the grey light of morning outside the porthole window. I must have slept here all night where I fell. There is terror at the edge of my memory; I brush it aside and look round.

The first impression is of chaos. The contours of the room are still dim, but nearer to me is the beaded foot-stool on which she rested her feet clad in those narrow laced black shoes. Lying on the footstool is the smashed photograph of my grandfather, the eyes, miraculously untouched, seeming to gaze at me with appeal in their depths.

My memory begins to return at the sight of the book and letter lying on the floor. I even remember some of the phrases he'd written in it. '. . . belief in your rightness which stripped me of my manhood', '. . . English first and foremost which is more important to me than being a husband, even a father', and '. . . encourage them to marry their own countrymen. Say it was their father's dying wish.'

He might have known she'd do the opposite, out of malice and bitterness. I thought of the sad, closed-in face of my mother, Aunt Berthe's coldness, an early withering of the spirit. And I'd never forget that saddest of all phrases, 'It is the final flurry of a weak man.'

Not weak, I think, neither in his living nor in his dying. As I bend down to lift the book it falls open and I read the pencilled note. 'Jolly good for Toadie.' My throat clogs with tears.

There is something white on the edge of my vision, and turning, I see it's the dead bird, its head on one side, the neck feathers soft and like white fur where it has bent over, the white wings streaked with soot. My heart fills with pity for it; I feel no fear, I even touch it gently with my foot and the head lifts and rolls to the other side. The round black eyes are hidden under purple lids. I owe it at least a decent burial, in memory of that other bird which saved me.

My memory floods back and I remember that knocking I'd heard last night which had struck such terror in me. I must have fainted, then fallen into a heavy sleep, exhausted. Had it been that man, following me like an evil shadow? If so, Tamaris must have frightened him with its brooding atmosphere, the broad overhang of the mansards like heavy eyebrows, just as surely as that bird on the beach at Dieppe had driven him off. I remembered him pulling up his jeans as he scrabbled over the whaleback of the shingle, fighting off its huge white wings with his flailing arms. I shuddered. But it hadn't been quick enough to save me. *Tant pis*.

Are we the victims of our heritage, or of circumstance? A strange question to ask at this early hour, but how many people must have asked it. My answer will be gentle, painless, and familiar. I've had plenty of practice, many small deaths . . . from which I've emerged later, as from the depths of the sea.

I should have liked a life with Don. We could have had another baby. I should have liked to see love in his eyes, instead of fear. But I am another. I am different, through no fault of my own, not even of my mother's. I don't blame her as Don did. She was a victim too, as are all the other people in the world like me. I hope they'll have more courage than I've had, that they'll find someone who understands . . .

What time is it? I look at my watch which luckily is still going; seven-thirty. The light is pale now through the porthole window. I know it's morning by my hunger. I walk about, feeling more supple, even think of going into the kitchen to look for food, realize how foolish that is. Even when *grand-mère* and mother and Aunt Berthe were here it had always been bare of supplies, only enough for each day was bought. So un-French.

I must go and see my mother for the last time. I straighten my clothes, lift my woollen cap and scarf from where I'd flung them on a chair and go out of the room. I lock the door behind me. I look at my watch again, and realize I'm going to be late for the bus. I must hurry, hurry.

I leave the beach, struggling through the soft grey sand of the dunes, half-running along the path through the *marais*. The rust coloured thyme is still tipped with white frost. As I bend to look, a brown bird whirrs up from a clump of grass in front of me and I remember the white one I've left behind in *grand-mère*'s drawing-room. Never mind, I'll come back and bury it. It must have come down through that wide chimney. Perhaps the wire netting has gone. Netting? What image does that raise in my mind? Image, or falling dream, a helmet, a camouflaged helmet . . . but the bird is real. I should have thought to lay it gently outside or bury it in the sand. Later . . .

When I got to the end of the path I saw the bus in the distance. I know the *Courriers Normands* runs in the morning to take the children to school, but that afterwards the service is poor. When it stops to my signal and I clamber on, there are only a few chattering women going to Cabourg or perhaps further round the coast to Trouville. I saw them looking at me curiously.

I pulled my cap straight, tucked in a stray strand of hair, wound my scarf tightly so that it covered the lower part of my face. '*Les Sapins*,' I whispered to the driver and he said loudly, '*Comment*?' I repeated it. I heard the silence round me, and then when I sat down the clucking started up again, like hens in a farmyard. I studied my ticket intently, *Ce billet doit être présenté a toute réquisition*. I read it again and again.

It's no distance, barely three kilometres, but I was glad when the driver pulled into the side of the road and worked his lever to open the door for me. '*Bonjour, M'sieu*,' I said as I got off, hiding my face in my scarf. I felt my back being pierced by the women's glances. I turned into the side road, started walking.

Now the white fence, the pines behind it, marching with me, the huge iron gate standing open, the long drive bordered by more pine trees, and the mounting fear and sickness which is so familiar. Don't run, I cautioned myself. Take your time. You'll become faint and then . . . I realized I shouldn't have come right away. The sensible thing would have been to have had a coffee at the bar in Cabourg where the juke box eternally plays that song of my namesake, '*Je sais dire* . . .' Haunting, beautiful. It would have calmed me.

'*Formidable*!' The bearded young man had said over his shoulder to me as he pressed the button yet again. 'She knows how to wring the heart, that one. It gets you here.' He'd put his hand to his tee shirt with 'Caen University' on it. I was sure he'd never seen the inside of it. He was a peasant with a Norman accent you could cut with a knife. Still, he had a soul . . .

Here's the great glass door. It's too late for anything. I push through it, so heavy this morning, like my head. I'm scarcely inside the hall with the black and white tiles like a chessboard when I'm stopped by that woman. So imperious. She comes from Nantes.

'*Bonjour, Madame*.'

'*Bonjour, Madame*.' I tremble, don't meet her eyes.

'Perhaps we can have a little talk in my room since you're so early.'

'Certainly.'

'You look rather pale this morning, if I may say so. Is the

visiting proving too much for you?'

'Not at all; I had a late night.'

'I could order you a cup of coffee.' A vision of the steaming cup rises in front of me, I can almost smell the coffee, see the thick cream making a pattern on top of its warm liquid blackness . . . I shake my head.

'Thank you, but no. Coffee in the morning disagrees with me.'

'Quite so.' She leads me to her room, a sanctum with her own books and comfortable chairs and cushions, photographs, a place she has made her own. 'Sit down, Madame, if you please.' She indicates a chair which is not as comfortable as her own.

'Thank you. How charming!' I murmur, glancing around although I've seen it before, have probably said the same thing.

She puts her fat elbows on the table, looks at me, composing her face under its starched cap into an expression of concern. 'I'm sorry to have to say this to you, Madame, especially as you've taken so much trouble . . .' She pauses.

'Yes?' I say to help her.

'I feel it would be better if you didn't come any more.'

'Not . . .' The dread moves closer. How could I tell her that this was to be my last chance, that I'd had a buried hope my mother would become lucid and would say, 'Don't do it. I need you.' 'I had hoped . . .' I can't go on.

I say it with regret. She speaks in a calming practised voice. I know she's made up her mind. 'It's doing no good. Indeed, it's making matters worse. My advice to you is to go back to England, forget all about it for the time being. I'll let you know when it's better . . . trust me.' But that's the point. I don't trust her. My head suddenly swims, I think, oh, God, not here, and through the mist I hear her say, 'Some spirits to revive you? Some cognac?'

I shake my head. 'No spirits.' I don't know whether I say it or not. I exert every particle of will-power I have in my body, and slowly my head clears, I see her fat, over-powdered face again in focus. 'A little faintness,' I say. 'Perhaps with hurrying to come here.'

'Let me give you some breakfast. I know you young girls, not eating. Although *you* have no cause to worry.' Her eyes on me are envious, God knows why. 'You could relax and rest before you leave.'

'No, thank you.' Desperation claws at me but I manage to smile. 'You don't think if I waited for a day, or even two days, I could come back? It's important to me. It's a matter of . . . life and death.' I see her alarmed face, and I smile apologetically, 'Well, in a way . . .'

She returns my smile, uncomfortably, then shakes her head. 'Impossible. It's too distressing for our patient. Take my advice and go back to England. You're a young woman. There must be plenty in your life. Your husband . . .'

'I'm divorced.'

'Ah, that's sad. Here it's the same. One wonders if there is sufficient . . . application. But there's your work. And your friends.'

'I had a friend,' I say, 'a girl.'

'Go back to her, Madame. Stay with her for a little. You need company. Try and build up your resources and then perhaps in the summer when you're stronger you can come back and see us. It's beautiful here in summer, especially inland. *Le Pays D'Auge*.' Why do they all say that?

'I prefer the coast; I've always liked the sea.'

'Well, there's the sea.' She prepared to be magnanimous. 'Bathing. The *Côte de Calvados* is salubrious in summer.' She speaks like a travel brochure.

I get up because my eyes are suddenly spilling over with tears. It's more than weeping, it's as if some inexhaustible source of tears had found their way through the eye-holes of my face.

'Try not to mind,' she says as we walk along the corridor together. Our figures make shadows on the shining surface of the floor, and I'm reminded of another shadow I've seen . . . somewhere. It had been significant: a helmet, a strap, a buckle. 'You'll realize later that I'm . . .'

'Madame Gauchet! Madame Gauchet!' We turn together, and there is a nurse gesticulating at the end of the corridor. She looks agitated, the usual calmness has gone. 'Come quickly!'

'Something has happened.' The woman presses my shoulder with her fat hand. 'I must go. *Bonne chance*.' She bustles away. I see I'm forgotten.

My feet lead me down the long drive guarded by pines and on to the side road which leads to the main road to Franceville. This time there is no bus to help me along the rest of the way. A big white Citroën draws up beside me after I've walked a few hundred yards, but my face must have frightened the man in it. 'Pardon,' he says. He has fair eyelashes, a Norman pig, and he drives away, laughing stupidly. A *commis voyageur*. In the distance I hear the screeching of a siren, and I think in a detached fashion how strange that is since there are no factories here. Perhaps the wind has blown the sound from Dives.

The soldiers struggled along this road in twos and threes, sometimes hiding in the ditches when the Boche was near. Further away, on Sword Beach, my grandfather didn't have to hide. His riddled and burned body would be lifted by his men and eventually buried in the British cemetery. You could say his suffering was short and swift. Mine, because of my mother's suffering, has been slow. In a way we, mother, Aunt Berthe and myself were war casualties, because of *grand-mère*'s hate.

People forget that on the whole soldiers are happy. Their lives are simple. They have a job to do and they do it. Most of them have come to terms with death. It is in many respects a strictly moral life, (I remember de Vigny's *Servitude et Grande Militaire*), and with it there is a camaraderie which isn't as stifling as the family circle. *Le foyer*, as the French call it, home, family, is the most important thing in anyone's existence. If the atmosphere isn't right there, nothing goes right for the rest of time. I've proved that. All my life I've been saddled by a poor, lonely ghost, an Englishman, Norman Sanctuary, who I now know as a false ghost, created in hate by my *grand-mère*. My mother lived in his shadow and wasn't able to love me. It ruined her life and drove her to madness. Perhaps I should have explained this to Karin instead of telling her she was dead.

When I reached Tamaris I unlocked the side door and went to *grand-mère*'s room again. The mutilated photographs didn't upset me now. What was left of Norman Sanctuary lies in the cemetery with the white crosses on the green lawns, at peace. I thought of putting the book and the letter back where I'd found them, but the bird was more important. It lay there, rigid in death, and I lifted it in my arms. So heavy.

It was difficult to open the side door, to lock it after me, to slip the key in my pocket, but I managed it somehow, and carried the bird to the dunes. My arms ached, and I was glad to place it down gently, to start digging a hole with my hands. The sand was soft and dry; it ran through my fingers. I placed the poor bird in the hole and scrabbled the sand over it, got up stiffly and walked towards the bathing cabin.

I tried not to think of my mother, of those restless black eyes which still held a flicker of recognition when they saw me yesterday coming into her room, whose hands stopped plucking at her dress, her far from elegant dress with the stains down the front. In time she would have enjoyed my visits, I know. She wouldn't have shouted at me, nor laughed behind her hand, her eyes wild, nor turned her back on me pettishly, like a child. In time she might have come to love me. She might even have said, like a mother, 'Don't do it.' *Tant pis*. One can't have everything.

Instead I'll think happy thoughts of the early part of my marriage when Don was loving and I had at last escaped from the shadow which hung over Tamaris. How can one love and hate a place at the same time? Tamaris is part of me, the joyous side of it: the clear air, the wide horizon, the feeling of being a bird on the wing; but so is the darker side: those interminable afternoons in the darkened drawing-room listening to *grand-mère* digging at the past with her old fingers, the long ridged nails. Falsifying it, crucifying my grandfather, and her daughters . . . and me. 'Done to death by slanderous tongues.' That's Othello. I remember we did it at school.

Life changed with Don. I discovered the joy of a man's body inside me, a man who could be a child at other times. We were happy until the accident. I mustn't blame him; it was my destiny. You couldn't expect anyone as immature as Don to cope with someone else's destiny, even if that someone was his wife. He thought 'in sickness and in health' meant something else altogether, or maybe he didn't think. I don't blame him. He taught me a trembling, caring kind of love.

There are different kinds. I felt love for Karin on that weekend in Dieppe, so far away now, but with those same vast skies and seas as are around me now. 'This is fun,' she'd said in that café, with those blue eyes beaming merrily on me. 'Merrily' is an old-fashioned word, but right. She was my schooldays. 'We'll have a really good cocoa-in-the-dorm time together, let our hair down, tell each other all our secrets.' Karin would have understood; she would have helped me.

I would have told her why I wanted to come here to Tamaris, and to Les Sapins, how my whole life had shaped towards this time. I would have opened my heart to her, I would have said, 'Do you see how it all stems from that dead soldier, from *grand-mère*, through my mother, through the accident, to now?'

But as it happened there was no point. It was finished for me before I got here. It was finished for me on the Dieppe beach. I knew it when I saw that terrible, familiar face which *grand-mère* had constructed from her hate and presented to us, colouring our thoughts, poisoning our lives. Mother had succumbed to a living death, Aunt

Berthe had an ice sliver in her heart . . . only I ever had a chance of escaping. There was a last chance with Karin. Then even that was taken away from me by that man. He took everything from me in violence, scrabbling over my body with his dirty hands, digging into the secret places with fingers whose bitten nails tore at the soft inner skin. When his body dropped into mine like a plumb weight, he took what was mine and had been Don's. But worse than that, he took all hope.

But he didn't take the earrings.

The key is difficult to turn in the padlock. The sea wind has rusted, and when I eventually get it to move there are rust marks on my fingers and on the palm of my hand. I push open the door and walk into my childhood. Oh, those remembered smells, seaweed, shells, the smell of the sea . . . if I open this shutter just an inch or two and close the door I shall be able to see my way about.

There are the limp bathing suits on pegs, and the striped towelling robes which pull in a pierrot frill at the neck. The rubber bathing caps have perished. They are stuck together like a row of bats. Perhaps I could ease one apart, gently . . . no, why bother if my hair gets wet?

I sit down on the bench with the faded cotton cushions and begin to strip off my clothes, thankfully; they smell. It's good to be clear of them, to lift down my own black bathing suit and pull it on. There's no real need to do so, but it's circumspect.

Now the towelling cape with its collar which frills like a pierrot's when it's pulled by the stained white cord. Perhaps if I pulled the ends tighter, tighter? No, the sea is cleaner. Now I am as I used to be when I went down to bathe on those long-ago summers, the trembling delicious anticipation of the first dip of the season, the lifting of my heart.

I've reached the important thing: the little box with the ivory earrings. If I'd sent them to Karin with the letter I might not be sitting in a bathing cabin on a deserted

Normandy coast . . . *tant pis*. If ifs and ans were pots and pans . . . how pretty they are on their scrap of blue velvet, like Karin's eyes! And how pretty they would have been against her short dark hair! The filigree work is so delicate, so painstaking, like lace. Didn't the man in the shop say there were still some craftsmen left in Dieppe?

That weekend in Dieppe . . . I must write to Karin first, and explain why I lied.

CHAPTER TWENTY-TWO

She wakened early in the room with the pink roses and white furniture, and lay with her arms behind her head, calm in spite of her sleepless night. It was over. She'd been unable to find Barbara, but in a way she'd found herself, or at least a part of herself which was unfamiliar to her, the reflective backward-looking part. She felt sad, but enriched. She would never be quite the same again. She'd go back to Saithe and Saithe, outwardly the same practical young woman, but there might be an extra dimension from which at least her clients would benefit.

She felt no bitterness towards Gerald. It was she who'd failed him, and he who'd taken the decision. There was no point in going on destroying each other. If he gave me another chance, she thought, I'd take it like a shot. I think I have my priorities right at last. Did one always reach that decision too late? Personal relationships were at the root of all problems. How omnipotent I was sitting behind my desk dispensing advice, a model of objectivity. It's necessary to stand back, as if from a painting. I've done that by coming here. Perhaps I've grown up, she thought, shutting and locking her case.

She went into the bathroom and removed her toilet bag, toothbrush and toothpaste. How quickly a place became home, one's hand went out to the same taps, the same handles, by habit. A part of her would go on living in this pink and white suite in this little hotel in Cabourg. Is that what memory is, she thought, checking drawers, and wardrobe, the shelf underneath the bedside table, under the bed itself, little parts of one left all over the place; was it like sowing seeds and then reaping the benefit by becoming richer in personality, deeper, more mature? Maybe when the next guests came to this room they'd think, I like this, it has an aura, something left behind, like perfume. She put on her anorak, her Michelin-lady anorak Gerald had called it.

When she went downstairs and paid her bill, the French language suddenly fitted her tongue and she had a short, pleasant conversation with the proprietor; she walked briskly out into the street. Her car was drawn up at the kerb where she'd left it last night. Nose to nose with it was Gerald's Rover. He scrambled out when he saw her, came towards her smiling, took her case from her, put it on the ground and took her in his arms. She needed their support; surprised delight made her head swim.

There weren't many people about, and those who were had that inward-turning look she'd already seen in the shops and cafés, as if she didn't exist. She was utterly happy, utterly shameless. Her hands were on the back of his head. She held up her face for his kisses.

'Hey, you've missed me!' He released her for a second to look at her, then drew her again into his arms. Why speak when this said everything? It became the clinging kind of embrace generally reserved for divans and beds.

'Gerald . . .' She came to her senses after a time. 'It'll be in the *Cabourg Chronicle*.' She was delirious with happiness. 'Where did you spring from?'

'I crossed on the Le Havre boat last night. I had breakfast there at the crack of dawn, then drove straight on here, or as straight as possible, it's a bit of a *corniche*. Even so, I had to wait till the *Syndicat* was open to try and track you down. There was a helpful girl there. She remembered you.'

'Stunned by my beauty, I expect.' She was facetious with joy.

'No, you'd been her only customer.' Gerald never threw compliments about. 'She gave me the name of two hotel restaurants. The first one I went to said there had been a young lady staying there but she'd left . . .'

'It could have been Barbara!' Her hand flew to her mouth. 'How could I have been so stupid! I had dinner there the night before last. I might have checked. I was so sure she'd be in her grandmother's house that I concentrated on that.' She bit her lip. 'I haven't found her.'

'We will. I was stupid too. I should have asked them for a description. We're not very good at this. Anyhow, to be on the safe side I came here and I saw your car. I was just going in to ask about you when you appeared.'

'Five minutes more and I should have been gone.'

'I'd have found you. Let's go and sit in my car.' He picked up her case. She noticed how pale and thin he looked. She followed him and said when they got in:

'Why didn't you reply to my letter? That hurt me.'

'It wasn't intentional. It hurt *me* when I realized how long it had been lying behind the door. Pete was away and I was in Tommy's.'

'In?' She was uneasy. As well as his thinness he had an indoor air.

'I was being investigated. Sounds very grand. I woke up with a pain in my gut and had myself whipped in by ambulance. I'm just out, more or less . . .'

She turned to him, conscience-stricken. 'I should have been there.'

'How were you to know? I tried to get you at the office, later.'

'But I'd gone. And I tried to get *you* at the hospital and the flat.'

'A stupid operator, and Pete was abroad. And all the time your letter was lying behind the door . . .'

'They didn't cut you up?' She was suddenly anxious.

'No, it was only a grumbling ulcer and they've put me on treatment. I knew it was there. It made me damned bad-tempered.'

'I should have realized . . .'

'Everybody told me, you included. I didn't want to listen to the truth. Anyhow I'm on sick leave now and I beetled off here as quickly as I could. That letter . . . you must have thought me a heel.'

'I was upset, disappointed, yes, even angry. Oh, don't look so woebegone, my darling. I shall have to feed you up.'

'No Normandy butter or cream.'

'There's sea-food, lots of it. That should suit you; full of trace elements.' She searched his face anxiously. 'Are you really all right?'

'Do you care?'

'I care very much.' She put her hand on his cheek. 'While you were in bed did you think of us much?'

'After the first day, or two, yes, a lot.'

'The same for me.' She leant forward and kissed him, kept her mouth against his for a second. I couldn't bear anything to happen to him . . . 'I'm going to look after you so well.'

'Don't overdo it. I'd die of delight.'

She drew away from him. 'I've missed you, really missed you for the first time in my life. I'm usually fairly complete. Not any more.' Her anxiety rushed back. 'And I've made a botched job of finding Barbara. That's why I'd decided to give up and go home.' She sat up straight. 'How did you get here, I mean, how did you know to come to Cabourg in the first place?'

'I've got so much to tell you.' He looked around. 'Is there anywhere we can go that's more private than this? We'll have a traffic warden along any minute.'

'They've gone to ground for the winter. What a pity I checked out! We could have gone back to my room.'

'I want to talk.'

'There's the bar across the road. It's a bit noisy but it'll be the only place open.'

'Right. Can we leave the cars here?'

'They're not likely to cause a hold-up.' She smiled, but he wasn't in the mood for jokes. She opened the door and got out.

The bar was deserted except for two youths leaning at the counter talking to the bearded young man behind it.

Gerald went to the counter, returning in a few minutes

with a cup of coffee and a glass of milk. 'I didn't ask if you wanted anything to eat.'

'No, thanks. You're on to milk?'

'Straight from the Normandy cows. I don't know the name of the breed. They're spattered brown and black, not in map shapes like ours.'

'*Vaches Normandes*. Is there something you're holding back? Are you all right?'

'As right as anyone can be who's been deprived of his wife.' His eyes warmed her. 'Barbara first?' She nodded, took a sip of her coffee than pushed it away.

'I'll tell you how far I got. I met a chattering French woman when I had dinner at the restaurant you called at. She said Barbara's grandmother had died of a stroke when she was alone in her house. There had been suspicions of an intruder but the police discounted that, I suppose because of the doctor's verdict. She told me the house was called Tamaris, and how to get to it. I went there yesterday but it was locked up, shuttered, empty. I didn't think Barbara was there, and yet there was a feeling of something moving, or at least, breathing. I walked around, and after a bit I banged and *banged* on the side door, used my fists, but . . . nothing. It was eerie, somehow. It frightened me, and I left. I had a look at the British cemetery before I came back to Cabourg, and that wasn't eerie at all, peaceful, and moving. Gerald, I saw her grandfather's grave, Norman Sanctuary; the whole thing was too much for me. I decided I was out of my depth, that I'd better go home . . .' She saw his grim face. 'Tell me what *you* know.'

'I got Don Sheldon's address from his doctor and went to see him, Sheldon I mean. His girl was okay, breezy, but he was cagey, even aggressive, at first. Of course I'd no right to ask questions, especially as I was pretty sure what was wrong with Barbara.' Her heart jumped.

'What?'

'In a moment.' A touch of the old autocracy. 'This girl, though, Chloe something, backed me up in a kind of way. She was shrewd. She saw Sheldon being difficult and said to me, 'Tell him *why* you're here.' So I did, and said if he could give me any address where I might find both of you, I'd be eternally grateful.'

She glanced at the bar, disappointed. She'd found Tamaris for herself. The two boys had gone, the bearded man was rubbing the counter. She looked at Gerald again. His paleness worried her. 'What did he say?'

'That I'd probably find her at *Les Sapins*, Cabourg, visiting her mother.'

'What?' She stared at him. 'But that's nonsense! She told me her mother was dead.'

'She told you she lived with a man in Surbiton.'

'I know, but why should she say her mother was *dead*?'

'It might have been one way of saying she was insane.'

'Insane!' She breathed deeply. 'Are you telling me . . .' she shook her head, 'I can't believe it . . .' Her mind went over all that had been happening, the feeling of mystery. 'Yes, maybe I can.'

'*Les Sapins* is a private mental home near here.'

The fog was clearing slowly. There was the strange behaviour of the aunt at Rouen, and Barbara's strangeness . . . no, that was different. She'd been withdrawn, devious, but she hadn't been unbalanced. Besides . . . 'It certainly doesn't apply to Barbara,' she said.

'Why do you say that?'

'I went to see her aunt at Rouen . . . I got her address from the school . . . and she told me I might find Barbara here.' She looked at him, speaking slowly. 'She didn't tell me about her sister being insane, but she did tell me she wasn't Barbara s real mother.'

'My God!' He buried his head in his hands. After a time he looked at her and said, 'Are you sure?'

'There wouldn't be any point in her lying, would there? John Charles had been married before his wife died in childbirth. He persuaded his second wife, Marie Malle, to adopt Barbara.'

'But Barbara didn't know of this?'

'No.'

'Nor did Sheldon. The awful part of it is that *she* didn't know. She'd think that . . .' His voice became curt. 'We've got to find this place and see if Barbara's been there recently.' He was on his feet. 'I'll tell you the rest on the way.'

'You haven't drunk your milk.' She got up too.

'There's no time.' He put his arm round her as they went out. 'When we get this settled, you and I have a lot of talking to do.'

'Yes,' she said. It seemed so trivial, compared with Barbara . . .

Dear Karin, I'm sorry I lied to you, about the little things like the man in Surbiton, and the big things, like telling you my mother was dead. Fear made me lie, and then there was the terrible compassion I felt for her. It's a living death to be insane, or to fear insanity. Can you imagine how I felt when I saw signs in myself, knowing I was her daughter? Don saw them too, and shouted at me, dreadful things. That was what broke my spirit. We'd been happy before the accident.

But it's all right now because I understand. *Grand-mère* passed on the hate she felt for her husband to her daughters. It made Aunt Berthe a bitter, unhappy woman, but in my mother, who was more vulnerable, it became madness, a kind of curse . . . the Malle curse, I call it in my mind.

But there's heredity, and I'm my mother's daughter. How else to explain my attacks after the accident, my inability to share my fears with Don! I made my last effort to conquer those fears when I phoned you. I was going to confide in you, to ask you to help me because you were the opposite of me in every respect and I'd always admired you. All that weekend in Dieppe I tried to summon up my courage to tell you.

But something terrible happened to me on the way

to the boat; a man attacked me. It was much worse than rape, and that has always seemed to me who hates violence, the ultimate degradation. It was as if this man was saying as he ravaged me: this is what you are, what you are worth.

I lost my chance to speak to you. I can't describe to you how I felt when I realized that. I think it was worse than death because of the hopelessness of it, but at least it helped me to make up my mind.

Karin, I can't tell you how fortunate you are not to have shadows in your past. Don't make them. Be happy, with Gerald. All my love . . .

They went in Gerald's Rover. Her car was still sitting at the kerb. Madame at the hotel would presume she was shopping in Cabourg before she left. She remembered their conversation about the desirability of taking back some specialities of the region, principally *confiseries de masse-pain*. When you bit into them, she'd said, you could taste the calvados running into your mouth.

Gerald seemed to know where he was going. He turned off the main road after he'd been driving for a short time, and then proceeded along a narrower road bordered by trees. 'The girl in the tourist office said I couldn't miss it,' he said. 'There's a white painted fence running alongside, pine trees, and then we'll come to iron gates at the end of a long drive.'

'You've got time to tell me about Don Sheldon,' she said. She closed her eyes, feeling tired, although it was only half-past ten. Something was rushing to happen. For a brief fanciful moment she imagined wings brushing her, the wings of a great bird.

'I'll go back to the beginning. I told you Sheldon was a bit truculent under that veneer of his.' She saw him in her mind's eye, his handsomeness which lacked a certain strength, a man for whom life had to run on oiled wheels. Gerald's voice, flat, emotionless, painted the picture as clearly as if she'd been there.

'He blustered a bit, looking aggrieved. "I'm not so sure I like people barging in on me like this, asking questions," he said. I looked at the girl in her pink blouse tied in a knot under her cleavage, quite a dish if you like the type. But her eyes were shrewd under that frizzy hairdo.

'"My God, how you men beat about the bush!" She smiled at me; there was no sting in her words. "Tell Don why you're here, Dr Armstrong. He's full of suspicions, aren't you, sweetie?" He glowered at her.

'"Right," I said. "My wife's very worried about Barbara, Mr Sheldon. I know she came to see you before but she couldn't get her out of her mind. She's gone off to France to try and find her, and I want to find my wife. I've got some time off from my hospital."

'"You look a bit peaky," the girl said. "Have you been ill?"

'"Yes, I have," I said, "peptic ulcer," thinking if it would help . . . Sheldon interrupted us rudely.

'"It's good to know someone else is worried about Barbara. By God, she kept me on tenterhooks after that accident. I can't be blamed, can I, for her getting . . . ill?"

'"I'm a doctor," I said, "I can appreciate that you've been through a bad time." He was so anxious to unload, poor sod, that he took the bait.

'"Only someone like you medics can appreciate what it was like, one minute fine, next minute staring at me, stiffening up, falling on the floor, writhing . . ." he let it all spill out. Chloe Boscombe was looking at me with those shrewd eyes.'

The blood had drained out of Karin's face as she listened, it seemed out of her whole body. 'She's an epileptic,' she said at last, 'it explains so much.'

Gerald touched her hand gently, 'It's a shock?'

'In a way I did know. There was always a feeling she was covering up something, that she lived on a knife edge. It vibrated round her, the fear, the apprehension. Little things come back to me. She didn't drive; didn't drink, much; she didn't want to share a room with me at Dieppe.

On the last night I know now I heard her having a fit next door . . .' She turned to him, 'Gerald, perhaps that's what prevented her catching the boat, another attack?'

'Two boats, remember. It's unlikely, although I thought of that.'

'She bought earrings for me. I spoke to the man in the shop. She meant to see me. She meant to ask me for help. I'm terribly frightened for her. Something dreadful has happened maybe on the way to the docks. I've known it all along.'

'You forget Sheldon said we'd probably find her at *Les Sapins*.'

'Yes, he did, didn't he? But then he couldn't know if anything has happened to her in Dieppe . . . unless he was putting us off the scent.'

He looked at her. 'Are you thinking he may have followed her, attacked her? No, that's stupid, he isn't the type.'

'I don't know what to think, except that now I feel there's a terrible urgency. Drive as fast as you can. I'm worried out of my mind.' She watched the speedometer, saw the hedges and fields flying past.

'No, he's a timid soul, Sheldon.' Gerald's face was grim. She could see his knuckles white on the wheel. 'He'd always run away from anything he didn't understand instead of turning round and challenging it. And then there are all the myths and preconceptions tied up with epilepsy, gods, devils, divine wrath, witchcraft, all the hobgoblins of the ignorant.'

'Maybe he read his Bible.'

'The falling sickness? At least there it gives you the drama, even the beauty of it, an awareness of the spinning of the cosmos, of being on life's turntable for a second or two. God-marked.'

'Some thought devil-marked.'

'Sheldon did. Worse than that, he thought it tied up with her mother's insanity.'

'And so would Barbara!' Her voice was anguished.

'That's the terrible part of it, she didn't know she wasn't Marie Malle's own daughter. Can't you see what this meant?'

'Only too well; poor kid. The thing is that her kind of attacks, caused by concussion, often go away. And she got no help from *him*. His beautiful doll-wife had been damaged. He shouted at me. "You doctors think you know everything! We were bloody well in the middle of making love once, and she had one, one of those . . . turns. Well, how would you like that?" He started pacing up and down the room, his hands thrust in his pockets.

'"Didn't the doctor help you?" I asked him.

He stopped pacing to look at me. "He did say something, but it wasn't me he was concerned with. About being sure to see that she took her pills. You just try getting Barbara to do anything she didn't want. She was convinced that they'd do no good, that the damage had been done long ago. Once when we'd had a nice dinner and it ended up with her on the floor, I shouted at her, 'You're just like your mother, you're mad, mad, mad!' It was the disappointment and everything. But I shouldn't have said that." He sat down and put his head in his hands. After a minute he looked up. "It's strange," he said, "after she came out of those turns she would hum a song under her breath, just the one line of a tune I never recognized. French, probably. Over and over again."'

'She did that in Dieppe,' Karin said. 'It was poignant . . .' Her eyes filled with tears and she looked out of the window again at the flying landscape. It didn't register. Her mind was full of Barbara. *Barbara . . . Rappelle-toi*. Had those words ever been put to music, or had she made up a little tune for herself, the way one did to the rhythm of trains? When you were in a fit did you have some deep fundamental awareness of the rhythm of your body, hum a little song to it? Great men and women had been epileptics. Was there a mark on them, something very special, an awareness which Barbara had shared, which made her different . . . ?

'*Les Sapins*.' She heard Gerald's voice, and realized that the pines had been gliding past for the last kilometre or so, that the blur of white had been a fence. He turned in through the open wrought iron gates and drove slowly up the drive. There was a fine drift of sand in the gutters as if it had been carried by the wind from the sea. She looked at her hands lying on her lap; they were trembling. 'Don't feel so badly, darling.'

'It's her having no one to turn to . . .' The noise of an engine, louder than a car, almost drowned her voice. 'Something's coming, a lorry maybe.' She looked at him.

'I can hear it.' He was pulling well into the side as he spoke. 'My God!'

Round the bend of the drive came a fire-engine, lights flashing. It crashed past them, the men sitting immovable, their eyes straight ahead.

'There must have been a fire!' The fear was back again, a dark familiar fear associated with Barbara. It seeped through her, forcing out the words, 'Something dreadful has happened. I have a terrible feeling it's connected with Barbara . . . or her mother.'

Gerald had rounded the last curve of the drive. Ahead of them was a scene of chaos, nurses, uniformed men, going in and out of the doorway of a huge red-brick pile of a house, carrying charred beds, odd pieces of furniture, plastic bags with tattered ends of what looked like curtains hanging from them. A grey pall of smoke clung round the turrets, the acrid smell filled their lungs. He parked the car at the side of the doorway. 'You stay here; I'll find out.'

'No, I'm coming with you.' They scrambled out and went up the wide flight of steps together. People rushed past them but nobody tried to stop them.

Inside the hallway it was more chaotic, a babble of French voices, some nurses assisting patients who looked frightened and clung pathetically to their helpers, two men with cameras. There was a porter in a dark blue uniform behind a desk and Gerald went to him, Karin at his heels. 'I'm Dr Armstrong. I'd like to see the doctor in charge, *le chef*.'

'I regret, monsieur.' The man looked harassed. '*Ce n'est pas possible. Regardez!*' He waved his hands, '*Catastrophe! Un incendie! Le docteur est très affairé.*' He shook his head decidedly. '*C'est tout a fait impossible!*' He broke into a further flood of French. Gerald turned to Karin.

'I'm not getting through to him. Could you try?'

'I'm no better.' She caught sight of one of the photographers watching them and smiled appealingly at him. He came over as if pulled by a string. 'Do you speak English, *par hazard*?' she asked him, keeping the smile going.

'A little.' He smiled too. He was young. 'I need it in my job. Can I help you?' His eyes stayed on Karin but Gerald broke in.

'I'm a doctor, a friend of one of the patients. My wife and I are anxious about her safety. Also that of her daughter.'

'Is she a patient too?'

'No, no, she was only visiting, but we can't trace her. Is it a bad fire?'

'Bad enough. But it was mostly confined to one room, I believe. Of course, in a place like this, the patients are easily alarmed, poor things.' Karin watched a weeping woman being led past by a nurse. She had dressed hastily. One stocking was snaking around her ankle, the yellow wig she wore was askew, and she was nursing a doll. '*Pauvre, pauvre bébé*,' Karin heard her say.

'The patient's name is Madame Charles,' she said to the photographer. 'Her daughter is called Barbara.'

He took out a notebook and wrote in it, his face eager. We'll be in the *Cabourg Chronicle*, she thought again, but it didn't matter. '*Bon.*' He looked up at Karin attentively. 'Perhaps something of your background, Madame, where you . . . ?'

'Look,' Gerald said, 'we're running out of time. Would you mind speaking to the porter and telling him we're very anxious to find out about them? It may be a matter of life and death.' The man nodded and shut his notebook regretfully.

They stood waiting while the two men had a dialogue in explosive French. At one stage it became acrimonious with much waving of hands, then the porter visibly softened, confining himself to nodding. His hand went out slowly to the telephone, he listened with his head on one side, said, '*D'accord*,' with a last decisive nod, and dialled a number. The young man stood back, giving a wry smile to Karin and Gerald. 'Those old ones,' he said in a low voice, 'it takes *finesse*.'

The porter put down the telephone and came from behind his desk. 'The doctor is still tied up but Madame Gauchet, the matron, will see you.' The photographer, translating for them, added, 'Lucky you!'

Madame Gauchet looked harmless enough, Karin thought at first glance: small, fat, amiable, but she took that back when she saw her eyes. They were those of a bright little animal, searching, curious. 'I can spare you only a few minutes, Dr Armstrong,' she said, 'you've come at a very bad time.'

'I realize that. This is my wife.' She shook hands with them and asked them to sit down.

'But when the porter told me you were friends of Madame Charles . . .'

' . . . and her daughter,' Karin put in.

'Quite so . . . Madame Charles, is, I'm afraid, very much involved in this business of the fire. You'd see signs.' Her little eyes snapped. 'Her daughter's visits have been the root of the trouble I'm sorry to say. She'd been seeing her for the last few days, but our patient's condition has deteriorated . . .'

Gerald interrupted her. 'Could you put us in the picture, Madame Gauchet, medically?'

'If you wish. Madame Charles is a paraphrenic, and in addition she has a weak heart. She's become extremely violent and abusive recently, talking incessantly about having to "find him." '

'Who could she mean?'

'Her dead father without a doubt. She holds imaginary conversations with him. I think her daughter's visits have stirred up memories. I had to order sedation yesterday, and this morning, when I met her daughter, I felt obliged to turn her away. Poor child, she looked so sad and pale. I was worried about her, but then this fire claimed my attention. I think she regarded me as an enemy. I should have liked to tell her that if she was looking for a mother's care . . .' she shook her head regretfully ' . . . she had no hope of finding it.'

'What time was Barbara here?' Gerald asked.

'Early, before eight o'clock. I was surprised. I happened to meet her in the hall, and took her to my room. I regret I didn't win her confidence. I was about to speak to her on the way out but I had to hurry away because of the fire.'

'In which Madame Charles was very much involved?' Gerald looked pointedly at her.

She nodded, her mouth pursed. 'More than involved; she started it. I could swear to that. The fire chief confirms that it started in her room and spread to the adjoining ward. Luckily there was only minor damage there, but her room was in a dreadful state.The seat of her armchair had been deliberately slashed, then set alight. The curtains were in shreds, her bed ruined. We have to face up to the possibility that someone might have given her a knife and matches.'

'Barbara would never do a thing like that,' Karin said.

'How can one tell? The terrible thing is that I'd given orders to allow the patient to sleep late this morning because of the sedation. You can imagine our feelings when we forced open the door . . .'

'She wasn't there,' Gerald said.

'I see you know paraphrenics too, their cunning. No, luckily she wasn't there or she would have been dead. But she's disappeared; it's almost as bad.' She half-rose. 'Now I really must . . .'

'Barbara didn't know she was adopted,' Gerald said, surprising Karin, 'did you?'

The woman looked surprised too. 'Well, of course. Dr Harauche always demands a full history. You mean the girl hasn't been told?'

'No.'

'I can't understand why her father didn't tell her.'

'He died when she was quite young. It's possible his wife may have extracted a promise from him when she agreed to adopt his child. She's an embittered woman, so many resentments stored up in her . . . her father, for instance. She won't accept that he's dead.' She shrugged. 'Who's to blame? The *grand-mère* had a . . . certain reputation around here.' She looked at her watch. 'But the main thing is that Marie must be found before she does herself any damage, or anyone else . . . please excuse me if I ask you to go now.'

Gerald and Karin stood up. 'We're terribly anxious about Barbara as well,' Karin said. 'Have you any idea where she might have gone?'

'I advised her to return to England. She said she had a friend . . .' She looked at Karin, 'Perhaps it was you, Madame. Poor child, she is the kind who suffers alone. I wish I could have helped her.' She paused. 'It occurs to me. She had the keys of the family home; I have a feeling she might have gone there. She had a strong attachment . . .'

'She wouldn't have gone to her aunt in Rouen?' The fear was back, choking her.

'Mademoiselle Malle?' Madame Gauchet sniffed. 'I hardly think so.' She got up as she was speaking, 'You should read our great author, Francois Mauriac. *He* could tell you about the tension within the family. No, she wouldn't go there.' She shook hands hurriedly, went towards the door with them. 'You will understand my first anxieties must be with my patient.'

'We'll try the house first,' Gerald said to Karin as they hurried along the corridor.

'You don't *think* Barbara would give her matches or a knife do you?'

'She's not mad.' She could scarcely keep up with his long strides. 'We've established she isn't a Malle.' But she thinks she is, Karin thought, that's the tragedy of it.

They rushed past two men sweeping the forecourt with

large brooms. The damaged furniture had been carted out of sight, and a gardener was busy amongst the laurels where tattered fragments of cloth still clung. Parked at the foot of the steps was an empty van.

'The police,' Gerald said as they got into their car. 'They'll be combing the grounds.'

'I wonder if she'll do herself any harm, I mean, the mother.' She had a vision of a body under the trees, a blood-stained knife.

'I doubt it.' Gerald drove carefully down the drive. A policeman in a flat peaked cap was speaking to two others in overalls, one with an alsatian on a lead. 'She probably got well away while the staff were having breakfast.'

'The house is called Tamaris,' she said.

'Is it? Tamaris . . .' He repeated the word.

Tamaris, where it all started. The fear was worse than it had ever been. Now the mother was involved, a deranged woman, roaming about, a prey to her delusions about a man who was dead.

CHAPTER TWENTY-THREE

'Karin . . .' I write more slowly, I'm shivering with cold and my hand trembles, ' . . . I can't tell you how fortunate you are not to have shadows in your past. Don't make them. Be happy with Gerald. All my . . .'

I raise my head suddenly, making the pencil skid on the paper. What was that noise, like feet scuffling in the sand? But feet in the sand wouldn't make a noise, would they? Then why is my heart beating rapidly, seeming to flutter against my ribs? Why do the words, 'The Malle curse' fill my mind? I scrabble through the letter to find where I'd written them . . .

'But in my mother, who was more vulnerable, it became a madness, a kind of curse . . .'

My mind goes back to the last time I was allowed to see her, her wild eyes, and how she clutched at me, saying, over and over again, 'I have to find him . . .' 'Who, Mother?' I said, 'who do you have to find?' Although now I know whom she meant. But as I looked at her, that dreadful emptiness came into her eyes again, and she plucked at her dress, smiling slyly up at me, then muttering, unintelligible words.

'Tell me, Mother please, please tell me . . .' I put my arms round her but she flung me off, her eyes glittering with hate. 'I have to find him . . . he'll tell me . . . why . . . why . . . it all went wrong . . .' She looked at me, and it was as if something about my appearance amused her. 'A secret . . .' she said, 'keep it a secret . . .' Then there was that terrible burst of laughter which brought the nurse into the room.

'Please go,' she said, 'her heart . . . it isn't strong.'

'She's saying terrible things . . .'

'They all do. Don't tell Matron or she'll stop you

coming. Just go and I'll calm her . . .' She seemed to be wrestling with my mother. I saw the thick peasant arms, my mother's thin ones, heard the wild laughter, and ran out of the room, my hands to my ears . . .

I listen again, intently, crouched in the cold cabin, but there is no sound now. It could have been the wind. The wind is a living thing round Tamaris, making strange noises of its own, and the wheeling seagulls add to it. There is one now, near the cabin. I hear its high screech, then a mewing, a wailing, a human sound, like the sound from my mother's room yesterday which followed me down the corridor. Poor, poor mother, how did I ever imagine she could help me when she can't help herself . . .

' . . . All my love, Barbara.'

I fold the letter and place it under the box with the earrings to anchor it, and get up.

Leave everything, my duffle coat, my clothes, my boots. Go out of the cabin and shut the door behind me. The padlock is lying on the bench inside but it doesn't matter. No one will come here now, or at least not until the season, the children with their buckets and spades, their shrimping nets, their mothers watching from their deck-chairs in front of their bathing huts.

'Why don't you play with Marcel, Barbara?' Poor, poor mother. That nurse with the strong peasant arms would hold her securely, perhaps put her to bed with a sedative. She had a kind face. And I didn't tell Matron, not that it mattered as it happened. She has forbidden me to visit. *Tant pis*. My last hope gone.

I cross my arms on my breast as the cold air strikes my skin. It doesn't matter. Cold is an attitude of mind and soon the wind will make me glow so that the sea will seem like a soothing balm on it.

Shall I run or walk? I've never done this before. Walk. Perhaps it's more fitting. How strange that there is no strangeness, as if since the accident I'd been practising.

Better to look around to make sure there's no one watching me. 'Like her mother,' they'd say in any case. 'Only someone mad would dream of bathing in *la Manche* in winter.'

Yes, that strange scuffling sound must have been the wind. The beach is deserted, cold, wind-swept. I look far away towards the sea which is soon to welcome me, as it welcomed so many of those soldiers long ago. It would be dyed red with blood as they fought with death there. There's something wrong with my eyes. I wipe them, they're streaming with the cold, or is it tears? I look again. There is one of them still there, a dark figure standing, its back to me.

The illogicality of my thinking clears my mind, and I know it's not a soldier, nor the ghost of a soldier, but someone else, a woman . . . '*I have to find him* . . . ' The words seem to burst, shatter into fragments in my brain. I know who it is. I begin to run.

'This is it,' she said. 'Slow down to turn. The surface is pretty rough.'

They bumped along through the rust coloured swamp, both busy with their thoughts, afraid to speak. Karin looked at the wide, flat landscape. You'd know we were within reach of the sea, she thought. I'll never think of this coast in sunshine, with people; only grey, wide, empty, but despite its flatness, hiding terrible secrets, a place of unhappiness caused by people, by old resentments . . .

'It makes me think of the war, this landscape,' Gerald said. 'Soldiers marching along, knowing they faced death. It makes you feel . . .' he laughed shortly, ' . . . kind of worthless, really. Our generation have never really been tested. Only vague threats which make you say, "To hell with it, let's enjoy ourselves while we can . . ."'

'Action may be easier than vague threats.' She put her hand over his. Her heart was full of love for him; it welled up, warm, enveloping, obliterating all their past mistakes. We've a bond now, she thought, an indissoluble bond. Whatever the outcome of this, Barbara has brought us together.

The tall back of the house was suddenly there in front of them, blocking their view of the sea. Tamaris. The coldness in her heart was back again, but this time she wasn't alone. He slowed down and she saw again the white stuccoed walls, stained with sea-damp. 'God,' she said, 'I wonder what we'll find.' She was trembling, but not from the cold.

'Let's find out.' Gerald was too matter-of-fact as they both got out. But he took her hand. 'Odd sort of place.'

'Wait till you see it from the front.' She tried to keep her voice steady, even light.

'It suits the bare landscape. The whirly bits make up for the lack of trees.' He was trying to calm her.

'Yes.' It was grimmer-looking than she remembered it, but then there had been the soft glow of sunset, not this cold grey light. Not even the wooden balconies, the decorative paint-work, the ornamental weather-vane, helped. The windows looked blind as if they had mirror glass in them.

'There's no sign of life. Let's start by knocking.'

They knocked loudly, then they both stopped pretending and battered on the door with their fists in their urgency. They tried the shutters but they were firmly fastened. Karin looked through the letter-box in the porch and there was the same motley collection, the sad relics of bygone summers.

'No one's been here,' she said, 'nothing's been touched. Even the same cobwebs trailing all over the place. We'll try the side door.' She had a sudden recollection of Barbara describing how she'd used the side door at Merriman's house. She almost heard the soft shy voice. 'Is there anything nicer than doing a good shop, putting away the stuff in cupboards . . .' Had that been based on her memories of Tamaris, how she'd driven back from Cabourg with her car laden? Before the accident, before she'd been told not to drive.

They knocked, banged and battered for about five minutes before they gave up. Several times Karin called her name. She heard the frantic note in her voice.

'She's definitely not here,' Gerald said. 'She might have been in there asleep the first time you came, but not now.'

'She *wanted* to see me. Unless she's decided to . . .' no, don't think that, ' . . . unless her mother has got here before us. Gerald!' She thought of a woman, tall, no longer elegant, hair loose, wild eyes, standing on the other side of the door listening to them, a knife in her hand, a blood-stained knife . . . 'The beach,' she said, 'we must go to the beach . . .'

When they were running through the dunes his foot kicked against something and they both got down on their knees. It was part of a bird's wing. He tugged at it; the dead bird came free easily; it was crawling with sand ants. Its head hung mawkishly to one side. The soft feathers at its neck had been gnawed away, showing the red raw skin.

'How horrible!' Her stomach turned.

'It's been buried . . . by someone.' His face looking up at hers was pinched, but not with cold.

'Yes, it's been buried.' The fear was steadily mounting inside her like a glass being filled at a tap. She watched him pass the palm of his hand over one of the wings. 'Why . . . are its feathers black?' She had to clear her throat to go on speaking. 'It's come down a chimney. We had the same thing at home once. We had to take out the whole fireplace. It got jammed . . .' He interrupted her.

'Someone *has* been inside the house. They've found the bird and brought it out here and buried it.'

'Barbara.' In the midst of whatever agony she was going through she'd take time to bury the bird. 'She could have gone away after that.' Why did her voice sound so strange. 'She could have gone away before her mother came here, caught a bus in Cabourg and then taken the train to Paris . . . or the *Courriers Normands* to Le Havre.' Saying the French words made the rest of it seem quite authentic. 'In fact,' she could hardly go on with these lies, 'we might see her on the boat when we go back . . .'

'Is that a hut?' He interrupted her again. 'It's pretty big

for a bathing hut.'

'Yes. I've been there already. Shall we have a quick look?' She was shaking as if with a fever as they ran. The dry sand might have been a swamp, a *marais* (another word she'd learned). Her feet seemed embedded in it. She stumbled and he put his arm round her shoulders. She leant against him, saying, 'It's difficult . . . the sand . . .' fear choked her words.

She noticed the padlock was missing and the shaking was worse than ever. He held her tightly against his side. 'Open it.' Her voice grated as if the sand was in her throat now. 'See if it opens.' She took a deep quivering breath as he pushed, then turned her head away as the door swung creakingly on its hinges. It scraped on the floor, like a knife on glass.

'Look,' Gerald said, 'look for God's sake. She isn't there!'

She had to make her head turn back again. Her eyes swept over the clothes on the bench, the boots neatly placed together under it. Their leather legs had flopped sideways, the way the dead bird's head had flopped sideways. There was a smell of seaweed and damp rotting wood. And a small white box.

She took it in her hands, read the inscription on the lid, 'For Karin', and her mind told her to open it while she was adjusting to the significance of the shed clothes . . .

The earrings on the bed of blue velvet were delicate ivory, chased, the small hollow drops intricately worked, the pendants shaped like a church spire. She knew Gerald was beside her. He was holding something. 'Read it,' he said, 'read the letter!'

CHAPTER TWENTY-FOUR

My senses were needle sharp as I ran. I saw the sand as if through a microscope; it seemed to be made of crushed shells and was so fine that it had the consistency of brown sugar. Little whorls erupted through it, like the worms which had made them. 'Mother!' I shouted. 'It's Barbara! Don't go any further, please, please! Wait till I get to you!' I knew the straight back, the black hair, the set of the shoulders, I even recognized the dress as the one she'd worn when I saw her last, and the grey cardigan. 'Mother!' I screamed, 'please look at me . . .'

She turned, and I saw her face, pale, eyes not belonging to the face, mouth open with shock. Her lovely teeth were rotted in one or two places and the cardigan was dowdy and stretched out of shape. 'The Malle girls were always smart,' she used to say, preening herself. She'd been vain about her appearance. 'Keep back!' she shouted. Her arms flailed, and I saw the glint of steel in her hand. 'I have to find him, I've looked all over . . . all over . . .' I saw it was a knife she was holding. And I knew immediately who she meant.

'He isn't here!' My foot caught in a clump of seaweed and I fell, full-length, but I managed to gasp out, my mouth half-full of sand. 'He isn't here any more. Don't move! I'll take you . . .'

'I know where you'll take me, back there . . .' she was brandishing the knife above her head and at the same time retreating into the water. Suddenly she turned round and plunged in. I heard her let out a loud keening wail, probably with shock. I got to my feet and ran the last few yards.

It was icy. The coldness gripped me behind my knees,

my thighs, under my breasts as I fell forward into the sea. I was half-swimming, half-walking as I tried to reach her, gulping water, choking. I shouted, teeth chattering, 'It's Barbara, your daughter! Stop, please . . .' She interrupted me, and now that I was close to her I saw the madness in her eyes. 'You were never my daughter! Don't come any nearer. I'll use this if you try . . .' I managed to grasp the arm which she was waving with the knife.

'We'll go back to the house, and find some warm dry clothes . . .' all the time I was talking I was struggling with her, struggling also against the weight of the water which was dragging me back. I looked down and saw the slash on my forearm which ran into a purple line. There were beads of blood along the length of the wound. Salt water's an antiseptic, I thought. It didn't matter. All that mattered was getting the knife. She was like an eel in my arms. I could hear her panting, choking, cursing.

My own misery, my own unhappiness, had gone. I realized it at that instant. I was in the sea for one purpose only, to help her. The original idea that I'd come here to end everything seemed farcical now, and with the realization came a great burst of energy. I flung myself on her, and as we both went back into the water, I managed to twist the knife out of her hand. We came up gasping, spluttering together, and as if my energy had drained hers, she stayed quietly in my arms, like a child.

'You've taken my knife,' she said, quite calmly. 'I needed it for him. He's the cause . . . the cause . . .' She swayed, and I saw how pinched and blue her face was around the nostrils. Her thin body was trembling against mine. Love flowed through me for her, and I clasped her closely like a child, like the child I'd lost.

'Come, Mother . . . I'll help you.' I kept one arm round her, pushing against the heavy weight of the water. I felt as if my chest had sharp slivers of ice in it, making it difficult to breathe. 'I'll tell you what I've found out,' I tucked a heavy strand of the black hair behind her ear, ' . . . how we shouldn't blame anyone . . . I even called it . . . the Malle curse . . . but it's just . . . how things were.' The cold seemed to be eating into my bones, making them ache, sickeningly. 'But we'll make a new life, the two of us . . .' All the time I was guiding her towards the shore, bearing her weight as well as my own. The water was still above our waists and it was like trying to walk through a swamp. I stumbled, and as if she'd been waiting for this, she wrenched herself free from my grasp, her body suddenly tense and strong.

'Leave me! Go back to where you belong!' She beat off my restraining hands and her voice rose in a wail. 'I looked everywhere . . . the dunes . . . I knocked, knocked . . . then I remembered . . . *she* told me they came out of the sea . . .' Her eyes were wild again, she screeched at me, 'Give me my knife . . .' she suddenly smiled, hideously, her head on one side, sang, 'Happy birthday . . .' then said in a mincing voice, 'Your own special birthday party, Marie . . .'

I took her by the shoulders, turned her towards the shore again. 'Tell me,' I said, 'tell me how you got the knife.' I began walking, dragging her with me, and she didn't resist. The smile was still on her face.

'That woman . . . like a fat squirrel . . . you've been a good girl . . . cake . . . blow out pretty candles . . . matches pushed under my fancy napkin . . . you cut it, Marie . . . take a slice to all your friends . . . the knife . . .' she laughed wildly . . . 'slipped it up my sleeve . . .' she suddenly clutched my arm in such a fierce grip that I dropped the knife. 'It's mine!' she shrieked. 'Give it to me!'

'I've dropped it. It's lost . . .'

She looked at me, mouth open, then she launched herself at me, spitting, scratching, and pulled me down with her, The knife gleamed beneath us. I saw her arm, the clutching fingers, and in my ears there was a drumming as I went down. My body seemed to fill with water, it filled my nose, my eyes and my mouth, I felt it swirling round my breasts, and I thought, as if in a dream, Don used to hold me there, cup my breasts as he kissed me. I imagined the sea like oil flowing all through me, and I thought again, we're drowning; it's what was meant after all, it will be better for her, better for me. I caught one of her trailing hands, and as the fingers closed over mine like a sea flower, my senses returned. Holding her tightly, I curved my body and took her up to the surface with me. Her face seemed to be twisted in pain as I looked at her, her eyes were closed, I felt her go limp in my arms. 'The knife,' she whispered, I had to bend my ear to her mouth to hear her, 'it's in my heart.' One hand clutched at her breast.

'No, no!' I looked at her bedraggled cardigan, the limp dress, but there was no sign of blood. Nor in the water around us. 'Lost . . .' I could hardly shape the words, 'don't need it . . . just let me help you . . . all I want . . . to help . . .' All the fight had gone from her. Her eyes were still closed, her face blue, dead looking. 'Mother!' I shrieked as she'd done. Her head fell on one side like that bird, that bird I'd buried . . . when was that? I began to babble incoherently as I dragged her the last few yards towards the shore. My eyes were blurred with the water. The beach seemed no longer empty, there were others there, perhaps the soldiers, or the ghosts of those dead soldiers . . . there was no division between reality and unreality.

I watched a man come splashing into the water towards me, jeans, sweater, of today, not of the past; then I heard a girl's voice, familiar, the voice of the one person I'd always trusted. Now she was there, in the water behind him. 'It's Gerald,' she called, 'and Karin. We're coming to help you. Hold on!' So confident that I knew it must be Karin.

The strange Gerald had reached me, he'd taken the weight of my mother's body from me, murmuring something which sounded kind, and lifted her in his arms. And then Karin, her kind face, her short dark hair, her rosiness. She put her arms round me and helped me to the shore. I noticed her light jeans go a dark navy-blue with the water. I watched Gerald lay my mother tenderly on the beach, and I said to him in a calm voice, 'Of course, I remember; you're a doctor.'

Karin had put a jacket round me. It smelled warmly of her, a lovely smell, comforting, fresh . . . I knelt down beside Gerald and looked at my mother. Her black hair had fallen away from her face. Her eyes were closed, and her fine mouth also, concealing the teeth which had once been fine. It's because she's been ill, I thought, tenderness flowing from me. She looked beautiful, calm and peaceful, at rest. I felt something warm running down my arm and saw the blood from the knife wound. I was living; she was dead.

Then the trembling started. I knew Karin put her arm round me and led me across the sand towards the bathing cabin. That she talked to me, softly, saying, not to worry, Gerald would see to everything. We'd get my clothes and then we'd go back to Cabourg in Gerald's car where she knew a little hotel where I could rest. When everything had been seen to, we could start off for home. I nodded from time to time, once I said, 'Thank you . . .'

CHAPTER TWENTY-FIVE

Madame showed admirable phlegm when Karin asked if she could have her hotel room back. Her husband had arrived here unexpectedly, she explained. They also had a friend with them who would require another room. She'd had an accident on the beach . . . she realized the news would come out in any case. The *Cabourg Chronicle* . . .

She took Barbara upstairs and helped her to undress. She was white and silent, but her hands had a fine tremor. When she was in bed Karin said to her, 'You've had a terrible experience, but try not to think about it yet. We'll talk later. You've to take this sedative Gerald gave me. He's attending to everything . . .'

The girl nodded dutifully. Her voice was low. 'She's dead, isn't she? My mother's dead?'

'Yes. But it could have happened at any time. She had a weak heart. Madame Gauchet told us.' She watched Barbara swallow the capsule, wash it down. 'The cold water would be too great a shock for her, you see. Close your eyes, Barbara. That's right. Lie down and I'll cover you up. I'll sit beside you until you fall asleep. Don't worry . . .' She stroked the heavy, light-coloured hair away from the girl's forehead as she spoke; peculiar, beautiful hair with the frosty glitter in the strands. She stroked it gently until she slept.

By some sort of osmosis, she told Gerald smilingly when he came back – their attitude towards each other had changed subtly; there was a tenderness, a lack of abrasiveness – she was able to talk easily in French with Madame of the hotel. He thought it might be a question of heightened awareness, a speeding up of everything, even learning capabilities, a clearer recall. They smiled a lot at each other in spite of the sad circumstances.

In any case, although Madame was not in the habit of serving meals, she'd listened sympathetically when Karin explained that Barbara was too weak to get up, and had said she would be more than pleased to waive her rules and provide a little supper for three in the young lady's room. She would bring it up herself.

Gerald willingly left the fraternizing to Karin. He'd waited with Marie Charles' body on the beach until Karin had alerted the Cabourg police on her way through the town with Barbara. Everything had been set in motion. There was to be an inquest, and they were free to go back to England once the date was fixed. *Les Sapins* had been duly informed.

He took Barbara's pulse and temperature, and said he was sure that physically there would be no ill-effects. 'I'll take you to the police station tomorrow,' he said, 'if you feel up to it. It may be possible to go back home depending on the date of the inquest.'

Madame arrived, smiling, with a well-stocked supper tray and asked Barbara if she'd recovered. She had the contained excitement of someone whose dull life has been unexpectedly brightened by outside circumstances.

'*Oui, merci.*' Barbara was pale but composed. 'I was trying to save my mother, you see.' Karin cast a fleeting glance at Gerald. Madame's face expressed only polite concern.

'You were successful. I hope?'

'*Malheureusement, non.*' Barbara's face was too calm. 'She drowned. She was a patient at *Les Sapins*. Perhaps you knew her family. They lived in a house called Tamaris. At Franceville.'

The woman's brows knitted together. She put down the tray, went over to the bed and took Barbara's hand. '*Chère Madame*,' her voice was compassionate, 'it's been a shock for you, a great shock. I can see that. I knew of your *grand-mère*, a lady of . . . principle.' She patted Barbara's hand, then went towards the door, where she turned. Karin could see she was deeply moved. 'My home is yours, Madame,' she said. 'Rest here as long as you like.' She nodded to Gerald and Karin, '*Bon appetit*,' then shut the door gently behind her.

Karin got up immediately and went to sit on the bed. Barbara was resting her head against the pillow. She looked deathly pale. 'You were quite right to tell her.' She stroked the girl's arm. 'Wasn't she, Gerald?' She looked across at him.

'Yes, quite right. Everybody will know soon.'

'Perhaps we should get everything over at once.' He nodded. 'You do it . . .'

'Is there more?' Barbara had opened her eyes. 'Don't worry, I'm very calm, Karin. I can't think why. Even last night, when I thought I'd have . . . dreams. Go on.' There was a serenity about her which was new.

'We think you ought to know. Madame Charles wasn't your real mother; she adopted you; your father was married before and his wife died giving birth to you.' She stopped, searching the girl's face. For a second the expression didn't change, then her eyes widened, seemed to grow darker. She let out a moan and pressed her hands to her face. The room was very still. I wish she'd weep, Karin thought, scream, anything . . . she put her arm round her. 'Are you all right, Barbara?' Waited, felt the girl's shoulders straighten.

'Yes.' She took her hands from her face. Her eyes looked dry and burning. 'There's a storm going on inside me,' she pressed a hand to her chest, 'here. A tornado. So many things to think about . . . Mother . . . I'll always call her Mother . . . and Don . . . he couldn't have known or he wouldn't have said what he did . . . but I thought it too. Never mind, it's over and done with . . .' she gave them a tremulous smile.

'That's the way to look at it,' Gerald said, 'over and done . . .' she interrupted him.

'But there's the accident, and what it did to me. Knowing my mother isn't my mother . . . how strange that sounds . . . does that alter things? Maybe you'd talk to me about that, medically, I mean . . . not now, Gerald, things are crowding in on me. There's the letter I wrote to you, Karin. I might never have written it, if I'd known . . . did you get it?'

'Yes. And the earrings.' She smiled at her. 'Take it easy. It's too much for you all at once. Have a look at these instead. Don't you thing they're right for me? Gerald did.' She shook her head and the ivory spires swung, milky-white against her dark hair.

'They look beautiful on you. I'm pleased . . . But so ashamed of the letter. I thought there was no hope. Don had said so, everybody . . .' her voice tailed away. She looked at them, her face drawn. 'I've just remembered the worst thing of all . . . that man . . . at Dieppe. How am I going to forget him, what he did . . . ?'

'Don't forget any of it,' Gerald said. 'You've got to have a clean sweep. Tomorrow we'll talk about everything. You'll be surprised how things will sort themselves out, how much can be done to help you. We'll talk till the cows come home, *les vaches Normandes*,' he smiled at her. 'Things are going to go well for you from now on, you'll see . . .'

'Well, on that note let's eat,' Karin said, trying to be the cheerful, matter-of-fact person she'd once been. 'You pour the wine, Gerald.' She kissed Barbara's cheek and got up, swallowing back her tears.

They ate Madame's supper: a good Norman pâté, some chicken which Barbara identified as *poulet vallèe d'Auge* and which Gerald ate sparingly because of its lemon and cream richness, cheese and fruit. Then they sat with her till she slept.

'Do you think she might waken during the night . . . and have a fit?' Karin asked when they were in their own room. She remembered the weekend in Dieppe when she'd heard the strange sounds . . . and the singing. *Barbara, rappelle-toi* . . . She must buy that book of poems, read it sometimes, and remember . . .

'I should be surprised if she did.' He was drawing the

curtains. 'Not a soul in sight. A quiet town. She's armed with knowledge now. It's the best thing for casting out fear.'

'Now at least we know why she missed the boat. You could kill people like that.'

'Yes. It was almost the last straw for her. It'll have to be reported, of course. And tomorrow I'll get a doctor here to examine her. It's not the end of the chapter yet.'

They got into bed and he took her in his arms. He made love to her, with passion, and a compassion she'd never known before, as if to say, I know how deeply involved you are with this girl but it's my involvement too, now. They came together with a new depth of tenderness, a oneness, as it had never been, as it might be from now on, if they were careful. They promised to be careful.

He sat up a long time afterwards and took a small book from under his pillow. 'What is it?' she stirred.

'Can't sleep; it's my pocket Hippocrates. Never travel without it,' he said shamefacedly.

'Oh, Gerald!' she laughed at him.

'There's been something niggling at the back of my mind throughout this business. I'm sure he had a word for it.' He riffled for a few seconds, then said, 'Here it is,' and began to read in his cracked voice, more cracked than ever with weariness.

'"Some people say that the heart is the organ with which we think and that it feels pain and anxiety. It is not so. Men ought to know that from the brain and the brain alone arise our pleasures, joys, laughter and jests, as well as our sorrows, pain, grief and tears."'

'Barbara,' she said, her face against his shoulder.

He nodded. 'The hell of the mind; but it's over for her, I hope.'

'Yes, I hope . . .'

They lay down, promising each other they'd go to sleep. Such a strange interval in my life, she thought. I've lived a dozen lives during it, learned something very important . . . she heard Gerald's voice in the darkness.

'There's not been a chance to tell you. I've been offered a job in Gloucestershire, general practice. The chief seemed to think it would be better for me, for my health, suit me . . .'

'Not you,' she said, not having to think.

'A house with a garden. You could grow things. And babies.'

'I can grow things anywhere, and babies. And how could it be good for your health when you'd be miserable?'

'You're so logical,' he said. She knew by the way he kissed her that it was what he'd wanted her to say.

THE END

THE THREE GIRLS
by Frances Paige

As the student quarter of Paris vibrated to the onset of the 1968 riots, three girls, attending a language school nearby, knew they would never forget their time together.

Tricia – child of a strict English Catholic upbringing, beautiful and intelligent, but inhibited by her background.

Jan – a free-spirited American from a wealthy Southern family.

Crystel – daughter of southern French peasants, with all the practical good sense of her rural forebears.

As Tricia chooses marriage, Jan forms a doomed liaison with a black American, and Crystel consoles herself with a successful career, they learn painfully and often tragically, that there is no freedom and that life is based on compromise and commitments . . .

0 552 12503 2 £1.95

THE DEBUTANTES
by June Flaum Singer

They are the golden girls. A quartet of blue-blooded beauties whose names and faces fill the society pages. Poor little rich girls whose glamorous exploits make international headlines – but whose tortured private lives are the hidden price of fame:

Chrissy, survivor of a notorious custody battle between her mother and her grandmother, with a fatal weakness for all the wrong men . . .

Maeve, daughter of the celebrated Padraic, and Daddy's little girl in every sense . . .

Sara, whose father could hide his Jewish origins from the world, but couldn't hide his taste for lechery from his blackmailing daughter . . .

Marlena, Sara's poor cousin from the South, swept into a world of affluence she couldn't quite handle . . .

0 552 12118 5 £2.50